PRAISE FOR
Find Me in the Blooms

Find Me in the Blooms

JONATHON ISLAND • SEASON 2

Find Me in the Blooms

ALYSSA SCHWARZ

Find Me in the Blooms
Jonathon Island | Season 2 | Book 2

Published by Sunrise Media Group LLC

Print ISBN: 978-1-966463-39-9

This book is a work of fiction. Names, characters, places, and incidents are either products of the author's imagination or used fictitiously. Any similarity to actual people, organizations, and/or events is purely coincidental.

Scriptures taken from the Holy Bible, New International Version®, NIV®. Copyright © 1973, 1978, 1984, 2011 by Biblica, Inc.™ Used by permission of Zondervan. All rights reserved worldwide. www.zondervan.com The "NIV" and "New International Version" are trademarks registered in the United States Patent and Trademark Office by Biblica, Inc.™

For more information about Alyssa Schwarz, please access the author's website at the following address: www.authoralyssaschwarz.com.

Published in the United States of America.
Cover Design: Sunrise Media Group LLC

To Lisa. I can never thank you enough for believing in me and this story and then reminding me again and again even when I doubted myself.

But he said to me, "My grace is sufficient for you, for my power is made perfect in weakness."

2 Corinthians 12:9a NIV

Jonathon Island

Season 1
Meet Me on Jonathon Island (prequel novella)
Meet Me at the Grand
Meet Me on Lilac Lane
Meet Me at the Fudge Shop
Meet Me on Blueberry Hill
Meet Me at Sunset Cove
Meet Me at the Christmas Cottage

Season 2
Find Me in the Story
Find Me in the Blooms
Find Me at the Table
Find Me in the Lyrics
Find Me in the Spotlight
Find Me in the Wind
Find Me in the Stars
Find Me in the Harvest
Find Me in the Silent Night

JONATHON ISLAND
N
W E
S
Jonathon Family Home
Sullivan Pumpkin Farm
Lake Shore Drive
Sullivan Way
MacBride Resort
State Park
Airport
Jonathon Blvd
Quinn Ranch
Sugar Maple Ln
Blueberry Hills Neighborhood
LAKE HURON
Sunset Cove
Barrett House
Partridge Ln
Dahlia Dr
Lilac Ln
Zinnia Blvd
Poppy Place
Rose Rd
Blueberry Blvd
Pinnacle Dr
Blueberry Hills Park
GRAND HOTEL
Main Street
Downtown Marina Way
Marina

One

SPINSTER OLDER SISTERS WEREN'T SUPPOSED to watch their younger sisters ride off into the sunset with Prince Charming. Especially when they were the ones packing up said sister's apartment like the forgotten twin from Cinderella.

Kate Sullivan stood on her toes, her full five feet four inches barely enough to reach the box on the top shelf of the closet. She slowly worked the box forward until it tipped and sprinkled a cloud over her like pixie dust, igniting a coughing fit. Roma, the orange tabby, watched indifferently from her roost on the corner of the bed.

"Careful, wouldn't want to accidentally get too close," she said to the cat, who merely looked at her. "Cinderella's fairy godmother only needed a pumpkin and a few mice. One sprinkle of this stuff and you might end up turning into a stepladder. Or better yet, a tall man with muscles to intimidate these boxes right into the back of Dani's golf cart." A giggle slipped out at the thought as Kate lowered the box to the floor beside her camera case. The soft thud made it sound like it was filled with blankets.

"At least it's not more travel books." They'd need to purchase at least another bookshelf to accommodate her sister's collection. But from the way Liam doted on her, it was obvious he'd build Dani an entire library if that's what she wanted.

Kate stood and observed the sparsely decorated room. Only a few photos remained on the walls—Paris, London, Rome—along with one propped on the nightstand, showing the happy couple at the Grand Sullivan Hotel's groundbreaking last spring.

She was happy for Dani. Proud, actually, of the way she was breathing new life into this island. Their family too. Only a wedding could get their parents to exist in the same room without something burning to the ground. Kate had secretly hoped hers would be the one to reunite everyone, but calling things off the night of the rehearsal dinner had hardly had a positive effect on such a strained family dynamic.

Faint music played from somewhere in the living room. After a moment of searching the couch cushions for her phone, she stood victoriously and tapped the screen. "Hey, Gabby. What's up?" Loud voices filled the background for a few seconds before Gabby finally spoke.

"Kate, hi!" She practically yelled over the other noise. "I know you're probably with your family right now, but I have a few questions on the Clarkson-Smith engagement photoshoot. Do you have a minute? I wouldn't ask, but they want these done as soon as possible, and they want the best. Which is you, by the way. In case there was any question."

Kate chuckled. "For you, anything." It was the least she could do for dumping things on her at the last minute. Not that the doctor had given Kate much of a choice, but leaving her business partner to deal with the early-wedding-season rush alone wasn't her idea of a stress-free vacation.

She waited for her laptop to power up and then navigated to the business's online Photoshop account. "Okay, I'm in," she said, already opening the RAW files. Set against an overcast sky, the muted colors hardly gave off that dreamy, romantic vibe they were known for.

Gabby stayed on the line as Kate softened the highlights and shifted the tone curve to bring a luminous glow back to the couple's smiling faces. A few more tweaks—bumping the peach undertone, brightening the mid-tones, and adding a bit more warmth—and suddenly, the photos looked like stills pulled straight out of the 2005 *Pride and Prejudice* movie.

"Thank you so much, Kate. That would've taken me at least an hour to figure out. They're going to absolutely love these." After a few more questions about an upcoming wedding shoot, she signed off, but not without leaving Kate's spirits more lifted than they'd been in days.

"Jane Austen had it right, Roma. What kind of affection would it create if Dani had to wait to find her happy ending, all because of me? One failed wedding shouldn't ruin it for all the Sullivans." She was bending to thread her fingers through the dense orange fur when a loud knock on the front door sent the animal streaking toward its tower.

Green-gold eyes watched from the shadows, as if the cat some-how knew about her prescribed medical leave and was silently judging her for taking on a new project.

"Don't look at me like that. This is what family does for one another. You know Dani would do the same for me." Sure, staying to photograph the island's flower festival in a few weeks wasn't the same as lying on a beach sipping umbrella drinks. But if anything would make her anxiety worse, it would be having nothing to do for an entire month. Dr. Weston might've been right about her needing a change after her most recent panic attack, but early retirement wasn't the answer.

She was fine. Really. Everyone got a little stressed now and again, right? Besides, she'd been finding ways to cope for years. This time would be no different.

A toothy yawn was Roma's only reply before Kate tugged open the door to the dimpled smile and designer haircut of her new brother-in-law.

"Who were you talking to?" Liam's chocolate eyes sparkled with mischief as he peered into the empty apartment. Crazy to think this tall man was her new brother-in-law, with his expertly styled brown hair and a watch that probably cost more than her monthly rent back in Petoskey. Yet he'd already fallen into the role of nosy younger brother with ease.

"Just Roma. She might not be the world's best conversationalist, but she's a decent listener once you get past the judgmental stares."

"Tell me about it. A year later and I'm still trying to convince her I'm not stealing Dani away from her." His chuckle was warm and relaxed. Shifting his weight, he cleared his throat, breaking the momentary silence. "Mind if I come in for a minute?"

"Yeah, of course."

Notes of garlic and freshly baked bread wafted from the pizzeria on the ground floor, reminding Kate she'd skipped lunch.

"Everything's still a bit of a mess, but we should have her all moved by tomorrow." That was, whenever her twin brother Oliver returned with the extra cardboard boxes. "Would you like some water or tea?"

Liam shook his head. "This won't take too long. I was actually hoping to ask you something. Although now that I'm here, I'm beginning to wonder if it's such a good idea."

"Oh?" She tried to soften his pensive expression with a smile. If it were Oliver, she'd have teased it right out of him. But she didn't know Liam well enough yet to know if he appreciated space or friendly prying.

"You know how we were planning a weekend honeymoon to Napa?"

Her sister had spoken of little else lately besides the wedding itself. "The Tuscany of America, right?" Short of the actual place, it sounded like the perfect trip for them. Dani had mentioned they were planning a longer one for later in the year, once her workload with all the upcoming festivals was over. A trip that was sure to impress with all of Liam's fancy hotel connections.

He nodded, but the sparkle had left his eyes. "That's what I told her. I wanted it to be a surprise when I gave her the real tickets this morning. For Rome."

"Italy?"

"One and the same."

"That's great, although I still don't see the problem."

His pinched lips said he had one. "The thing is, it's for a few more days than a long weekend."

"Like, a week?"

He winced and bobbed his head side to side. "Plus two more."

Wow, three whole weeks in her dream destination with the man of her dreams. Dani should be knocking down the door to tell Kate the news herself, and instead, Liam was standing there with his hands in his pockets. "What did she say when you told her?"

His flat expression and raised eyebrow seemed to say *You know Dani.*

"Just wait here a sec. I'm going to call her." Kate grabbed her phone from the charging station and punched in the number. Two steps into the bedroom, she heard Dani pick up.

"Hey Dani, this is Kate."

"Yeah, I kinda figured from the caller ID." The humor in her voice fell flat, replaced with a stubborn edge Kate knew well. A grunt, followed by the squeak of moving furniture, and then a moment of silence. "Is Liam over there?"

The crack of vulnerability broke Kate's heart. Only days into their marriage, and they were having their first fight. She reminded herself that it was nothing serious—not like a broken engagement. But the pain was still real, no matter how small the disagreement. A reminder for Kate to tread lightly.

"He is, and he's told me about the trip he's planned for you two. You've wanted to go to Italy forever, and now you're going. No ifs, ands, or buts about it."

Dani sniffed as if she'd been crying. Either that or she'd been wrestling with her own dust-encrusted boxes all afternoon. "What about the Apple Blossom Festival? I'm supposed to organize the vendors, not gallivant across Europe. Not to mention the interview with *American Wanderer*. And with Holly leaving soon for a wedding, we still don't have an event florist. I've called nearly every business in northern Michigan, and they're either too busy or not interested or haven't responded at all. This festival will set the tone for the entire year, which means if it doesn't work out and bring more tourists to the island, the hotel remodel will be for nothing."

Kate softened her voice. "You only get married once." God willing. "It's your right to be happy and make us all insanely jealous by going on an amazing trip."

Dani didn't respond right away, but neither did she argue, which had to be a good sign. For as much as Kate had loved getting reacquainted with her baby sister this past week, no amount of late-night ice-cream runs or family dinners could make up for the years they'd already lost. She wanted to be a good sister, and even more so, a friend. And if that meant seeing Dani off to the ferry herself, that's exactly what she'd do.

"What if I handle things here while you're gone?"

"Did you just volunteer to manage the festival? Don't you have a business to run?"

Which would have been a fair point if not for a stubborn doctor and Oliver's worried tone when Kate had called him from the urgent care clinic in Petoskey last month.

"That's exactly what I'm saying. And it won't be a problem." She coughed into her sleeve to loosen the tightness from her throat. Darn dust allergies.

She could almost hear Dani tapping her foot in thought until . . .

"You'd do that, really?"

Success. Kate couldn't help but smile as Liam's gaze locked with hers, realization, then relief washing over his clean-shaven face. The hope in his expression made a different kind of lump form in her throat, one she worked to swallow down.

"What are sisters for? And if that's not enough to convince you, I'd owe you one for letting me take the lead with *American Wanderer*. A mention in a magazine like that could launch my photography business for life." And save her and Gabby from any lost business while Kate was away.

An excited squeal pierced Kate's ear, and she held the phone away.

"You're the best, Kate."

Chest swelling with satisfaction, she pasted on her best poker face before hanging up and rejoining Liam in the kitchen. But one look at his crooked grin had her slipping. "Pack your bags. You're going to Italy."

He jumped from the chair and caught her in a twirl. Giggling as her feet landed back on solid ground, Kate looked up at his sheepish grin. Little brother, indeed.

"Thank you, Kate. Dani's been so focused on everything but herself lately. First with the hotel and now the festivals. This is exactly what she needs."

"Consider it my wedding gift." This was far better than a gravy boat any day. "Just promise to take lots of pictures and eat your weight in pasta and gelato."

"I fully intend to." His warm chuckle filled the space, the weight from earlier visibly gone. He was halfway out the door, presumably to start packing, when he paused and turned. "Some guy's gonna be lucky to find you one of these days, Kate Sullivan." A wink and then he was gone.

The soft click echoed in his absence as surely as his parting comment.

Little did he know, finding a guy wasn't the problem. Lincoln St. James had found her five years ago and sealed their relationship with a promise. But that was before he'd walked out on her the night of their rehearsal dinner, shattering her visions of her own happily ever after.

At least one Sullivan sister would have hers. Kate would make sure of it.

All Dr. Weston had said was to take some time off from work. Which she had. But that didn't mean she couldn't call a few vendors and oversee a meeting or two in her free time until Dani got back.

Sparks rained down on Lincoln as flame and steel met in a ring above his head.

Form and function. Destruction and beauty.

He moved the blue flame across the red surface, touching the beaded wire solder to the final joint. Too little, and the entire frame could snap under the flowers' weight. Too much, and he'd be accused of shoddy craftsmanship.

"Not that a single member of Detroit society would be able to spot the flaw once tipsy on champagne and doing the cha-cha slide," he mumbled to himself.

But he'd know.

If you can't do something right, don't bother. His dad's words flowed uninvited, echoing as the hiss of the flame fell silent. He ripped his goggles off and set them and the torch aside.

The smell of hot metal mingled with roses, delphinium, Sumatra lilies, and the white Duchesse de Nemours peonies he'd ordered specially from a boutique farm near Edwardsburg. With no place for water in the live floral chandelier, he'd have to work fast. Silk flowers would have afforded him more time and flexibility, but they wouldn't catch the attention of the Great Lakes Bloomfest selection committee. They considered only the most exciting and innovative of florists for their yearly showcase.

Fortunately, Felicity had the delivery trucks and phones under control, allowing him to do what he did best.

Starting at the edges, he worked in circles as the halo of green began to take shape. The chocolate Queen Anne's lace came next, followed by hanging tendrils of burgundy amaranthus, as if heaven was extending its blessing over the happy couple. The rest of the flowers would have to wait until he had the floral chandelier suspended from the rafters of the Shinola Hotel's famous Birdy Room—a conservatory of vaulted glass and city views worth the six-figure price tag this wedding surely carried.

The distant chirp of a phone barely cut through the piano music from his Bluetooth speakers, followed by Felicity's melodic voice. His mother's oldest friend and the best assistant he could've ever asked for, Felicity could talk down the most flustered of brides while color-coding the entire year's calendar as if it was nothing more than a church picnic. The day she no longer needed this job was the day he'd close up shop. Just the thought of having to interview for a replacement made his skin itch.

"Mm-hmm, yes ma'am. Yours is the only wedding we have on today's schedule." Her blonde waves bobbed through the open door linking the studio to the back of the flower shop. "I have three thirty on my calendar, but I'll double-check."

Right as the piano piece was about to reach its climax, the volume plummeted. Felicity stood beside the now-silent speakers, her pink-and-lime-green kimono swishing around her knees as her blue eyes lifted from the workbench to the forest above. "My, doesn't that just take your breath away?"

Lincoln grunted his agreement.

An artist at heart, Felicity viewed everything as a miracle. A few more awestruck moments later and she finally spoke. "I have an anxious mother of the bride requesting an update about the arrangements."

"Tell her I'm almost finished here and should have everything loaded and ready to drive over to the hotel within the hour." He twisted another length of wire around a stem before climbing down from the stepladder.

She relayed as much before smiling and ending with enough overly profuse compliments to choke him. Hanging up, she returned her gentle smile to him and the flowers.

"How do you do that?"

"Do what, dear?" A quiet patience threaded her words. He'd have thought it impossible to appear so cheerful all the time had he not known the woman since before he could walk.

"How do you manage to turn every client into a friend? You and Mom always made it look so easy."

She twirled a single blue daisy that he'd set aside earlier between her fingertips, the creases of her forehead softening. "We all have our God-given talents. For some, it's hospitality, while others can make masterpieces out of nothing but fronds and florets."

She made him sound like some horticultural genius. "Mom was the real artist." Elaborate displays were one thing, but she'd had a gift for touching strangers' hearts with her bouquets. Lillian's Lilies had been a real-life Garden of Eden, the true inspiration behind his own flower business, Lily & Stone Floral Designs. If he could honor a sliver of her memory through his work, that would be enough.

"I miss her too. But she'd be so happy with what you've created." Felicity lifted the daisy and placed it in the palm of his scratched and calloused hand. A paltry remembrance of the woman who'd loved them. But a reminder, all the same.

The tiny brass bell dinged above the shop door, signaling an end to their conversation.

Felicity returned to her post inside the shop, taking her smiles and sunny disposition with her.

Lincoln reopened his music app and scrolled to a new playlist, then turned up the tropical lo-fi, the simple melody pushing back April's soggy cityscape as he got to work. He'd just swiped a pair of wire cutters from the bench when a pair of high heels stomped over the music.

He turned in time to see a smartly dressed woman barge in through the studio door with Felicity in hot pursuit.

"Mr. St. James. I need to speak to you immediately." She stopped short of the workbench, scrunching her upturned nose at the scattered mess.

"Mrs. Howard. How can I help you?"

Designer sunglasses perched like a crown on her short hair. Only snatches of sunlight had broken through the past week's drizzle, yet she was dressed like she was headed to a fancy garden party. "You can start by explaining what happened with the flowers for my daughter's engagement party. I specifically ordered apricot roses, not peach. Nora Carmichael already did peach last year for her daughter's wedding. I will not be accused of imitation. And don't get me started on those gaudy vases." She pronounced it *vahses*, casting a disdainful glare in Felicity's direction.

Lincoln felt as if he'd accidentally swallowed a stray spark, but he schooled his mouth into a straight line. "Yes, I remember the order. I had to call over a dozen vendors to find apricot roses in April." He'd done it without complaint, as the Howards were one of the most influential families in Detroit. But now he was beginning to think he should've listened to the rumors before taking her on as a client.

"Well? *Something* went wrong, didn't it?" The woman's burgundy lips dipped at the corners. "If you think I'm going to pay for these, you're mistaken. I expect you to rectify this by tomorrow and refund the money I've already wasted."

The spark grew to a small flame. He clenched his fist around the wire cutters to keep his anger under control despite the rushing in his ears. "Mrs. Howard, I'm sorry you're not satisfied with the arrangements we agreed on." Or had she already forgotten about their meeting last week? "But asking me to drop everything and redo a perfectly flawless order when I have other commitments is unreasonable." Not to mention it would cost him the biggest wedding of the season.

Her gasp was worthy of the stage at Fisher Theater, her mouth opening and closing like a kid playing with a snapdragon. "Of all the insolent, ill-mannered . . ." She huffed, as if remembering Felicity was still there. "Alistair was right. I should have gone with Nora's recommendation instead of taking a chance on some up-and-coming amateur. And don't think I won't be telling my friends to steer clear as well." Her gaze dropped to the table, nose scrunching as she sneered at the blue daisy beside the other exotic flowers. "Any florist who uses *weeds* isn't worth my time."

She turned on her heel and stormed out of the studio. The room fell silent except for the soft beat of the music and the jangle of the bell above the door.

Fire burned the back of his neck, his forceful inhale and exhale doing little to quench his temper.

This was why he didn't work directly with the clients. He couldn't be trusted not to lose his cool. Not only had Mrs. Howard walked away with a veritable steal of apricot roses, but she had the power and influence to make good on her threat.

"She still has the entire order," he said through slowly unclenching teeth.

"Let her keep it," said Felicity with a slight wave of her hand. "I doubt she'll be able to find another option with less than twenty-four hours. Besides, her daughter still deserves a happy day, no matter how difficult her mother might be."

"I sure hope the groom knows what he's getting himself in for," he said with a heavy sigh. An indentation of the wire cutter reddened his palm as he finally set the tool aside, looking up only to see Felicity's frown.

"Children aren't their parents." Her hand rested lightly against his arm. She meant it as reassurance, but all he could hear was his mother's voice making excuses for another of his father's drunken outbursts.

So maybe he wasn't his father, but he might as well be. After all, it was because of them that she was gone.

Two

KATE WAVED FROM THE DOCK AS DANI AND Liam's ferry disappeared on the horizon.

Despite the cool temperatures, blue skies and only a fistful of wispy clouds overhead gave Kate hope that the second half of April wouldn't bring any more surprise storms.

A northern breeze licked off Lake Huron and through the open knit of her sweater. She turned and wound past rental bikes and the sprinkle of tourists on her way to historic Main Street. Already, a line was beginning to form outside Good Day Coffee as doors popped open one by one down the row of quaint Victorian storefronts. Wrought-iron streetlamps flickered out one by one as the sun rose over the rooftops, causing the whitewashed walls and green-accented beams to glow like a forest in spring. If she'd had her camera with her, she'd have stopped to take a few pictures.

Hard to believe that only a year ago, over half of the stores had been all but vacant. The town had come a long way since then, with the hotel renovation underway, and the quiet street of preseason tourists hinted at more to come.

"God, what have I gotten myself into?" She released the prayer on a sigh. But then she thought of her sister's radiant smile as she'd waved goodbye from the ferry deck, and the doubts faded a little more.

Kate shuffled past Kelley's Bar & Grill, stomach gurgling at the lingering smell of last night's fried chicken, and ascended the few steps to the century-old Tourism Bureau building. Warm air welcomed her down the hall to Dani's office, labeled *Director of Tourism*.

Kate smiled. For once, her sister could finally be a tourist herself.

Her smile dimmed the moment she opened the door to overflowing bookcases, mismatched chairs, and a desk she could only assume was an antique. She couldn't quite confirm that due to the piles of paper, tabbed books, and empty coffee mugs scattered across its surface, only the corner of what she thought might be a corded phone peeking through the jumble. "Heaven help me."

"Knock, knock."

Kate turned, surprised but happy to see her twin brother standing in the doorway, a to-go mug from Good Day Coffee in each hand. Maybe God really had heard her prayers. "Wow, that was fast."

"Hmm?"

"Oh, nothing."

He gave her an odd look before handing over what smelled like an oat-milk latte with a dash of cinnamon. How had he known it was a coffee sort of day and not chai?

"I figured you could use some reinforcements this morning. I've got a little time before I open the bookstore and thought I'd offer my services..." His blue eyes widened at the mess behind her. No doubt he already wished he could rescind his offer but was too polite, as always, to say as much.

"Thanks, Ollie, but I've got it under control."

His raised eyebrows said otherwise, yet he didn't pry. But that was Oliver. She could always count on him to be there for her, even when that constituted a late-night call in tears to tell him she'd been ordered to take a month off work. Or supplying her with caffeine to make it through the day.

His crisp polo and chinos indicated he was on his way to work, even if the Dockers still reminded her of the lovable but quiet book nerd from their childhood. For twins, they had little in common aside from their brown wavy hair. Oliver ran his fingers through his, accentuating the six inches he had over her and some surprising muscles for a bookworm.

She sipped the cozy blend and closed her eyes in a moment of bliss. "Mmm, they make the best coffee."

"Good enough to move back here, I see."

"It's only temporary," she said a little too forcefully. April might be a slow enough month for weddings in the upper Midwest, but June would come soon enough. "Dani needed the help, and I have nothing but time. Plus, who else was going to watch Roma while the two of them are in Italy?"

"Mm-hmm." A man of many words, her brother. Which was just as well. She could read his microexpressions like one of his beloved books. The slight tilt of his mouth and the crease between his eyebrows said, *Just don't work yourself too hard, okay?*

"I'll be fine. I know Dani's office might look a bit of a mess at the moment."

His grunt said that wasn't an overstatement.

"It's a festival. How much different can it be from working a wedding?" she continued. "I guarantee I'll have this place whipped into shape by lunchtime."

"I just don't see why it has to be you. The doctor said to rest. Do you even know the definition of the word?" Oliver might be younger than her by a few minutes, but he'd always assumed the role of her protector when they were kids. Thirty-six years later, not much had changed.

"I'll be fine."

A frown, then, "Remember that panic attack you had before the state golf tournament? You said you were fine then as well."

"That's hardly the same." Yet the memory of that day still haunted her. "Besides, the exposure in *American Wanderer* will do far more to promote the business than staying in Petoskey would have. This couldn't have come at a better time."

"Right. A *vacation*." His sip of coffee lasted a whole four seconds, in which he said, *No shame in admitting you're in over your head.*

"I'm not in over my head."

"I never said you were."

"But you were thinking it."

As much as the movies loved to glamorize twins and their telepathic communication, it was a lot less fun in real life. Knowing a person's tics and tells only made it that much more difficult to skirt the truth.

"Should've gotten you decaf," he muttered under his breath. "If you change your mind, I'll be at the bookstore." He turned to leave, then paused outside the open door. "Oh, and Kate?"

She didn't need another lecture about taking on too much, or her borderline caffeine addiction, but she looked up anyway. Lines she hadn't noticed before creased around his eyes as he truly smiled at her for the first time that morning.

"Welcome home."

Home. The word slipped around her as quickly as his footsteps down the hall. Jonathon Island hadn't been her home in almost fifteen years—a lifetime, really. Yet the sentiment warmed her all the same.

"I love you too, oh brother of mine." He was too far away by now to hear it, but it didn't make it any less true.

By eleven thirty, she was placing the final scrap of paper into a new binder. The books were back on their shelves, and dirty dishes were clean and in the cabinets where they belonged, but no amount of sorting and reorganizing of Dani's sparse notes could sugarcoat the truth.

Her brother was right.

"Ugh, the florist. Why didn't I start there?" Even if the island's apple blossoms were the main showcase, there were additional displays and flower talks and classes to think about. Tourists loved that sort of thing. The devil may be in the details, but all the cider tastings and historic tours in the world wouldn't be enough to impress the readers of *American Wanderer* when they'd been promised flowers in abundance.

Just breathe. Dani had to have those notes here somewhere. A quick raid through the ancient rolltop desk revealed nothing but a drawer of pens and a bag of saltwater taffy from the Fudge Shop on the Corner. Kate popped a yellow one into her mouth and cringed when what she'd expected to be pineapple turned out to be banana flavored instead.

In need of a serious serotonin boost, she pulled out her phone and scrolled through videos of puppies and baby pandas. An arrangement of orange and white roses in front of a green velvet backdrop snagged her attention. She paused on the image by her favorite florist, Lily & Stone Floral Designs, and immediately tapped the heart beside it. Many floral influencers shared more about themselves than the flowers, but she appreciated the singular focus. The flowers should sell themselves.

A deafening ring made her almost drop her cell as she scrambled to silence the ancient landline on the desk.

"Jonathon Island Tourism Bureau, how may I help you?"

Despite the poor cell reception across the island, the female voice came through loud and clear. "Hi, I'm Mrs. Shepherd. I'm responding to a call we received last week about the Jonathon

Island Apple Blossom Festival. Is this the right number to inquire about the festival florist position?"

Talk about miraculous timing. Kate did a little dance in her seat—one Oliver would no doubt roll his eyes at—before resuming a more professional demeanor.

"Yes, this is the office in charge of the event. May I ask which vendor you're calling from?" The filing cabinet jangled as she slid open the top drawer and skimmed the file names. Where was that list?

The sound of a door closing echoed in the background of the call, followed by a long pause before Mrs. Shepherd continued. "That would be Lily & Stone Floral Designs, based out of Detroit."

Her hand froze over a folder of antique blueprints. "*The* Lily & Stone?" It was either the most unbelievable timing, or the woman on the other end of the line had seen her stalking the Instagram page and decided to give her a right scare.

"I realize this is a little last-minute, but is the position still available?"

Was it still available? More like a dream come true.

"Absolutely!" She winced and tried again. "We'd be thrilled to have you partner with us. The festival doesn't start for another couple of weeks, but you're more than welcome to arrive early and get acquainted with the island."

"I have a few things to work out on our end, but how does April the eighteenth sound?"

Saturday? That was . . . she checked the wall calendar . . . only three days from now. She'd asked God for help, but even this was moving a little fast. "Saturday sounds perfect." Kate scribbled the date onto her calendar, then dug into the pile of sticky notes on the desk. She thought she recalled reading a note somewhere about using an old outbuilding at the livery in town. If only she could remember which sticky note it was on . . .

"Wonderful. I'll put it into his calendar and book the ferry for then." The clack of a keyboard trickled over the receiver. "All set. He'll be on the noon crossing. Between you and me, he's not much of a conversationalist, but I'm sure you'll get along just fine."

"I look forward to meeting and working with him when he gets here." Kate returned the phone to its cradle, hardly able to believe her good luck. Feeling adventurous, she popped another taffy into her mouth—red this time—and savored the tangy watermelon candy.

Take that, Oliver!

Not even lunchtime, and she'd both organized Dani's office and jumbled notes *and* secured their frontrunner for the festival. This called for a celebration.

Purse in hand, she practically skipped out the office door and down the building's front steps in search of the bookstore so she could tell him just how wrong he'd been.

This had to be a joke. A cruel trick that only people who laughed at drunken college pranks might find funny. No one was laughing, least of all Lincoln.

"This is slander. She has no right posting something like this on her social media account." He glared at the screen as the *Like* count continued to skyrocket on Mrs. Howard's post. "It's already gotten over two thousand hits in the past forty-eight hours. She even tagged us with *#BadServiceAlert*. If the Bloomfest selection committee gets wind of this, I can kiss my chances at the showcase goodbye."

"Everyone has a right to their own opinion," Felicity defended from the kitchen. It was just like her not to take sides.

"Even if that opinion is a load of—"

"Language, please." She cut him off with a pointed look from behind a refrigerator door covered in funky magnets and a handful of photos of him growing up. She might not be his mom, but she sure acted like it at times. Down to insisting he come to family dinner with her and her husband every Wednesday night. Not that he minded hamburger casserole and homemade cheesecake for dessert. But he could do without the moral lessons every second.

"I was going to say *manure.*" However, a few other choice words came to mind.

"Sure hope you're not talking about the food." Felicity's husband Daryl appeared around the hallway connecting the condo's kitchen to the living-dining room that was decked out in potted plants and brightly colored artwork that screamed *Felicity.* Dressed in a blue button-down and slacks, the man still looked every inch the tax lawyer he'd been for forty years before retiring. His bunions must've been acting up again based on the way he plopped onto one of the high-backed barstools and proceeded to rub his argyle-stockinged foot.

"Lincoln's stressing about how Mrs. Howard's comments might affect the business. Orders have maybe been a little slower the past day or two, but these things eventually blow over."

Yeah, if half his clientele didn't cancel on him before then.

"Mind if I take a look?"

"Be my guest." Lincoln handed over the phone, knowing he would only get more angry if he kept looking at the post.

Daryl peered down his nose and squinted at the screen with a lawyerly *hmm.*

"What would my chances look like if I were to file a defamation suit against Mrs. Howard? Get her to retract her statement and the post."

The man grunted as he lowered the phone. "Might make more a mess of things than you'd want. However, I never did much in civil law. Now, if you had a question about navigating an audit, I could be of more use." Daryl went back to massaging his big toe. "It's usually best to settle disputes outside the courtroom and public eye. No use exposing all your dirty laundry to the world when it's only one grungy sock in question." He wiggled his toes for effect, chuckling at his own joke.

Lincoln wasn't in the mood. This wasn't some smelly piece of laundry. This was his livelihood. His mom's legacy. If he'd simply agreed to Mrs. Howard's terms earlier, none of it would be in jeopardy.

His phone buzzed on the counter, cutting his pity party short. One glance at the familiar number on the caller ID and his appetite disappeared.

"Are you going to answer it?" Felicity prompted as she shredded a head of romaine lettuce. There was no way she could know it was Nancy Kensington from the Great Lakes Floral Association, but a person didn't say no to Felicity Shepherd.

He downed another swig of root beer before answering. "This is Lincoln St. James of Lily & Stone Floral Designs."

"Mr. St. James, I'm glad I caught you. Do you have a moment to talk?"

Lincoln steeled himself. A woman asking a man to talk was akin to an officer telling a prison inmate to walk the green mile. Palms sweating, he wrapped his hands around the cool glass bottle. Maybe it was good news after all. Maybe they hadn't seen—

"I'll get right to the point, Mr. St. James. In our industry, reputation is everything, as I'm sure you're well aware. A couple of our members have expressed concerns, so the committee has decided not to proceed with your application to this year's Bloomfest."

"I see." He nodded numbly, then realized she couldn't see his contrition through the phone. Feeling the heat of Felicity's and Daryl's gazes, he dropped his to the flecks of gold and red within the granite countertop. "What can I do to convince you otherwise?"

The pause was so long he thought she'd hung up on him. But then . . .

"It's not normally done, but we'd be willing to extend a probationary period of thirty days. If you can prove your participation won't jeopardize the Bloomfest name, we'd reconsider."

How was he going to convince the committee when all his clients were pulling out?

"Thank you, Mrs. Kensington. I won't let you down." Why he promised her that, he wasn't sure, but it sounded like the right thing to say.

"So? What did they want?" Felicity asked when he hung up.

Lincoln repeated the ultimatum, ending with the thirty-day deadline.

"Sounds like they believe in you," Felicity said, clearly trying to soften the blow.

"That or they want to make themselves feel better by not turning me down outright."

"Think of it as a growing opportunity." Daryl was as much an optimist as his wife. "A chance to broaden your scope and step outside your comfort zone."

Hadn't he been doing that the past few years already? When his mom had died, he'd taken her small neighborhood shop and turned it into a sought-after floral design business. No more prom corsages or flowergrams. That might have been enough for him five years ago, but he wasn't the only one to consider in this equation.

The timer on the oven went off, the smell of tomatoes, garlic, and cheese filling the kitchen. "Have you thought any more about the email I forwarded to you last week?" Felicity asked as she set the dish on the stove to cool. "Participating in a community event like that would go a long way toward showing the kind of man you are."

"The Apple Blossom Festival?" He'd read the short article, more than a little impressed by the larger-than-life description. However, it seemed like a lot of inflated promises to him, and he wasn't an entertainer by any stretch of the imagination. "I keep away from the customers for a reason. Look what happened last time."

Her uncharacteristic silence had his neck tensing. "Felicity?"

She wrung her slender fingers around the towel hanging from the oven door before finally speaking. "What if I told you . . . I already accepted the invitation on your behalf?"

Lincoln's eyebrows shot up. "You didn't."

This time Felicity had gone too far. He didn't care how well-intentioned she was. She shouldn't have signed him up without at least discussing it with him first. "I can't just drop everything and leave at a moment's notice. I've already made commitments. There's still the Waverly wedding next week, and I should really clean out the storage room behind the studio. You've been on at me about it for months, and now I finally have the time to take care of it."

The tiniest shake of her head ground him to a halt mid-stride. "Mrs. Waverly called while you were out earlier today. She canceled, didn't she?"

He didn't need Felicity's apologetic nod to confirm it.

"Which means"—she jumped ahead of him—"your schedule is wide open. You were the one who said you needed something to impress the judges. So, impress them."

His focus bounced from her to her husband and then to the golden-brown casserole between them. It wasn't the *worst* plan, but . . .

"Daryl?" Felicity asked. "What do you think?"

Despite the blue-and-gold argyle sock propped against his knee, he looked every bit the seasoned lawyer. He was quiet for only a moment before his mouth twitched into a smile. "I think I married a very wise woman. Crafty, I'll give her that, but wise."

So that was it. Not that he had many other options. Slumping against the back of the seat, he swiped his pop and downed the remainder of its contents.

"So, where is it that I'm going again?" Please say somewhere tropical and warm. Anything other than this dreary spring they'd been having.

Felicity's smile wavered only a fraction before she aimed those sunny eyes at him. "The pride of northern Michigan. Jonathon Island."

The root beer churned in his stomach. It had been a popular tourist destination back in the day, but it also happened to be the childhood home of his ex-fiancée, Kate Sullivan. "Are you sure that's a good idea?" Five years might be a long time, but surely not enough for her to forget his leaving her at the altar for reasons he couldn't bring himself to admit to.

Felicity's face softened. No doubt she could read every reservation bubbling inside of him, despite his clamped jaw. "If you're worried about running into Kate, you should know she's been living in Petoskey the past few years."

"I wasn't worried." *Liar.* But after nearly losing his reputation and business all in a few days, his personal pride was the last thing he had.

Felicity gave him the same look his mom had always worn whenever she knew he was being stubborn. "Good. Then there shouldn't be a problem, right?"

There was no use arguing with her. He'd only embarrass himself further and end up giving in eventually anyway. That didn't mean he had to like her underhanded tactics, but she needed this to work as much as he did. And as she'd said, Kate was in Petoskey, hours away from where he'd be going. And seeing as she'd never taken him to visit the island when they were together, there was no reason to think she'd be there now.

"Fine, you win." It was difficult keeping his frown in place when her smile grew so large, even if she was right about everything.

"So, what time does my ferry leave?"

Three

H E'D EXPECTED A CHILLY WELCOME, BUT THE frigid Canadian winds licking off Lake Huron were something else entirely.

With temperatures barely hovering above forty, Lincoln slipped right past the open deck of the ferry to the more sheltered seats inside with the other passengers. A middle-aged man with a padded rod case sticking out of his bag took the seat across the aisle from him, behind a group of young adults decked out with trekking poles and backpacking gear. All dressed in down jackets and heavy boots, it appeared everyone had received the memo to pack winter clothes except for him.

"Welcome aboard, ladies and gentlemen," the captain's voice crackled over the ancient intercom. "It's a balmy forty-two degrees outside on this lovely Saturday. Perfect time to visit Jonathon Island before the busy season picks up."

Balmy, indeed.

As they began to pull away from the dock, the speakers crackled back to life. "In a few moments, a member of the crew will come around with a visitor's guide. It's a little publication put out by the island's historical state park commission with detailed maps that show her bicycle routes, walking trails, and other noteworthy sites that are hidden throughout the island."

A minute later, a guy in a navy hat and fleece vest made his way down the rows, a stack of papers beneath his arm. Lincoln took one look at the yellowed trifold pamphlet and waved the crew member on. He was here for work, not a vacation. No matter how hard the captain was working to entertain his guests.

"Well, folks, there she is." As if on cue, they turned, and the massive green-and-white bridge came into view. "Opened to traffic in 1957, it's just shy of five miles long, connecting Michigan's upper and lower peninsulas. It's also the dividing line between Lake Michigan and Lake Huron. We are currently sailing on Lake Michigan, but once we cross back underneath the bridge heading toward the island, we'll re-enter Lake Huron."

Lincoln popped in a pair of earbuds and closed his eyes as the gentle beat pulsed to the rhythm of the waves. He tried not to fixate on the bounce of the boat, focusing instead on the past two days of research. As far as he'd found, this was Jonathon Island's first Apple Blossom Festival in years, which provided him very little to go off in putting together design ideas. What exactly did festival florists do? He'd asked around, but the other business owners knew about as much as he. Not a great start if he hoped to impress the journalist from *American Wanderer* who was expected to cover the event.

The one upside to this arrangement.

Something bumped his shoulder, and he opened his eyes to a nearly empty cabin. They were there already? The man with the rod case gave him a ruddy-faced smile, as if waiting for Lincoln to follow him out onto the deck with the others.

One step off the platform felt like he'd passed through the wardrobe only to stumble upon a dollhouse village rather than wintry Narnia, but it was no less a contrast to Detroit's modern cityscape. He stared at a horse-drawn carriage as it lumbered down Main Street, the clip-clop of the horses' hooves the echo of a bygone era.

And not an apple blossom in sight on the bare trees.

"It sure takes your breath away," said the older fisherman. He seemed amused at Lincoln's first impression as he brushed a hand over his thinning gray hair, doing little to tame it against the breeze. Something about the man gave the impression of a seventy-year-old Boy Scout. "Name's Dwight. Been coming here for nearly twenty years, but it still gets me every time." He held out a beefy hand that Lincoln hesitated only a moment to accept.

"The fishing must be really good to keep you coming back every year. Trout?"

"That and some carp. But I come mainly for the whitefish. Grill it up with a little butter and lemon and you've got yourself a feast to remember." He patted a protruding stomach that indicated he knew what he was talking about. "You staying at the Island House Inn," the man stated more than asked, eyeing Lincoln's duffel bag. "It's a bit of a trek up the hill. Mind if I join you?"

"Not at all."

Dwight proceeded to give Lincoln an unofficial tour of the island as they walked. Lincoln listened with mild amusement as the man pointed out the fudge shop, going on about something called the "fudge wars" before pivoting mid-sentence to tell him about the old hotel and that it was a shame it had burned all those years ago. "They're rebuilding it, I hear. Just hope they do her justice."

Not that Lincoln didn't appreciate the attention to detail, but his morning coffee was beginning to wear off, along with his patience for small talk. Surely this town had a decent café. His gaze wandered up the street when Dwight stopped to comment on a new fish and chips place and whether or not they might have any good fishing-hole recommendations.

"Hey, Dwight, why don't I meet you at the inn?" With any luck, Lincoln could refuel and ask for directions to the tourism office in one go.

"I'm sorry. My wife always warned me I get a bit long-winded whenever I'm excited. Say no more. I'll leave you to discover for yourself what makes this place so special." With that, he turned and continued down the street, only making it as far as the fish and chips shop before stopping to talk with someone else.

Lincoln shook his head. He'd never understood the need for constant chatter. Give him a quiet room and a table full of flowers any day.

He waited for an older couple to pass before stepping from the sidewalk in the direction of the coffee shop. A woman loaded down with binders and what appeared to be rolls of paper was struggling to talk on the phone and walk at the same time, which was probably why she didn't hear the tiny bell of the oncoming carriage.

"Hey, watch out!" Lincoln raised his voice over the street noise, but nothing. Without thinking, he set down his bags and hurried forward.

She yelped as he grabbed her by the elbow, spilling her coffee down both their shirts as the carriage lumbered past. The papers scattered to the muddy street as she fell against him. Hooves skidded as the driver pulled back on the reins and swerved, crumpling a few of the paper rolls but thankfully missing the two of them entirely.

"My schedule!" She immediately dropped his arm and retrieved a rather grungy-looking page from the gutter.

"Better that than a leg." He swiped at the brown stain dripping down his sweater, only smearing it more. Less than five minutes here, and he was already caught in the middle of a new mess. But at least the woman was unharmed, thanks to him.

"I just finished organizing the layout, and now it's ruined."

When she turned to face him, it was her large brown eyes that struck him first. The same eyes that widened in recognition a second after they locked with his.

The street noises blurred to a static hum, muddling his senses like one giant down pillow over his head.

Kate Sullivan as he lived and breathed.

Her earlier bluster disappeared. "Lincoln? How? Why . . . ?"

It all came flooding back. The whirlwind romance. Plans for a big, fancy wedding. That look of confused betrayal when he'd called it off after fighting with his dad.

"I'm here for the flower festival. What are *you* doing here?" He didn't mean to bark at her, but he was too busy trying to blink away the apparition to censor his tongue. The commotion had drawn a few curious stares, and Lincoln tried to rein in his galloping heartbeat before he did anything to make matters worse.

Of all the coffee shops in all the world . . .

"You two know each other?" asked Dwight, who'd suddenly reappeared at Lincoln's side. He must've heard the noise and doubled back to investigate. He looked ready to launch into a recitation about the virtues of equine travel, while Kate stood gaping at the two of them like a fish caught on a hook.

He could only imagine what was going through that head of hers.

"Wait, *you're* Lily & Stone Floral Designs?" she squeaked out. Her face turned the color of a grey ghost agapanthus, and for the second time that day, Lincoln caught her in his arms.

Kate blinked as something strong and warm supported her back. She had the oddest sensation of being carried on a cloud.

"Should we call the doctor?" said a nearby voice.

"I think it was only shock. It looks like she's already coming around."

Why were her pants wet? Oh, right. She'd been on her way to the island art center to discuss doing a pop-up art market in the park when someone had nearly tackled her . . . Her eyes flashed open to a handful of faces peering down at her, along with the one she'd hoped to never see again.

"See, right as rain," said an older gentleman she didn't recognize.

Despite the reassurances, Lincoln's drawn face stared back at her. A few more wrinkles than before, and hair wild and curling above his shoulders, but she'd never forget those stormy eyes. The hard line of his brow bunched as she registered that his arms were still wrapped around her. Heat flushed through her, and in an instant, she was pushing away from him and his annoyingly concerned expression.

"Kate, are you all right?" Oliver's voice preceded him through the dwindling crowd as she scrambled to her feet. He was breathing heavily, as if he'd run all the way from the bookstore in his Dockers—*bless him*. She gave him a wobbly smile meant to say, *I'm fine, see?* But instead of relaxing, his face darkened the moment his gaze landed on Lincoln beside her. "What are *you* doing here?"

One of Kate's papers crinkled in Lincoln's fist. He stood to his full height, drawing even with Oliver, who was standing on the raised sidewalk with his own jaw set. "I was only trying to help."

"Haven't you done enough already?"

Who was this person, and what had he done with her quiet, noncombative brother?

Normally, she'd have appreciated him standing up for her, but all she wanted was to disappear inside a dark cave and never show her face again. At least, not until Lincoln left the island. Throw in a desk, a few lamps and rugs to fend off the damp, and a Wi-Fi router so she could work remotely, and she'd have a perfectly suitable office safe from unwanted intruders.

Maybe she was a troll after all. Why else would Lincoln have tucked tail and run the night before their supposed-to-be wedding?

She ignored Oliver's outstretched hand, along with the unspoken questions zinging off him. "I might've had a bit too much caffeine this morning. No more lattes for me today." Her chuckle felt as lifeless as the scattered papers currently lying in the road. Three days of work literally in the gutter. At least her heart rate was finally beginning to slow back down.

"You weren't supposed to be here until this afternoon." She brushed a hand over her sweater as she tried to switch to a more professional tone, then remembered the fresh mud stains.

Oliver's gaze swung from the man to Kate, eyes growing wide. "You mean you *knew* he was going to be here?"

Where was that cave when one needed it? "I, uh . . . think I sort of . . . invited him?"

"You what?" The question echoed between the two men.

Lincoln moved back a step, hand running through his overgrown hair. The dark waves fell nearly to his shoulders, making him look more like a pirate than a florist. "Wait a minute. Felicity said the island's Tourism Bureau reached out to her regarding the position in the first place, a Dani—"

"Sullivan. Yes, that's my sister." Maybe it was the mix of caffeine and adrenaline coursing through her, but she could hardly contain the shiver in her voice when his blue eyes locked with hers. Her face grew warm. "I'm filling in for her while she's on her honeymoon."

Oh, why had she been so insistent on taking Dani's place? *Because you love your sister and want to make her happy, that's why. That, and for the interview.*

"Kate . . ." Her name stretched on Oliver's long exhale.

"I'm sure we can find a way to make this work." They had to. Dani was counting on her to do so. Not that she didn't have a few choice words for her sister at the moment, but now was neither the time nor place.

She pasted on a smile. "The Apple Blossom Festival is still in need of a capable florist. Lily & Stone Floral Designs will bring a level of sophistication to the event, a fact which I'm sure will go a long way toward impressing *American Wanderer*." A fact her business was also counting on.

Oliver didn't seem to share in her thinking, but at least he remained silent.

Coming through for Dani and the town was of far more importance than her feelings about Lincoln. Old or otherwise.

"Maybe coming here was a bad idea." Lincoln looked like a caged animal ready to flee.

It wasn't like he didn't have the experience.

She mentally chastised herself for the ungracious thought. Five years was a long time. They could act like decent, civilized adults. "If you're worried about us getting in each other's way, don't. I have a to-do list that's a mile long, and I'm sure you'll be busy wowing tourists with show-stopping displays at your studio at the end of the street." Never mind that his "studio" was currently blanketed with dust and cobwebs. She'd meant to clean out the old tack room earlier but had lost track of time with this morning's paperwork.

Which was maybe just as well.

Lincoln only stared at her.

She had the sudden urge to hide, but kept her head up and shoulders back. Not so severe that she'd look stubborn, but enough to make him understand this was a business arrangement and nothing more.

Oliver glanced at his watch and released a forceful sigh. "I'd better get back to the bookstore while it's still standing. I've already been gone too long." Yet his Dockers remained glued to the spot.

"Don't want to keep your customers waiting. I'll be fine," she added. Too forceful a smile and he'd know she was faking it. "I can handle showing him to the Quinns' property on my own."

"Do you mean the livery?" The older gentleman with the kind eyes reemerged, unapologetically keen to join their conversation. Had he been there the whole time? "I know the place," he said with a general wave up the street. "The young man and I were already headed toward the inn. It'll just be a short stop along the way. Isn't that right?" He beamed a smile first at Kate, then Lincoln, who only frowned in response.

Had they traveled here together? The two couldn't be more different from one another. The older gentleman was shorter and soft around the edges, with wrinkles that said he laughed a lot and often, while Lincoln's stony expression and chiseled shoulders could have been etched from the island's limestone.

Oliver's microshrug pumped next to her, and like a coward, she took the easy way out.

"That's a wonderful idea, Mr. . . ."

"Driscoll, but you can call me Dwight."

The name made her think of the character from *The Office*, but that was where the comparison ended.

She wasn't throwing off her responsibilities if someone else offered to help. Besides, Lincoln would want time to settle in before they dove into specifics for the festival. And God knew she needed all the time she could get to wrap her brain around what had just happened.

Lincoln smoothed the crumpled page against his thigh before handing it back to her. "Sorry, again, about the mess." He looked at his feet, then behind him as if searching for an invisible bag.

"Right here." Dwight lifted a black duffel and handed it to Lincoln.

"Thanks."

"Sure. Anything for my new friend."

Lincoln seemed to cringe at his kindness. Odd. The man she

remembered from five years ago might've been a mystery in many ways, but never standoffish. *What happened to you after that night, Lincoln?* Not that she cared. Not really. If he hadn't opened up to her back then, he sure wouldn't now.

"Shall we?" Dwight turned, narrowly missing Lincoln with the padded rod case protruding from his bag.

Without so much as a backward glance, the two men slipped across the street and up the hill.

"Want to tell me what that was all about?" Oliver still hadn't moved from the sidewalk except to pick up a few of her lost papers. He kept stealing glances up the street, either making sure Lincoln made it to the stables or that he didn't double back. She wasn't sure.

"Not really?" She was still struggling to make sense of it all herself, including why she hadn't sent the man packing the moment she realized who he was.

From the tense set of his jaw, he looked like he wanted to press further, but he didn't. "Well, if you want to talk about it . . ."

"I'll know where to find you." Her shoulders relaxed. She snatched up page three of the schedule she'd spent all morning on and added it to Oliver's soggy pile before the breeze could carry it away. "I can handle the rest if you need to get back to the store."

"You sure?"

"Positive."

She swallowed down the desire to ask him to stay. While she appreciated the help, his time was far better spent pursuing his own dreams than picking up the pieces of hers. She'd managed the last five years on her own. What were a few more weeks here on the island?

Four

AT LEAST THE PLACE HAD RUNNING WATER. Lincoln flipped the hot-water valve, stanching the murky flow. A few minutes ought to clean out the ancient pipes, so long as the brown color was from buildup and not rust. But he'd deal with that later.

The rest of the workspace?

He sighed once again at the derelict storehouse. At least, that's what it had become in the last hundred years, based on the assortment of tack gear, yard equipment, and machinery in varying stages of disrepair. The enameled iron stove in the corner thankfully appeared to be in decent condition, but probably needed a good clean before he dared fire it up.

If he'd wanted an impossible project, he could've just as easily stayed home to deal with the Mrs. Howard fallout rather than driving four hours and taking a fifteen-minute ferry trip back in time.

"It's got character," Dwight had said after Terry Quinn, the owner of the livery, had shown them to the northernmost outpost of the property. Far enough away from the horse stables that the noise wouldn't be distracting, but surrounded by a cluster of wild apple trees that made it feel like the middle of nowhere. "All it needs is a little elbow grease. Kids nowadays don't know what it means to do hard work. God gave us thumbs to work this earth, not sit around and play video games all day."

Tugging on a pair of gloves from his bag, Lincoln knelt beside a cracked buggy wheel and rolled it—cobwebs and all—through the open door to the growing pile out back. The junk alone would take him at least a couple of days to clean out if he had any hopes of transforming this into a respectable studio. He picked up one of the blacksmiths' hammers left on the workbench, only for a startled mouse to cause him to drop it on his big toe.

"For the love of—" He bit back a couple of words Felicity would surely frown upon as the pain pulsed through his foot. A fresh scuff marred the dried mud already caked to the leather upper of his shoe, the rounded edge like a smile laughing up at him.

First the incident in town and now this?

Kate had seemed just as surprised as him, but maybe this was some complicated plot to get back at him after all these years. Flower festival with no flowers, ramshackle workspace . . . He deserved that and more after what he'd put her through, calling off their wedding as he had. But hadn't he already suffered enough?

St. Jameses aren't quitters. His dad's unwelcome voice collided with his moment of self-pity. What did the man know about it anyway? He'd been the one to walk out on Lincoln and his mom, after all.

"I'm not my dad. I'm *not* my dad."

Saying the words out loud did little to ease the knot in his gut, but at least it broke the awful quiet. *God, I'm really trying to be a better man. But You're not making it easy on me.* First with the problems at the shop, and now this.

He stripped off the gloves, pulled out his phone, and began to type out a list of supplies. If he was going to make this work, he'd need trash bags and plastic drop cloths to start, extension cords plus more lighting to make up for the single window, Murphy Oil Soap for the wood floors, and at least one roll of chicken wire.

He jotted down a couple more items to take care of the pest problems and then started off toward town. Surely this place had a decent hardware store.

A row of apple trees lined Blueberry Boulevard, skeletal arms adorned with a few sprigs of green. It would only be a matter of weeks before they leafed out in full, dripping with delicate pink-and-white blossoms. He could only imagine the harsh winters these trees had to endure, and hoped the colder temperatures didn't push back their peak bloom until after the festival.

Up ahead, the road forked in a V with Marina Way and Main Street. He took the second, and immediately, the historic town rose before him in all its painted glory. At the corner, a bookstore stood next to a local market, followed by a boutique and nail salon on the left, a couple souvenir shops, an Island Outfitters, and a pizzeria. His stomach grumbled in protest over the protein bar he'd eaten an hour ago, and he made a mental note to check their menu later. It wouldn't be the Detroit-style squares with the cheese-encrusted corners that he liked from Mario's back home, but pizza was pizza.

Down the street, a woman with wavy brown hair and slim shoulders disappeared inside another shop. Kate? She didn't look up from her phone, but he was almost certain her gaze flicked toward him for a fraction of a second.

He stood on the corner, torn between wanting to go after her and giving her space. The ding of a bell tore his attention from the closed shop door and to a white two-story Victorian in front of him. A man was walking down the steps beneath a sign reading *Smith's Hardware*.

"Bingo."

Wheelbarrows and stacks of potting soil rimmed the covered wraparound porch as if to say spring was already here. He took the wooden steps two at a time, a tiny brass bell above the door announcing his arrival as he stepped inside.

A man at the front counter looked up from behind a newspaper before Lincoln could slip unnoticed down the first aisle. "Good afternoon. Anything I can help you with?"

"Thanks, but I just came in for a few basic supplies. I'm sure I can find my way around."

The man's shrug said *suit yourself* before he returned to his paper.

Lincoln swiped a cart from the front and made quick work of the list. A box of disinfecting wipes went in, along with black duct tape, a couple mouse traps, and a box of fireplace matches for the stove.

He brushed past a clothing rack on his way to the counter, then doubled back. No use sporting a stained sweater all day long. The navy crew neck with *JONATHON ISLAND* in white block letters across the front went into the cart with the rest of the items.

"Will that be all?" the man asked as he rang up Lincoln's haul.

"Not unless you have a way of scaring off spiders." Indiana Jones was afraid of snakes, and no one questioned his manhood. He knew creepy crawlies were mostly harmless, but he had absolutely no desire to have one skitter into his glove when he wasn't looking.

"You could always try a bug bomb." Having rung up the sweater, the man reached over the side of the counter and plopped what looked like a can of spray paint in front of Lincoln.

Lincoln frowned at the tiny can. "You sure that'll be enough?" The outbuilding might not be large by normal standards, but it wasn't a sock drawer either.

"Yeah no, for sure." His head bobbed in agreement. "Just make sure to point the can away from you when you start, and then leave it for a couple of hours. Been using them for over twenty years myself and never had a problem."

Sounded easy enough.

"Great. I'll take two."

The man bagged the items and loaded Lincoln down for his trip back up the hill.

Once inside, he dragged a chair to the center of the room and placed the can on top. Even with the extra lighting, he had to squint to read the tiny print on the label. "'Open all cabinets and doors inside the area to be fumigated.'" He crossed to the built-in sink, hinges squeaking as he followed the instructions.

"'Remove all food items and dishes before proceeding.'" Check. Any food still in this place was already beyond saving. "'Lastly, make sure to close all windows and exterior doors to ensure a thorough clean.'"

Now it was time to get to the good stuff. Heeding the man's advice, he tilted the sprayer away from his face and clicked it open, then did the same with the second can. Two streams of high-powered mist shot toward the ceiling. Even with the face mask, he held his breath as he backed toward the open door and clicked it shut behind him.

Now to wait for two hours.

Plenty of time to check into his room and switch into more work-appropriate clothes. Maybe even order a pizza.

He set a timer on his phone and, grabbing his bag, went in search of the Island House Inn.

Five years she'd had to get over him. *Five years.* So why did every thought seem to yank her right back to Lincoln?

Kate waited behind a display of antique enamelware and hand-painted ceramic lighthouses until she saw Lincoln exit Smith's Hardware. This was silly. She was a grown woman in her thirties.

She definitely shouldn't be hiding inside Miller Antiques like some heartbroken teenager.

He paused and looked down the street in her direction, and she ducked behind a well-placed Tiffany lamp, holding on to her last scrap of pride.

Fine, so maybe that had fallen to the street this morning with everything else, but what would she even say to him? *Hi, I know it's been half a decade, but apparently I'm still not over you and would prefer it if you'd leave on the next ferry.*

"Hello, earth to Kate." Her brother Zachary's voice cut through the phone's speakers, and she lifted the screen to see a close-up of him in his chef's uniform in front of a brick wall.

"Sorry about that. Where were we?"

Dark brows slanted over his green eyes as if she'd asked whether to use sugar in a cake. "The festival menu? I only have a few minutes before I need to be back in the kitchen."

"Right, sorry about that." Another look through the window confirmed that Lincoln was gone. Placing the festival binder on a nearby table, she flipped to the correct page and rattled off the list of possible ideas for the gala.

"Skip anything that's too trendy or fussy," he said once she'd finished. "This is Jonathon Island we're talking about, not the Met Gala. People don't really like salmon mousse as much as they say they do."

"Nothing overly fancy. Okay, got it." She scribbled the note at the bottom. "And what about for the dessert?"

"For an apple blossom festival? You gotta go with apple-pie bars."

"With vanilla ice cream?"

"Better yet, Lily's cinnamon ice cream. But whichever you choose, make sure to hold off on serving it so it doesn't melt." He turned to talk to someone else for a second, showing off his perpetual five-o'clock shadow until he was back. "Gotta go. The dinner rush is starting to pick up. Let me know how it turns out."

"Thanks again. You're a culinary genius."

She tucked the phone back into her purse, then placed the binder under one arm and dashed the rest of the way down the street, to the last building on the left.

Martha's on Main was as much an island staple as the Grand Sullivan Hotel. Little had changed from the white clapboard siding to the row of stately windows out front. Bikes leaned against the building's exterior, where people stood waiting for their tables.

Kate checked her phone and cringed at the time. Had it not been for the slight detour, she'd have gotten there early as planned and not at the beginning of the three o'clock happy-hour rush.

"Table for one?" The hostess hardly looked up from the guest check-in sheet in front of her.

Kate tried not to flinch at the dismissive tone. She could be meeting up with friends for all the girl knew. Not that she was, but that was beside the point.

"Actually, I'm here to talk with Martha Kelley about the festival. Dani, my sister, left a note about following up on doing the catering for the gala." It might be the final event of the festival, but it was important that it went well.

Kate followed the girl's directions past the bar and the sign that read *Check your guns, politics, and religion at the door* to where a squat woman with gray-streaked hair stood chatting at the far table.

Martha looked up mid-sentence and beamed. "Kate Sullivan! I thought that was you I saw talking with your uncle yesterday. But why are you still here? The wedding was over a week ago. Unless . . ." Forgetting the couple she'd been talking with, she grabbed Kate's hand and tugged her toward the bar, a satisfied grin overtaking her soft face. "I knew it. I told Elise it was only a matter of time."

"A matter of time before what?"

"Before you decided to move back to the island." Her eyes glittered almost as much as her gold earrings. "And who was the young man I saw you with earlier this morning? Did you go and get married without telling me?"

Kate gulped. The last thing she needed was Martha spreading rumors. "No, it's just me. I'm actually stepping in for Dani while she's away. That's why I'm here. Do you have a moment to go over some details for the Apple Blossom Festival?"

Martha's face fell at the less-than-juicy news. "Oh, I'd just thought . . ." She waved a hand as if to shoo away a fly. "Never mind. You were saying something about the festival?"

Remember what you rehearsed. Kate opened the binder and pulled out one of Dani's flyers—she'd somehow found an old photo of one of the black-tie events held at the Grand Sullivan Hotel before part of it had burned down—then handed it over.

Eyebrows peaked in interest, Martha inspected the flyer. She scrunched her mouth. "You sure the Grand will be ready in time?" She sounded none too certain. "There've been an awful lot of crews up there recently, working on the repairs and renovation."

"The ballroom was unharmed in the fire, so there's no need to worry." Kate had been skeptical herself until her Uncle Seb—who was also the town mayor—had taken her on a tour of the place the other day. There were a lot of workers, as Martha had pointed out, which meant they were ahead of schedule.

"I know Dani was insistent on holding the event there when she talked with me last month."

Kate braced herself for whatever unsolicited advice Martha was about to dole out.

"That husband of hers might have won over this town with his designs, but that doesn't make him a miracle worker. Even if the ballroom is in decent shape, nobody wants to walk through a construction site in high heels and fancy dresses to get there."

"Yes, but Dani and Liam had their wedding reception in the Rose Room only a couple of weeks ago, and I didn't hear any complaints." Aside from her mom when she'd cornered Dani in the women's bathroom after the cake cutting. Apparently she had sat their parents next to each other at the same table, which, according to their mom, was comparable to the end of the world.

"Hmm. I suppose you make a valid point." Martha wrinkled her nose but refrained from making any more objections.

For the next ten minutes, they discussed a possible menu, settling on whitefish beurre blanc as the main and apple-pie bars for dessert, until a crash of dishes in the kitchen had Martha begging her apologies. "That's the third time this week," she huffed in lightly veiled distress. "Are you sure I can't convince you to come work for me again while you're here? Only a day or two per week—just long enough to whip the summer crew into shape."

"Thanks for the offer, but I'm afraid this is going to keep me pretty busy." Kate tapped the binder filled with her sister's dreams for the island.

"Oh, I suppose you're right. But it never hurts to ask." After disappearing into the kitchen for a few minutes, she sent Kate away with a to-go bag of her famous meatloaf sliders—and a square of bumpy cake, based on the decadent chocolatey aroma tickling her nose.

Living above a pizza parlor had its advantages, but three nights in a row of the stuff was her limit.

Kate thanked Martha for the generous offer and slipped outside past the growing crowd.

It was only a couple blocks' walk back to Dani's old apartment. She dodged a bicycle tour group, picking up her pace outside Good Day Coffee until she was near the other end of the street, where Lincoln had disappeared earlier. Island Pizzeria and her home were immediately to her right, but guilt tugged beneath her ribcage in the direction of the livery.

"You're not that same girl anymore."

The man may have broken her heart, but that didn't mean she should give him the cold shoulder forever. Nor could she dump their celebrity florist in a subpar workspace without at least offering to help. If her sister wasn't all the way in Italy right now, she'd call her up on the phone and ask what she'd been thinking by inviting her ex-fiancé to showcase in the festival.

"It's for the town. This is what Dani would want." Never mind the way her legs turned to jelly with each step up the hill.

Silence greeted her as she slipped beneath the canopy of trees surrounding the property.

"Hello? Anybody here?" Tiptoeing over the crunchy gravel, she wound her way through the series of outbuildings until a sound like cannon fire followed by shattering glass had her ducking for cover. "What in the world?"

What looked like smoke rose from the building in front of her through the trees, filling the air with a distinctive chemical odor. "Lincoln?" Her voice wavered as she picked up her feet and ran, a siren starting up in the distance. "Lincoln, are you there?"

The smoke stung her eyes, and she wiped the moisture away with the back of her sleeve. But since when did smoke smell like cleaning solution? She was about to burst through the open door when a hulking shadow cut her off, wheezing like the big bad wolf suffering from hay fever.

She ground to a halt, relief at seeing him unharmed mixed with an unexpected anger she could no longer keep shoved down.

"Leaving me at the altar wasn't enough? You have to blow up my hometown as well?" she yelled, flinging her arm at the building hard enough to make her wince.

His head jerked toward her, the blue of his eyes even more striking contrasted with the red rings around them. He froze momentarily, then swiveled his head as if he didn't know where to land his gaze. "I had it perfectly under control."

"Clearly."

"The stove must've had a pilot light or something that ignited with the bug bombs." He looked a little lost as he took in the shattered window and dissipating cloud.

"Bombs? As in plural?" Her mouth dropped open. "You really are trying to blow up the island."

"Only the eight-legged critters camped inside." He grabbed one of the larger pieces of intact glass and carried it to the growing pile outside.

Despite her better judgment, she joined in. She might be angry with Lincoln, but that didn't mean she was going to leave the Quinns' property a mess either.

Working together, they managed to sweep up the rest of the broken window in a matter of minutes along with the worst of Kate's fuming frustrations. Not that she wasn't still livid with Lincoln—she was—but it was difficult not to appreciate his thoughtfulness when he handed her an extra dust mask to stave off at least some of the chemical fog still drifting through the open door.

"You do realize there are less toxic ways of cleaning a room, don't you?" She inspected the rest of the building's perimeter and, so far, it appeared the window had taken the brunt of the hit. "What possessed you to risk contaminating the island's entire ecosystem instead of using a fly swatter like a normal human being?"

Once the fog cleared enough that they could finally see inside, he ducked back in for the two empty cans and chucked them into a garbage bag. His back was to her, but she didn't miss the stiffness in his shoulders as he tied the bag onto the door handle.

"Spiders."

Kate just stared at him. And that's when it started. The twitch in her diaphragm moved up her throat until she could no longer hold back the giggle that shot out.

Lincoln's face darkened, but she couldn't help it. She'd all but forgotten about his arachnophobia. She used to tease him about a big guy like himself being afraid of such tiny creatures. However, the old bug traps he used to place around his mom's flower shop were nothing compared to this.

"I'm sorry, I shouldn't be laughing." She wiped a tear from the corner of her eye even as a weight seemed to lift from her. "It's just, you have to admit this has been quite the reunion today."

"You can say that again." He didn't join in, but neither did his frown seem as set in stone as it had before.

Kate knew how to handle the explosive Lincoln who spoke whatever was on his mind, but she didn't know what to do with this pensive version. She'd played their reunion out a hundred times over the years—what she would say to him, all the questions left unanswered. But now that her chance was here, she couldn't seem to think straight.

Someone cleared their throat behind them, and Kate spun to where a man in a fireman's jacket stood frowning at them and the building.

"Not to interrupt, but someone called about a fire at the Quinn property?" His gaze shot between the two of them like they were a couple of teenage troublemakers.

She'd never even participated in Senior Ditch Day, let alone destruction of private property. But then again, the teenage version of Kate hadn't known Lincoln St. James. Somehow, things just seemed to happen around him, and when they did, she was caught right in the crossfire.

Five

KATE COULD NO LONGER BLAME THE FUMES from Saturday's explosion for why she was currently standing on Lincoln's doorstep. A paper coffee cup in each hand, she pushed open the door with her shoulder and stepped inside. Only a tinge of the chemical smell remained two days later. "Thought you might need a caffeine boost." She raised her voice over the music as she squinted against the bright flame of a torch in the far corner.

Lincoln looked up from where he was welding the hinges back together on the potbellied stove and cut the gas. He looked like Han Solo dressed as a low-budget stormtrooper with that face shield of his—even more so when he raised the visor to his tight-lipped expression. He'd rolled his sleeves above his elbows, revealing muscular forearms that could take Darth Vader any day. The same arms which had held her close more times than she could count.

You're supposed to be working *together, not casting the next Star Wars movie.*

"You bring coffee to all your festival vendors?" He turned down the volume on a portable speaker.

"Only the ones prone to pyromania," she teased.

"So you're my babysitter now?"

"Got to make sure the town is still standing by the end of the month." She raised an eyebrow at the torch in his hand. At least he was using his powers to fix something this time. "You sure come prepared."

"This?" He set aside the torch and tossed his heavy leather gloves on the workbench. "I went back to the hardware store this morning for some steel epoxy. Russell, the owner, and I got to talking, and before I knew it, he was lending me his welding kit."

"You seem surprised." She handed him one of the coffees, trying not to flinch at the brush of his fingers against hers.

"That's because I was. Back in Detroit, I'd be lucky to get a nod from the man behind the counter if money wasn't involved, much less his personal tool kit." He took a tentative sip and almost smiled. "Black with two sugars. You remembered."

"Like I could forget the most boring drink in the history of the world." The cinnamon notes of her oat-milk latte clashed with the pungent odors inside the workshop as she raised her own cup to her lips.

Lincoln chuckled, though his eyes held a seriousness she wasn't sure how to interpret. "As much as I appreciate the gesture, you don't have to keep checking in on me."

"It's called being neighborly," she said a little too brightly, and cringed. *Remember why you came here in the first place, Kate.* The festival folder weighed heavy inside her bag, tugging her back to reality. "A meeting."

"Huh?" His brows pitched downward.

At least try to sound like a somewhat coherent adult, Kate. Gripping the strap of her bag for support, she took another breath and tried again. "We should set up a time to meet so I can walk you through the festival."

"Oh, right." Now he was the one who appeared lost for words.

At least they had that in common.

She'd normally suggest Good Day, since they had the best coffee. While that was fine for talking with the other vendors, she didn't have a complicated history with any of them. And no way was she about to invite him back to Dani's place. What they needed was someplace neutral yet away from prying eyes. "There's a conference room down the hall from the tourism office. How does ten tomorrow morning sound?"

He dipped his head in a slight nod. "Tuesday at ten. Got it."

Silence draped over the room, replacing the unusual banter of moments before.

"This place is really coming together. Hard to believe it was a storage shed only a few days ago." She walked over to the workbench, her eyes searching for anything to land on other than Lincoln's intent gaze. The broken window had been replaced with a new one, and there wasn't a bug in sight. She frowned at the rolls of chicken wire stacked against the opposite wall, then shrugged as she turned to face him again.

Lincoln watched her, something unreadable in his expression. "You've got enough on your plate with the festival, Kate. You don't have to stay." It was the closest thing to him telling her to leave him alone. But now that she was here, he wasn't getting rid of her that easily.

"I know."

He was right about both. She still had a million and one things left to do, not to mention finalizing her presentation to the festival committee on Wednesday. But then again, she'd never be able to handle the next few weeks if she kept running from her problems. If she could take a flooded wedding venue and a tear-streaked bride in a wet dress and turn it around with the most gorgeous sunset beach photos, she could handle Lincoln's moods. Anything for Dani and the festival's success.

He grunted, but raised eyebrows aside, he didn't argue. "Then I'd say you'd better put on some gloves. I'd give you mine, but they might be a bit big."

"Good thing I brought my own." Or Dani's, to be precise. She'd already commandeered her sister's apartment and job. Why not her work gloves as well? Her list of duties could wait another hour or so. Besides, helping Lincoln was in the festival's, and therefore the town's, best interests.

This was really an extension of her managerial duties. And the thought of working closely with the man was in no way responsible for her overactive sweat glands.

"Uh, earth to Kate?"

She blinked at Lincoln, who was watching her with an amused tilt of the head, and her cheeks suddenly warmed. Maybe Oliver had a point about her needing to switch to decaf.

"Do you have a broom and dustpan?" she asked a bit sheepishly.

He stepped to a small closet she hadn't noticed until now and withdrew a heavy-duty straw broom, sans dustpan.

"Perfect. I can sweep the dust right out the door. That's far more efficient than going after all those pesky dust lines."

He covered a cough, and she had the sense he was trying not to laugh at her.

She swiped the broom and gave him her sweetest smile. *Watch out, buster. Tomorrow, you're getting an extra packet of sugar in your coffee.* "Well, this floor isn't going to sweep itself." She wanted to slap herself the moment it was out, and from the grin splitting across his face, it was too much to hope that he hadn't heard it as well.

To his credit, he didn't laugh this time. At least, not audibly. "No, I suppose it won't."

He turned the music back up as they both settled into their

tasks, her with the floors and him reattaching the stove door. They worked quietly for fifteen minutes, the gentle instrumentals filling the space between them where words would only get in the way.

Every so often, Kate stole a glance at his corner of the room. Forehead mashed into a V, he filed and hammered away on the cast-iron hinge as if he were Moses striking a rock for water. Any more and she feared it might cleave off. But the next time she looked up, he was swinging the door back and forth without a squeak.

From him or the door.

Which was fine. It wasn't like she was looking to pick back up where they'd left off. Far from it. They were ancient history. A galaxy far, far away kind of history.

There was no reason his silence should make her oat-milk cinnamon latte churn in her stomach.

Lincoln stood outside the conference room, notebook clutched under one arm as the other hovered within reach of the handle.

Last night's all-nighter better be worth it. After realizing he'd accidentally left his notes back in Detroit, he'd stayed up well past midnight piecing together ideas to present to Kate for the festival. Not that he even knew what sort of venues he was supposed to be designing for. Indoor or outdoor? Fancy or casual? Lots of little arrangements or a few showstoppers?

The moment his watch flipped to ten, he turned the handle and stepped inside. The door bounced against something solid—a box of old string lights, apparently—making Kate look up from the long table in the center of the room.

"You made it." She seemed surprised. Her face dipped in a slight frown at his faded jeans and Detroit Red Wings T-shirt, but then she was clearing a space on the table for him to join her.

"And with sustenance too." He set down his notebook along with the two cups he'd stopped at Good Day for on the way. "I asked the barista to make your usual. I hope you like it." She'd always taken her coffee extra sweet with some flavor. Who'd have thought she'd still be hooked on cinnamon after all these years?

"You didn't have to do this, but thank you." She eyed the drinks for only a moment before taking a sip of the latte. Read the label. Then took another, longer sip.

"It was the least I could do." Literally. Thank goodness for small towns and chatty baristas.

Somewhere overhead, the heating kicked on. Between that and the coffee, it was a warmer reception than he'd anticipated. Especially when Kate set down her drink and gave him a timid smile.

"Can we start over?" She held out a hand, at which he raised an eyebrow. "Hi, I'm Kate Sullivan. Temporary event coordinator for the Apple Blossom Festival."

She couldn't really be serious. Yet the plastered-on smile and slender outstretched arm said she was.

Her hand was soft in his, exactly how he remembered it. Same with the zing that shot to his chest, warning him just how difficult keeping things professional might be. "Lincoln St. James. Florist and killer of spiders."

"Destroyer, more like." She matched his grin, and something seemed to shift between them. Nothing earth-shattering like lightning, but he felt it all the same.

Shoving his hands back into his pockets, he followed her to the end of the long table, where she'd already set up shop for the morning. Coffee from Good Day, a partially opened laptop, and a three-ring binder like the ones used in the college business classes he'd finally finished with last year. All reminders of how ill-prepared he really was.

"I'm kind of flying blind here, Kate. What exactly does a florist do for an apple blossom festival, anyway?" She'd all but banished him to the outbuilding-turned-studio without so much as a welcome packet. Not that he could blame her—he deserved far worse for what he'd done. But maybe they could table their issues until after the festival.

"Well, loads of things." She opened the very large binder in front of her, which thudded against the table, and flipped to the first page.

"I don't need the whole island history," he said, interrupting her. "But I do need to know what kinds of flowers to order and in what quantities."

"Of course, just one sec." Setting down her cup, she began flipping through the pages. "Originated in the twenties . . . officially started in the seventies during the Fudge Wars . . . Ah, here we are." She jabbed a finger at the packet and smiled. "As festival florist, your job will be to provide arrangements for all the major events. There's the apple blossom queen coronation the last Friday of April—to start off the festival—then there's the pop-up art show Monday and Tuesday, a still-life watercolor class that'll need some bouquets, and of course the gala that Sunday night. You won't have to worry about the vintage bicycle rally or the walking tours, but you'll be busy teaching the floral arrangement classes most days."

Lincoln froze. "Nobody said anything about me teaching a class." He didn't mean to raise his voice, nor to make Kate flinch.

"Oh, um . . ." Face falling, she turned to the next page and bit her lower lip. "Yes, arrangements. It won't be every day, but visitors will want to take a piece of the festival home with them. And seeing as it's illegal to pick any of the island's flowers, that's where you come in."

What exactly had Felicity gotten him into? He had no business standing in front of a room full of students. Especially the touristy type who didn't know a rose from a ranunculus. He could almost kiss that spot in the Bloomfest showcase goodbye right now. "I can handle the arrangements for everything else, but you do not want me dealing with people."

"Because you know exactly what I want, right?" she shot back. Face growing pink, she dropped her gaze to the rows of text and bullet points on the page in front of her, but she didn't apologize.

She didn't have to.

Lincoln rubbed his hands against his thighs and released a measured breath. "I probably deserved that." He hadn't come here to fight. Yes, this whole thing was uncomfortable, but a job was a job. And this was one he couldn't afford to lose. "Listen, Kate . . ."

He should've rehearsed his apology beforehand. He couldn't think straight with her sitting so close to him.

Luckily, he didn't have to.

"Oh, Kate. There you are." A woman's voice, and in a hurry, based on her fast-approaching footsteps. The woman's large glasses, tweed skirt, and matching cardigan made her look at least fifty, despite her somewhat youthful complexion and red hair.

"Hi, Janine." Kate shoved an unruly curl behind her ear, giving the woman her undivided attention. "What can I do for you?"

Janine's lips flattened into a pink line as her gaze not-so-subtly flicked to Lincoln and back. But whatever it was, it apparently didn't warrant them going into a separate room to talk. "I'm having a bit of trouble with the displays at the historical society. At first, I thought it might be prudent to showcase the history of the island's apple blossoms. They are, after all, the state flower of Michigan. But then I remembered we've already done that before."

"We have?" asked Kate. "It's been years since the last flower festival. When would we have—"

"You remember—2015. It was the same year your father burned down half of the Grand Hotel."

Kate winced, but she didn't appear to let the woman's comment get to her.

She'd never talked much about her parents, but he knew enough to recall that was the same week of their divorce and her mom's marriage to the guy she'd cheated on Kate's dad with. Had it been his own family's dirty laundry the woman was airing, he wouldn't have been so stoic about it.

"Anyway," Janine continued, "I was thinking that instead of the blossoms, we might take a different approach and instead focus on how the trees have provided for the island in other ways over the centuries."

Kate just nodded politely. "Whatever you think is best."

"Good, because I've already started pulling things out of storage to make the necessary changes." Smiling at both of them, Janine turned to leave but paused at the boxes of string lights by the door. "You're not considering putting those up around town, are you?"

"Blueberry Hill Park, actually." Kate's whole countenance shifted from unnervingly submissive to engaged at the change in conversation. "I think they'll give some nice atmosphere to the park, especially as the sun starts to go down later in the evening."

"People come to Jonathon Island for a unique and special experience. An escape from all the trappings of the twenty-first century, if you know what I mean. Aren't you the least bit concerned these might detract from the natural beauty?"

Lincoln grunted. What, was she the fun police as well? "It's just a few string lights."

But based on the way she narrowed her eyes at him through those glasses of hers, she didn't agree.

See? He was terrible with people. Case in point.

"I'm sorry, but you are?"

"Lincoln St. James of Lily & Stone Floral Designs." Not that he expected her to know about a Detroit-based company like his, but the blank stare he got in return was anything but impressed. "I'm in charge of the flower arrangements for the festival."

"I thought that's what the trees were here for. It is, after all, an apple blossom festival, is it not?" He'd have laughed had her head not tilted in innocent confusion. Then to Kate, she said, "We can add the lights to the list of things to discuss at the meeting tomorrow."

It was as if he were back in elementary school, being volunteered by the teacher to stay after school and clean chalkboards and then abandoned by said teacher as Janine turned around and walked away as fast as her heels allowed over the gravel path.

"What was that for?" Kate hissed the moment the woman was out of earshot.

"What?"

He'd never seen her like this, all tense and worked up—nothing like the docile creature of moments ago. "The way you practically goaded her with that comment about the lights."

He was lost. "Uh . . ."

"Janine hates anything modern. If she'd had her way, the island never would've replaced the underwater power cable between here and Port Joseph when it went out. She had a petition ready and everything. She probably thinks I'm out to destroy the town one electric light bulb at a time."

"I thought I was helping."

"Well, I didn't ask for your help. I know how to handle myself."

"By caving to what other people want?" He might not be an expert at communicating, but he knew an avoidance tactic when he saw it.

"It's called compromise. It's what adults do. You should try it sometime." Her eyes rounded in shock the moment her words were out, but she didn't take them back.

He clenched his teeth to keep from saying anything else that might make the situation worse. She was right. She did know how to stand up for herself. Only, it wasn't Janine she had a problem with, apparently. He and Kate never used to argue. But now, it seemed that was all they were capable of.

One look at her sparking chestnut eyes—the ones that used to smile up at him with pure adoration and trust—and the tension drained from him. It was only right she was angry with him.

A few days of teamwork would never be enough to make up for a lifetime of regret. Who was he kidding? Her brother was right. He shouldn't be here.

He pushed back his chair to stand and reached for his notebook and pen. "I don't think this was such a good idea after all. I should just go."

"Wait." She grabbed his arm to stop him, then released it just as fast, eyes growing wide. "I—"

Another jolt of electricity. The shock alone made him freeze, but it was the strained look on her face that really kept him from walking out the door. The way she somehow grew even smaller in the padded office chair.

"I need you. I mean, I need this. The festival." Her gaze flitted to the computer and open binder as if they held an explanation she was reluctant to give. Again, her shoulders seemed to drop under some heavy weight, and the sudden spark inside of her went out. "I need the festival to go well," she finally admitted, talking to the table instead of Lincoln. "My photography business could really use the interview in *American Wanderer*." She looked like she was about to say something else, but didn't.

Huh. "Then it appears we both need the same thing."

She finally looked up from the page detailing the gala, eyebrows raised, and actually scoffed. "You've got, like, twenty thousand followers on Instagram. I'm sure you're doing fine."

Yeah, especially considering those followers had probably seen Mrs. Howard's post by now as well. "Let's just say I've recently had some not-so-good publicity that could hurt my chances of getting into a showcase I've been working toward for years." If there was any chance this festival and the article could change that, he had to give it a real try. No matter how much he might want to walk out that door right now. "You can go back to hating me after the festival. But until then, is it possible we can somehow put our differences aside for a few weeks? At least until after the interview."

Another long silence stretched between them, but at least she wasn't glaring at him anymore.

"I don't hate you, Lincoln. It's just . . ."

"It's hard letting go of the past. I get it. And I'm not asking you to forget—just to defer it for a while." There had to be a way to make this work for both of them. Otherwise, what was the point?

Six

THE TRUTH WAS, KATE WAS IN WAY OVER HER head and needed help.

Just not from Lincoln.

Phone glued to her ear, she listened to it ring before the international messaging app bumped her over to voicemail.

"Hi, Dani. I know you're probably off sipping wine in some Tuscan villa while Liam hand-feeds you pizza and gelato, but if you could give me a call back when you get this, I'd really appreciate it."

The twelve-person table stretched down the middle of the modern conference room, flanked on three sides by the projector, pull-down screen, and harbor-facing windows. She was supposed to present the schedule of events at the town council's open festival meeting in twenty minutes, but all she could think about was Lincoln making her look like a helpless damsel who couldn't even handle someone as harmless as Janine Dirks.

"Knock, knock."

Oliver stood in the doorway to the tourism building's conference room, wearing jeans and a graphic T-shirt that said *To quote Hamlet act 3, scene 3, line 92, "no."* Despite the nonverbal message, he grabbed the stack of handouts for today's meeting and chuckled. "Did you create a schedule to plan out another schedule?"

"There's still a lot to pin down for next week. I'm just trying to be thorough." The binder landed with a thump on top of the pastry boxes, followed by her laptop and HDMI cable. "Anyway, I really appreciate you coming to the meeting last-minute."

"Kate, take a breath." He demonstrated a long inhale and exhale until she flicked his shoulder.

"I'm serious, Ollie. I don't want you to feel like I'm taking advantage of your time or pulling you away from Eliza."

"You're not. Eliza is working today, and seeing as I've already read *The Return of the King* four times, I'm not missing much. Besides, I enjoy being your yes-man."

"Your shirt says otherwise."

"Or does it? Maybe it's trying to say you don't have to keep making excuses to ask for help. Even Éowyn needed Merry's help when fighting the king of the Nazgûl. Or Leia when Luke and Han rescued her from Jabba the Hutt."

Kate flinched, then reminded herself there was no way Oliver could actually know her earlier thoughts.

"That's all well and fine, except I'm not some heroine in one of your books." If she were, she'd have found her happily ever after by now. Of course, that didn't mean God couldn't drastically change her story, but after thirty-six years, she'd learned to accept the one He'd already given her and not ask for more.

"Speaking of accepting help, the meeting will begin in a few minutes. We'd better get this stuff over there and set up before people start arriving." She ducked past him before he could laser her with another thought-provoking question.

She itched to escape down to the water and disappear in a world of candid photos. She'd take a crying flower girl covered in mud any day, so long as she didn't have to stand up in front of everyone and pretend to know what she was doing.

Kate sensed Oliver's hovering presence behind her and did an about-face toward the back table, where she laid out the muffins and sticky buns she'd grabbed from the newly reopened Hudson Bakery on her way in. Good food could cover a multitude of wrongs. And hopefully keep everyone occupied enough not to see the way her hands were shaking.

The nutty aroma of coffee teased her empty stomach, but she reached for a cup of water instead. Best not to add caffeine to her already jittery nerves.

Oliver was spreading out the last of the handouts when Uncle Seb stepped into the room with Patrick Kelley and Tommy Macintyre, the fire chief, in deep conversation.

"All I'm saying is we might need to bring on a few more volunteers to the station house with the influx of tourists we're expecting this summer. Dani's already talking about fireworks for the music festival this summer, and we're stretched enough as it is. I won't have another major fire on the island under my watch."

The three men migrated to the end of the table after getting their coffees. Uncle Seb gave Kate a nod of encouragement across the room before being sucked back into his previous conversation. His salt-and-pepper hair and broad shoulders commanded respect, whereas Kate had always preferred to blend into the background. He should be leading the meeting instead of her.

She brushed a hand over the wrinkled front of her shirt. When she'd come for Dani's wedding a couple of weeks ago, she couldn't have anticipated stepping in at the helm last-minute. Which meant the light-blue blouse and dark-wash jeans were the closest things to a blazer and dress pants she was going to get.

The projector, as well as the room, buzzed with energy. Still waiting for the machine to warm up, she opened her laptop and navigated to the right PowerPoint presentation.

The rest of the town council, plus a representative from the police department and a few last-minute volunteers, trickled in over the remaining ten minutes. And still no sign of Lincoln. Kate couldn't decide whether to be relieved by his absence or annoyed at him for not keeping his word.

Arms tingling, she swallowed against the tight lump that had suddenly formed in her throat. On second thought, maybe she could use a coffee after all. One step from her laptop was all she managed before Uncle Seb's booming voice brought the chatter to silent order.

All eyes turned toward her.

The dual hums of the percolator and projector seemed almost deafening until she cleared her throat once to speak. Then twice.

"Welcome, everyone. As you know, Dani is on her honeymoon. And while I'm still working on getting up to speed on everything, I want to assure you I will do my utmost to see this festival succeed."

Uncle Seb's calm smile put her at ease, and for the first time all week, she felt as if she might actually be able to do this. But before she could continue, the door creaked open, drawing everyone's attention away from Kate and the front of the room.

A whole two minutes late, Lincoln slipped into one of the empty seats, ignoring Oliver's and Janine's stares from across the table. So much for moral support. Uncle Seb's slightly downturned expression seemed to linger on the newcomer as well. He wouldn't remember Lincoln after five years, would he? After all, he'd only ever met him once, at the family brunch before the rehearsal dinner. But then his eyes locked again with hers, and his furrowed brow said otherwise.

Never had she wanted to disappear behind her camera more than now.

The knot in her throat grew twice as large. *Not now.* There was never a good time for anxiety to get the better of her, but if there were, in front of a crowd of people definitely wouldn't be it.

"As I was saying, there's still a lot left to be done before next Friday. We already have the permits for the different events to be held at Blueberry Hill Park, and I'm still waiting to hear back from John York at the police department about the Main Street closures."

"Got them right here," said Tommy from the back. "Talked with him this morning and we're all clear to move ahead."

"Wonderful." Okay, things were going better than planned so far. "Which brings me to the next item on the agenda. Would you all please turn to page two in the packet in front of you?"

She waited for the rustling of papers to die down before continuing.

"As you can see, I've taken the liberty of drafting up a schedule for the festival. Here, you'll find a detailed breakdown of all the events, along with our current volunteer list. We still need more help with the bike rally, and I need to coordinate with the Jonathon Island Center for the Arts to see where they are in planning the pop-up art show."

She hazarded a peek from her notes and instantly regretted it. Lincoln was the only one looking at her instead of the packet. Never mind the flush that crept up her arms as she recalled their earlier argument and truce. He'd since changed out of his dirty T-shirt and jeans into a clean navy button-down that seemed to accentuate his broad shoulders as well as his dangerously blue eyes.

A girl could get lost in those eyes, sucked out to sea before even realizing she was miles from shore without a life jacket. She would know. Yet she had the sudden desire to slip down to the cove and dip her toes into the lake's frigid waters.

Festival. We're here to talk about the festival.

"Of course, there's the matter of ordering flowers for the displays and floral arrangement workshops Mr. St. James will be leading. He'll be providing us with a list to ferry over from the mainland."

At the mention of Lincoln and flowers, the energy of the room shifted.

"What's the point of an apple blossom festival if the apple blossoms aren't the center of attention?" said Martha to Janine for everyone to hear. "First, it's daisies and Queen Anne's lace, but then a hogweed gets into the mix, and before you know it, our island will be overrun by harmful plants that don't belong, choking out those that do."

Seb frowned. "Now, Martha. That's a bit extreme."

"I agree," said Chief Macintyre, shifting in his seat. "Last summer, I saw nearly three dozen cases of poison ivy. Now, maybe it's a bit to assume something as harmful as hogweed could slip in unnoticed, but I'd rather err on the side of caution myself."

These were *flowers* they were talking about. How could they be so divisive?

Lincoln sat a little straighter. "I assure you, the farms I work with are the best in Michigan. They'd never let anything like that happen."

Kate flipped to the next slide, hoping to defuse the tension with the apple-themed menu, when Janine turned toward her.

"What about poor Holly?" asked Janine. "Did you ask if she'd be interested in the position? We should be focusing on making sure the businesses we already have can succeed. Not outsourcing jobs when we think it's convenient."

"Dani did ask Holly," said Oliver, coming to Kate's rescue. "However, she'll be off island for a family wedding the first half of the festival. And seeing as the festival's dates were already set, Dani had no other option but to outsource."

Just because he'd defended Lincoln's spot at the table didn't mean he wasn't still frowning at the guy. Oliver muttered something under his breath that Kate couldn't quite hear, but apparently Martha did.

"Of course! *That's* where I know you from. From the wedding announcements." Her face lit as if she'd been given the juiciest bit of town news since the ban on motor vehicles back in 1898. "You're the man who walked out on our Kate."

They really ought to employ a chiropractor for all the head swiveling happening at today's meeting. And if Oliver's red ears were any indication, they might require a doctor to reset Lincoln's jaw soon.

"Is that true?" asked Tara with delicately raised eyebrows. As the pastor's wife, it often fell to her to keep the peace.

The muscle in Lincoln's jaw pulsed as if he were trying to hold in whatever defense was on the tip of his tongue. A commendable effort when boxed in by the entire council.

Any longer, and Martha might just pull a pitchfork from her handbag and convince the others to run him from the room. As much as Kate enjoyed the mental image, she couldn't sacrifice him like that. Like Tara, she wanted to hear his explanation, but the sharp ache in her chest when she looked at his guarded expression refused to let go. He was right. The past would always be there, but at least for now, they had to find a way beyond it.

She reached for Oliver's cup, then rapped it against the wooden table to regain control of the quickly spiraling meeting. The reverberation rang all the way up her arm, colliding with her earlier jitters. Their curious stares held her captive, most of all Lincoln's, as she gathered her emotions back into their well-contained box.

Just . . . breathe.

"Lincoln is a professional, and while yes, there might be some history there, he's the best florist for the job. We are lucky to have him here." And she meant it. He was watching her with rapt attention, eyebrows drawn together as if confused by her defense of him. Well, that made two of them. "A big name like his is our best shot of impressing tourists as well as the readers of *American Wanderer*. Imported flowers or not."

Janine's grumble said she thought otherwise, and Martha's cluck was more than disappointed. Oliver still looked like he wanted to slug Lincoln, but all Kate could see was Lincoln's quiet exhale and the slow smile that communicated a million little things without a single word.

Kate never ceased to amaze him.

Lincoln hung back as the others filed out of the room. One would've thought he'd set off another bug bomb from the pinched faces and curt farewells.

"Hey, Kate. Wait up." He swiped the box of leftover pastries and paper plates from the back table before jogging after her. The other footsteps faded down the hall as he stopped in front of an open office door.

Kate was already inside, twirling a piece of hair between her fingertips as she dropped the notes packets onto the desk. The faint scent of lavender and jasmine beckoned, taking him back to five years ago, when he would have tugged her into a reassuring embrace for handling that meeting with such grace under pressure.

Instead, he lingered in the doorway, half inside and half in the hallway.

"Where should I put these?" He wobbled the half-empty box and looked around the tidy space.

"Oh. I completely forgot. Thank you for cleaning all that up." Pink tinged her cheeks as her fingers brushed his and she took the box and placed it next to the stack of papers. She slipped the wisp of hair back behind her ear, then clasped her hands in front of her. Did his presence really make her that nervous? "I'll take them with me when I go to Island Outfitters to inquire about the bikes for the rally."

The dark jeans accentuated her slim legs, and the pale-blue ruffles around her collar reminded him of a bouquet of forget-menots. As if anyone could forget a face like Kate's, with her long, dark lashes, pink lips, and almond-shaped eyes. "They're lucky to have you."

"Wasn't that my line?" Her smile reached her eyes this time, creasing the soft skin at the corners as she brushed off the compliment. "I meant what I said. Your work with flowers is . . ."

"Over the top? Unconventional?"

"I was going to say *enchanting*."

Now it was his turn to squirm under praise, but surprisingly, the questions and self-doubt that usually followed people's comments didn't come. "I don't think anyone's ever used that word to describe my work before."

"Well, they should. That floral chandelier you made a couple of weeks ago was stunning."

"You saw that?" Had they somehow both been hired to work the same event? "I thought you lived in Petoskey?"

"I did. I do." Her cheeks flushed again at the matrimonial phrasing, a delicate peony pink spreading across her face. She began to fidget with the decorative silver band on her middle finger. "I follow your account on Instagram."

What? How had he not known this? Maybe he shouldn't have insisted Felicity manage the social media accounts for him.

"It's completely out of professional interest," she rushed to explain. "And as we've already established, it's not like your name is listed on the main site or anything."

"An oversight I'm seriously beginning to rethink."

"Plus, it's my job to keep up with wedding trends and popular vendors."

"Of course." Yet her pragmatic explanation did nothing to stop the warmth spreading through his chest. So maybe she hadn't known exactly who Lily & Stone was, but he had to think that more than just chance had brought them back together.

Was that You, God?

He'd never had much use for another father in his life, what with how poor the first one had turned out to be. All the man had ever taught him was to bury one's emotions before they exploded. That and never to mix beer and liquor.

What would God want with a broken person like Lincoln?

Yet the very fact he was standing here, of all places, working once more with Kate, must prove that this Father hadn't given up on him, despite all the mistakes he'd made over the years.

Either that or God was still punishing him.

"So, Mr. St. James. What do you intend to do about the flowers for the festival?" Dimples he'd thought he'd never see again framed her mouth, which tilted playfully to the side. "Mind you, the apple blossoms *are* the centerpiece of the festival, as Janine and Martha so graciously pointed out. But short of hogweed, I think everyone will love your designs."

He didn't give a flying carnation what other people thought about him. He'd cover the island in sunflowers if it would make Kate happy. Even if he had to call every last greenhouse from here to Kalamazoo.

"I've got a few ideas." An entire notebook full, actually. And with her by his side, he couldn't wait to get started.

Seven

LINCOLN RETURNED THE BROOM TO THE HOOK inside the closet and stood back to survey his newly restored studio.

Fresh pine floors gleamed in the mid-morning sunlight beside a long table that stretched down the length of the room. A fresh coat of paint covered any evidence of the window he'd had to replace, and not a single bug or dust bunny could hide under the additional lighting. Just in time for the opening weekend of the festival. The peaceful quiet was only punctuated by birdsong and the faint clop of horses' hooves from the livery next door.

Amazing how things could change in just under two weeks.

Kate would be here any minute. She'd offered to help him transport the flowers from the ferry to the portable coolers he'd installed out back. He'd told her not to worry about it, that he'd find a way on his own, but her insistence knew no bounds.

He rolled up his sleeves, then slid the box of ceramic and glass vases into the corner with the wire mesh, scissors, and floral tape.

Janine was right. The apple blossoms would be the star of the show, but that didn't mean he couldn't supply an immaculate supporting cast to make them shine.

Outside, something like a toy car horn beeped in quick succession.

Checking the time on his phone, he stepped through the open door to find Kate watching him from behind the steering wheel of a brown golf cart.

Lincoln couldn't help but smile. "This takes me back to the first day we met. Only I'm not delivering the wrong order of flowers to the country club, and you're not here to politely escort me off the property."

"Aren't I?" She pushed a pair of sunglasses above her head, securing her wavy hair like a spray of chocolate solidago. "Hop on in. The freight ferry will be here in a few minutes."

Even her honk was polite as she zipped them around corners and down Main Street. The Victorian storefronts stood in picturesque rows, like a postcard from the 1800s.

"So, horse-drawn carriages and golf carts, huh?"

"Don't forget bicycles. And then there's the snowmobiles in the winter once the snow begins to pile up."

Chuckling, he held on tight as she zigged and zagged around bike racks and vendors.

Her brown waves flew and twisted in the breeze, tugging at something beneath his ribcage as they fluttered near his face. Maybe it was the way she charged through the early-morning stillness of the island or the way her eyes lit up as the water came into view, but this Kate was free, fearless, and alive.

This Kate—the one who had dreams bigger than the sky and wasn't afraid to chase them—was the Kate he remembered. The one he'd fallen in love with.

He shook away the thought as the cart suddenly stopped and he lurched forward. On reflex, he shot out his arm to steady her as well, the contact of his large hand on her small waist like an electric shock.

"Sorry about that. I guess I'm a bit rusty." Her chuckle came out a bit breathless. "It's been a few years since I've driven one of these." Before he could ask when she'd made the switch from working at a golf course to photography, she jumped onto the concrete where the first passengers were already disembarking from the ferry. "I'm going to check with the port office real quick and make sure your delivery made it this morning." She disappeared down the wharf into a sea of backpack-toting tourists.

As he was waiting, a man in a navy hat and fleece vest ducked through the rear hatch behind the last of the island visitors, a stack of yellowed packets with a map of the island protruding from his back pocket.

Lincoln immediately recognized the man as the same crew member from his ferry ride over. And from his friendly wave, so had the crew member.

"Hey, man, you're still here." He clipped a chain behind him, sealing off the pedestrian ramp to the boat as he walked over to greet Lincoln. He seemed close to Lincoln's age, mid-thirties, based on the faint crow's-feet around his eyes, yet built like someone who'd spent their entire life working on a boat. Or bumming it on the beach and surfing all day, based on the man's tanned forearms and sun-bleached hair.

"Sure am."

Lincoln's ears perked at the familiar sound of Kate's short but quick strides against the wood. Good. Hopefully she'd found the right loading dock and they could get on with transferring the flowers.

"Birdie Sullivan. Is that you?"

Lincoln was about to correct the guy that it was in fact *Kate* when a flurry of arms and squeals cut him short. He stood awkwardly off to the side as she wrapped the man in an all-too-familiar hug for his liking.

"Noah Rampart. I thought you were leading kayaking or rafting tours out in Colorado. What brings you back to Jonathon Island?"

"Same as you, I suppose." He tilted his head toward the island, arms relaxed at his side. "As much as I wanted to get away from the small-island life as a teenager, it turns out it's in my blood. However, I do miss the sound of 'Noah's Ark.' 'Noah's Ferry' doesn't have the same ring to it."

Lincoln grunted at the lame joke.

Yet Kate's giggles said she thought otherwise. "I'm sorry. Lincoln, this is Noah. We went to high school together and played on the men's golf team."

His eyebrows dipped.

"I know what you're probably thinking," Noah jumped in. "But she could play circles around most of us. Did you know she broke the state record for most birdies in a high school tournament when she was a junior?"

Hence the nickname.

"You don't say?" He raised an eyebrow toward her bashful shrug.

"And this is Lincoln." His name on Kate's lips made him freeze. She was quiet for a few seconds, her relaxed stance hardly betraying what she'd say next. Then . . . "He's an old friend."

The breath seeped from his lungs in a relieved exhale.

"Nice to officially meet you, Linc. Any friend of Kate's is a friend of mine." Noah took Lincoln's hand and gave it a hearty shake.

"So, what did you find out about the delivery?" Lincoln asked Kate.

She answered his question with a sigh. "Not much, I'm afraid. The office was closed."

"Yeah, we've all been running a bit shorthanded lately. But I've got a few minutes to spare right now. Maybe I can help."

"That would be great," Kate chimed enthusiastically.

Yeah, just peachy.

Against Lincoln's better judgment, he and Kate followed Noah as he led them down a maze of docks and boardwalks, where small boats bobbed in the water.

In under two minutes, they'd reached the other side of the harbor, where a smaller ferry quietly floated in place. A couple of men were unloading boxes when Noah called out to one of them. "Hey, Luke. These two are here for a pickup."

"Name?" the man shouted back over the roar of the small forklift. He finished transferring a final pallet to the growing mound at the end of the dock, then parked the machine at the base of the ramp.

Now half deaf, Lincoln withdrew the shipping receipt from his jacket and handed it over for the man to inspect. "It should be under Lincoln St. James or Kate Sullivan via the Tourism Bureau."

"Yep, got it unloaded just this morning." He pointed his chin at the smaller stack of boxes on the other side of the pallet tower.

Following his direction, Lincoln found the boxes easily enough. He peeled the lid off the peonies to Noah's low whistle.

"It looks like you raided every garden south of Lake Huron. The flowers are for the festival, right?"

No duh, Sherlock.

Lincoln clamped his mouth shut and got to work inspecting the next one. Good. The lisianthus and ranunculus appeared no worse for wear. Same with the quince, dogwood, and apple blossom cuttings he'd specially ordered from a family-owned farm in Ann Arbor.

"If you need any help moving them all, just let me know," said Noah. "I'll be in and out of here all day but would love to lend a hand."

"Thanks, but I think we've got it covered." Lincoln ignored the look Kate shot him as he reached for the nearby dolly. "Mind if we borrow this?"

Luke tucked the signed documents under his arm and shrugged. "Knock yourselves out."

To the point, not unnecessarily friendly toward a certain brunette . . . Lincoln liked the guy already.

"Thanks, man. We'll be sure to return it as soon as we get these in place."

"No rush. We've got more on board, so take as much time as you need. Just have it back here before dark."

Perfect.

And hopefully by then, the passenger ferry and its crew would be long gone. He didn't have a right to be upset about Kate with another guy. But that didn't mean he wanted a front row seat.

It took them a total of five trips to unload all the flowers. Six if Kate included the bundle of baby's breath they'd had to go back for when Lincoln jumped the curb by the real estate office on the last run.

"Remind me to drive next time," Kate joked as they unloaded the last of the flowers from the back seat. The way he'd acted down by the docks had almost been comical. But she knew better than to laugh at him when he was upset.

Kate stifled another giggle at his expense.

"It was just a curb. Nothing a hundred other drivers probably haven't hit over the years. And why it has to stick out so far into the road is beyond me." He mumbled something else before swinging the refrigerator lid closed. A rainbow of colors filled each of the two coolers, making them look like they might burst in a shower of petal confetti with one wrong touch.

She really shouldn't take such delight in his misery, but he made it so easy. A breath of crisp air filled her lungs, and she released it along with the tightness in her chest. Maybe Dr. Weston had been right about needing a vacation.

Lincoln gave her a slanted look, yet he failed to hide the twitch at the corner of his mouth when he ran a hand through his overgrown hair.

The unruly hair had grown on her, much like Brendan Fraser in *George of the Jungle.* She could easily see Lincoln taming a wild stallion while wearing a billowy white shirt. He'd shed the heavy jacket twenty minutes ago and had rolled up his sleeves to reveal muscular forearms marred by rose thorn scratches and a few other faint scars. Odd that such a rugged man would make a career caring for the most delicate of flowers. Helping his mom with the shop was one thing. But striking out on his own?

Even stranger that she didn't feel the least bit intimidated by him. Maybe his saying no to her all those years ago when he left her at the altar had empowered her to feel free to say it right back to him.

"Well, that's the last of them." He stood nearly a head taller than her, his shadow engulfing her in the late-afternoon sun.

It wasn't fair that men only grew more attractive with age. It would be easier if he'd gone bald or developed a gut, but there wasn't an inch of flab on him. Something the snug fit of his gray T-shirt confirmed with a single glance.

"Do you have everything you need for tomorrow? Your first workshop isn't until Saturday afternoon, but I could always . . . stick around for a bit if you'd like." She shouldn't be volunteering—she had more than enough to keep her busy back at the office, like checking last-minute details for tomorrow's festival queen coronation.

And she *definitely* shouldn't tilt her head back to better look into those soulful eyes that could see straight through her. The shadows obscured most of his facial features except for the subtle pulse of his jaw.

"There's really no need. I've already taken enough of your—"

A horse's whinny interrupted whatever else he'd been about to say, and Terry Quinn appeared from behind a row of trees. A slight tug on the reins brought a dappled gray horse and the freshly painted carriage behind him to a stop. "Afternoon, you two. Lovely day for a ride."

Kate felt the space widen between them as Lincoln took a step backward. She wasn't disappointed. She was just . . . surprised.

"Yes, it is, especially with the apple trees nearly all in bloom." Again, she wished she hadn't left her camera back at the apartment. Of course, she'd snapped a few pictures with her phone while she and Lincoln were transferring the flowers, but it wasn't the same.

"Actually, it was you I was hoping to find." The man was tall and lean, with tan skin from spending years working out in the fields with his horses. Deep lines framed pale-blue eyes that always seemed to be smiling even when his mouth wasn't.

"Oh?" She hadn't forgotten about a meeting with the Quinns, had she? She'd double-checked her list this morning, but between finalizing the festival menus and helping Lincoln, it was possible she'd accidentally let something slip.

"It's nothing, really," he continued, rubbing the leather reins between his rough fingers. "Asher, Angela, and I got to talking yesterday, and while we still love the existing carriage route, we thought maybe it would be nice to try something special for the festival. Make the most of the apple blossoms while they're here, you know?"

Kate released a sigh of relief. "You're the expert. I'm sure whatever changes you make will be lovely."

"If it's all the same, it would make me feel a lot better if I could walk you through it. Get your thoughts and all." He turned to

Lincoln and added, "Both of yours, if you have a few minutes to spare."

Her gaze shifted to the carriage and the blanket spread across the bench seat for two. Driving flowers back and forth in a golf cart with Lincoln was one thing, but a romantic carriage ride around the island was something else entirely. "Oh, I really shouldn't."

Lincoln shoved his hands in his pockets and took another backward step toward the shop. "Yeah, and I ought to get started on some arrangements, myself."

"It'll only be around the block," Terry countered. "A quick clip-clop and Bob's your uncle."

The idea of telling the man no a second time physically made her chest hurt. "I suppose I can spare a few minutes. After all, it *is* for the festival." She turned to Lincoln for support—or to talk her out of it. She wasn't sure.

He lifted a shoulder and let it fall. "I guess a little inspiration couldn't hurt."

"That's the spirit."

A soft tug on the reins brought the large draft horse into full view. Its shoulders were a good two inches taller than her, making even Lincoln seem less of a giant as he came nearly eye to eye with the animal.

She could feel the muscles around her throat begin to tighten as she swallowed. It wasn't that she didn't like horses, but that was a lot of animal. Far more intimidating than her sister's cat Roma or the geese that pestered golfers.

"If you think Gus is big, you should've seen his father. Largest horse I ever laid eyes on, but as sweet as they come." Terry brushed a hand over the dappled coat. "Hop on in, and we'll get this tour started."

After only a moment's hesitation, she willed her feet to move. Lincoln gave her a hand up into the carriage, making sure she was settled before climbing in behind her.

The warmth of his hand lingered long after they began to move, yet she clutched the edge of the blanket as they turned away from the park entrance. She hadn't realized how small the bench seat was, and his wide shoulders nearly filled the space beside her, making it impossible to keep her distance.

At the corner of Main Street and Blueberry Boulevard, they turned right, heading north toward the center of the island. Pink-and-white apple blossoms peeked through the wispy branches, perfuming the air with their delicate floral scent. One inhale and a lifetime of memories came to mind, each nearly as sweet and fleeting as the flowers themselves.

"It must've been idyllic growing up in a place like this." Lincoln kept his voice low and inviting. "*Enchanting*, I think, was the word you used."

She looked over to see him smiling at her, the kind that reached his eyes and made it difficult to look away.

But not impossible.

"It wasn't all perfect. We had our issues like every other family." Despite her and Lincoln's shared history, she'd had little opportunity to share this part of her world with him. Some might have called it a whirlwind romance, dating to engaged within a few months. "Being part of such a large family, I sometimes wondered where exactly I fit in. I'd thought I'd found that with golf, especially when I made it to state freshman year. But even then, something came up, and Oliver was the only one who came to support me."

"Your panic attack." Lincoln held her with his gaze. "I remember how scary you said that was."

Scary was an understatement. It wasn't until after her coach had gotten her checked over for heat stroke that their athletic trainer had declared her perfectly healthy. But perfectly healthy people didn't feel lightheaded and have a racing heartbeat for no apparent reason. She'd experienced some anxiety before then, but nothing like that. And in front of so many people too. Somehow, that was when things always seemed to turn south for her. The tournament, their rehearsal dinner . . .

A panic attack was such a small thing in the grand scheme of it all, yet the recent memories still made her chest grow suddenly tight.

"What about your mom?" she asked, feeling awkwardly vulnerable. "I remember the way she could turn even the simplest thing into something magical." She'd love this—the flowers, the fairy-tale carriage, all of it.

Lincoln shifted beside her, his shoulder bumping hers as a weight settled heavier in her stomach with the long silence. "So do I." It was so quiet, she nearly missed it. Then . . . "She passed. Two years ago."

"Oh, Lincoln. I'm so sorry." Here she'd been trying to deflect from her own family drama and instead jumped right into his. It suddenly all made sense why he worked with flowers. It was his way of keeping his mom's memory close. Lillian St. James had suffered from lupus flare-ups for years, but she'd always recovered. Always bounced back like a beam of light in a dark mirror.

"I know how much you adored her."

A length of hair fell over his face as he nodded. "As did everyone. And thank you."

"For what?" She hadn't done anything but put her foot in her mouth since he'd arrived.

"For caring."

Her lower lip fell. "Of course I care about you and your family. She might not have been my mom, not really, but she was in every way that counted. Did you know she came with me to all of my dress fittings and gave me a shoulder to cry on when my own mom canceled last-minute? Lily even insisted on doing the flowers, no matter how many times I told her she didn't have to." Her way of welcoming Kate into the family she hadn't known she'd needed until it was gone. Even with their breakup, she still wished he'd told her about his mom's passing.

His hand lingered near hers on the bench, but he didn't do anything to close the gap.

A part of Kate wanted to take his hand in hers and gather up all his pain, while the other part knew that such actions would send the wrong message.

Something the next pothole in the road didn't seem to care about.

The carriage tipped, throwing Kate against Lincoln's solid body. Arms like sturdy branches instantly wrapped around her, making her feel exposed yet oddly safe.

"Whoa, easy there, Gus." Terry pulled on the reins, steering them across the uneven road as they jostled back and forth in the back seat. "Sorry 'bout that. I suppose the winter did a number on the road here. Maybe I should take Lilac Lane next time instead of Dahlia Drive."

"Sounds like a good idea," said Lincoln. His pleasant voice rumbled through Kate's chest, doing funny things to her mind and stomach.

Faint warning bells urged her to replace the earlier space between them, but she couldn't bring herself to separate from his warmth. Neither did he remove his arm from around her shoulder, where it draped for the rest of the ride back to the stables.

It didn't matter that they hardly spoke for the remaining ten minutes. Terry more than made up for the lack of chit-chat with historical tidbits and stories about the island. But an entire conversation seemed to pass between them with the simplest of touches.

One where Kate's brain fought to rein in her runaway heart, lest she risk Lincoln breaking it all over again. In another couple of weeks, they'd both go back to their respective lives *not* on Jonathon Island. Saying goodbye had been hard enough once before. Starting anything now would be an invitation for disaster.

It would be better for both of them to keep things friendly but professional. If only her heart thought as much as they hit the next bump.

Eight

LINCOLN TOOK A SWIG OF HIS LUKEWARM coffee and grimaced.

He'd almost forgotten what regular drip coffee tasted like. Flat and disappointing compared to the stuff Kate had been bringing him the past two weeks. He was addicted. One day without, and he already wanted more.

Like a glutton for punishment, he took another sip of the bitter brew to warm his fingers inside the frigid studio space. He'd start the stove in a minute. Just as soon as he got the vases unpacked for today's workshop.

His plunky ringtone interrupted the gentle piano music coming through his Bluetooth speakers. That was probably Felicity calling with an update on her ETA. Main Street was closed all morning for a vintage bike rally, so he'd have to allow extra time to get to the dock. An hour was plenty of time to set up, pick her up, and give a short tour on their way back.

Leaving the vases, he reached across the table for his phone and flinched when, instead of Felicity, the name *Dad* flashed across the screen. He quickly silenced the phone and dropped it into his tool kit by the sink. It landed with a satisfying clunk beneath the rose strippers and wire cutters.

He hadn't seen the man in nearly five years. Not since Thomas St. James had been escorted from his mom's house with a black eye in the back of a police cruiser. His mom might've been able to forgive his drunken outbursts, but as far as Lincoln was concerned, his dad had deserved as much if not more after what he'd put them all through.

Lincoln released a sigh, a puff of fog forming around his face in the chill morning air. Last night's rain had washed clean the sidewalks as well as the insulating cloud layer from yesterday, which meant cooler temperatures and a biting humidity not even his new jacket from Jonathon Island Outfitters could ward off.

The buzzing started up again as he flipped on the pellet stove.

"Call all you like, but I'm not falling for your lies and excuses again." This time, he ignored it by turning up the volume of his music and getting back to work.

Each of the twelve place settings along the large farmhouse table received one vase, a roll of floral tape, and a strip of coated chicken wire. The simple task of cutting calmed his hands, if not his mind.

I wonder what Kate's up to right now.

He snipped the wires one by one, imagining Kate with her clipboard in one hand and camera in the other as she oversaw the race preparations. She'd be wearing one of her heavy knit sweaters—possibly the cream one—as she coordinated volunteers. He hadn't thought to check the race route ahead of time, but a few well-placed flower baskets out front ought to brighten the cyclists'—and a certain event coordinator's—day.

You know. Just in case.

Lincoln dug inside his tool bag for a pair of needle-nose pliers as his phone started up again. "For the love of . . ." He drowned the rest of his response with a gulp of bitter coffee, then smashed his finger against the green button.

"You've reached the voicemail of Lincoln St. James. If this is Tom, Mrs. Howard, or a reporter looking to capitalize on misinformation, you can take your story and—"

"Lincoln Thomas." Felicity's reprimand cut through him like ice, making his face suddenly burn despite the cold. "I hope you weren't intending on finishing that sentence."

He could count the times he'd heard Felicity raise her voice on one hand. Once when he accidentally tracked mud through her clean kitchen, and twice when his dad had shown up at the shop. The man had been half drunk and slurring angry words at him and his mom. Who knew what might've happened had she not stepped in when she did and sent him packing.

An awkward silence washed over him.

And then in a softer tone . . . "I've been trying to call you all morning."

"Sorry about that. Spotty reception." He scuffed his foot against the hardwood floor, studying the knotted grooves and scratches. No matter how many coats of wax and cleaner he'd applied, it would never be enough to smooth out the imperfections. A hundred years of foot traffic and dropped horseshoes would do that to a place. No wonder the Quinns had abandoned the old yet spacious building years ago.

"How close are you to the island?" Maybe if he changed subjects, she'd forget all about his short welcome.

"Actually, that's what I wanted to talk to you about."

"You got the ticket I emailed you, right? If they give you any trouble about it, tell Noah I've already got it covered." He might not like the guy, but some things about small-town life and knowing people came in handy.

"No. No, I got the email."

"Then why do I get the feeling there's a *but* behind that sentence?" He might as well cancel her reservation at the Island House Inn if her hesitant reply was any indication. "It's the business, isn't it? We lost all our clients and the game is up."

"That's a bit overdramatic, even for you."

"I don't hear you jumping to correct me." He winced the moment the words left his mouth. She was only trying to help. After all, it was he who'd landed them in this mess to begin with. Not her. "How bad is it?"

"It's nothing we can't handle. But that does mean I won't be able to make it to the island to help with your workshops, I'm afraid."

He mentally crossed off *Pick up Felicity at the marina* from his to-do list.

"I'm really sorry I can't be there. But we've got a potential client coming in at one to talk about estimates for a summer wedding. I couldn't turn them down, considering…" If she knew about Kate, she didn't say as much. "But if anyone can enchant people with flowers, it's you. You don't need my help to do that."

One corner of his mouth curved then fell. That was the same word Kate had used. And it filled him with the same unexpected warmth.

Outside, the crunch of gravel drew his attention as the first few cyclists sped by on mint-green cruisers.

"Lincoln, are you still there?"

He sucked in a reviving breath of cool air. "Sorry, it's the—"

"Spotty cell service. I know." And that she did. "Lincoln?"

"Yes, Felicity?" He could picture her trying not to smile at his mimicked reply of her serious tone. But her long pause this time left him feeling deflated rather than relieved.

"I've been praying for you."

Here we go again. It wasn't that he didn't believe in God. Of course he did. But the thought of bringing every problem and request to Him seemed like a waste of breath. He hadn't listened during all those late nights spent in the hospital chapel asking for a miracle. Why would He start now?

"I know how you roll your eyes when I say things like that, but that's one of the beauties of a phone conversation."

Besides the fact he could hang up whenever he liked. Not that he would . . .

"Now, before you hang up, I want you to remember something."

"Yeah, and what's that?" He was in no mood for one of her sermons, yet a part of him wanted to hear what she had to say nonetheless.

She was silent for so long, he thought the call had dropped, but then . . .

"Blue daisies."

The half smile from earlier returned, along with the special memory. "Blue daisies, huh?"

"Precisely." He could almost hear her dangle earrings clink with a mischievous nod. "Whenever you find your thoughts going down a dark path, I want you to remember that God turns all things for His good. Whether it be a bad review, a missed ferry, or an accidental truckload of blue daisies. You can either choose to dwell on the negative or open your eyes to the possibilities."

"Aunt Fee, you really missed your calling as a motivational speaker. Your talents are wasted answering phones and handling my messes."

"Nonsense. I'm only reminding you of what you already know. It's getting it from your head to your heart that's the difficult part."

He snorted. "You can say that again. Well, I'd better let you get back to fielding phone calls. Give Daryl my best."

"You know I will. Oh, and Lincoln?"

"Yes, Felicity." There was a little less tease in his voice this time. As much as he disliked talking about his feelings, it had been good for him.

"Tell Kate I say hi."

Kate? But before he could ask if there was really a client waiting for her, the call disconnected. He checked his phone only to see the roaming signal in the upper corner.

"Great. *Now* the signal decides to go out." At least he didn't need to worry about ignoring any more unwanted calls, but the next time he got her back on the line, he'd have a few questions.

Firstly, how did she know Kate was there on the island?

And secondly, why hadn't she warned him?

A batch of bicycles flew by in a blur outside his window, accompanied by cheers from the migrating crowd of onlookers. Through the trees, others were busy setting up tables and chairs in the park beside an inflatable bounce house that currently looked more like a melted box of crayons than a castle.

Wow, this place sure took its festival events seriously.

Sunlight flashed from beside the food table, where Janine Dirks was busily arranging napkins and paper plates while another woman loaded up the table with hot catering pans, based on the rising steam. Only a pair of large glasses like Janine's could act as a homing beacon, which was probably why she was now waving off a persistent goose that seemed entirely too interested in the hem of her tweed skirt.

Lincoln didn't even bother to hide his chuckle. Especially when Dwight rushed over from the grill, flapping his arms at the poor creature.

The goose, not the woman.

That's when Lincoln saw her. Clipboard tucked beneath her arm as a camera swung in front of a white cable-knit sweater. Gone was the worried frown of Thursday, replaced by a pleasant smile that said she was comfortable and in her element.

The very same smile that was now turning his direction as she cut across the grassy field.

Kate ignored Lincoln's soft stare as she walked into the studio, and instead focused on the white flowers lining the table behind him. As if that could make up for his unwavering eye contact.

Like a groom gazing at his bride as she walked down the aisle.

No, she wouldn't go there. Not now. Not with him. He was her ticket to a raving review in *American Wanderer*, that was all.

"Ready for your first workshop?" she asked.

"I'm ready if you are."

Her eyes flicked up to his, which were studying her with far too much attention. Or observation. Both made her feel awkwardly exposed and comforted at the same time. "I didn't see you at the race earlier."

He shrugged—a mountain of a man, who should have been intimidating if not for the half apron tied around his waist. "Been here all morning. I assume all went off without a hitch?"

"What makes you say that?"

"Because you're smiling," he said without missing a beat.

Was she? She tugged at the sleeves of her sweater, despite the warmth radiating from the stove. Goodness. And why was he still looking at her like that? Half serious, half lopsided grin.

"I'm just happy there's been such a good turnout so far this weekend. With Dani still in Italy until Monday, and the weather so cold for the first week of May, I was afraid no one would show." Or worse, that the whole thing would implode before her sister got back.

"Well, from the looks of that checklist of yours, I'd have thought you'd done this hundreds of times."

"Oh, which reminds me . . ." She flipped to the next page of names, grateful for the work-related distraction. "All twelve slots have already been filled for your first workshop."

His eyebrows dipped. "All of them?"

"Mm-hmm. There's even a waitlist." She didn't miss his measured intake of air as he looked over the full page of names. She also didn't miss the partially prepared workbench behind him when there was less than twenty minutes until his first class. "Is it only you today? I thought you said you had someone coming up to help you this week."

"Change of plans."

"They're not coming?"

He shrugged again. "Looks like you're stuck with just me."

"No one's *stuck* with anyone." Okay, so maybe she'd thought otherwise a couple of weeks ago, but she'd be lying now if she said his presence wasn't welcome. For the festival, of course. No other reason.

Her gaze dropped to the roll of chicken wire and the vases strewn about the floor, and she tried not to frown. "Are you sure you've got everything under control here?"

"This your idea of a pep talk?" Face relaxing, he studied her with a raised eyebrow.

She recalled the afternoons spent in his mom's flower shop assembling boutonnieres and bridesmaid bouquets for their wedding. The wedding might not've worked, but she'd enjoyed the time making something beautiful. She could still smell the jasmine-scented centerpieces, now mingled with Lincoln's spicy aftershave as he stood silently watching her.

"It's just . . . well . . ." *Spit it out, already.* "If you'd like, I could stick around and help."

"You'd do that? Why?"

Because I need this to succeed as much as you do. Because I don't trust myself not to be distracted thinking about you when I should be working.

"Why not? That is, unless you don't want me to—"

"No."

His curt interruption had her mind scrambling for any coherent reply. "No?"

"I mean, yes." He grimaced.

Well, that made things less confusing.

Then . . . "As long as you're sure it's not a problem."

Hmm. He seemed sincere enough. Despite the unusual politeness. "I wouldn't have offered if it had been." She paused, realizing that hadn't always been true. "I mean, what I meant to say is . . ." His hand on her shoulder silenced the rest of her thought, but it was his steady presence that had her arms relaxing at her sides. Her diaphragm eased, and she released a soft laugh. "Look at me with my runaway mouth."

"At least it's not your feet." His chuckle turned into a cough as his lips flattened against each other.

Clipboard still under her arm, she turned toward the open door as his hand brushed her arms once more. She understood Lincoln's body language well enough to answer the silent question. "I'm just going to check the refrigerator. That is, after all, where you keep the flowers."

"Right. Flowers." His shoulder grazed hers as he stepped around her and into the hazy sunlight. "I was thinking about starting off with something small and simple. Roses and peonies, mostly. If people seem to like those, we can go from there. What do you think?"

What did she think? He was the expert. But then again, maybe he wasn't only talking about the flowers.

"I think that sounds perfect."

Thirty minutes later, Kate couldn't help but smile as Lincoln demonstrated the best way to fluff a rose.

Around her, the class of overly attentive ladies took their turns twirling the trimmed stems between their palms—to varying success. Doris Poe, the seventysomething woman who worked at the island's small airport office, had already destroyed two, the mess of petals at her feet sweetly perfuming their corner of the studio.

"Gently. You don't want to bruise the petals, only encourage them to open naturally." Lincoln plucked a fresh one off the table and spun the creamy flower in one fluid motion, making it spread like a frilly gown. "See? A nice, full rose."

The other ladies flocked around him, oohing and aahing over his airy bouquet.

Content to remain in back, Kate reached for another stem of white sweet pea and threaded it between the wire mesh into her own vase. It wasn't going to win any awards—not with the eucalyptus branching out to the left and the ranunculus bud that kept drooping like a marble on a string. But her mind hadn't felt clearer in weeks, and the nagging tension in her chest had all but vanished under the flowers' heady scents.

Someone bumped her elbow, and she looked up from her work to the older woman beside her.

"Could you be a dear and hand me the floral spray?" Annabelle Kennedy—retired librarian and known gossip—pointed to the large bottle at the other end of the table. Her artsy pink-and-white shawl matched the flowers in front of her, which glistened like wax. Probably were, actually, after the half bottle of preserving spray she'd already used on them.

"Any more of that stuff, and those things will outlive both of us," quipped Doris, on the other side of Kate. "Isn't that right, Mr. St. James?"

He flinched only a millisecond at the formal address before pasting on a patient expression. "Lincoln, please." He smiled at Doris, who practically swooned under the weight of it, before turning to address Annabelle. "And while I'm all for flowers lasting more than a few days, I think those are beyond well protected. I'd hate for you to run out of time when you could be finishing your lovely bouquet."

Oh, he was good.

Neither woman questioned him, and soon, everyone was quietly working on their own arrangements.

After picking up another sprig of sweet pea, Kate went to push back the other flowers when something pricked her finger. A spot of red stained her skin from a stray thorn. In search of a rose stripper, she left her vase and circled to the other side of the room, where the tools sat in neat piles. It also happened to be the one empty station beside Lincoln.

Not wanting to disturb him, she waited as he took special care with the blush peonies, wedging something small and blue between their tightly packed stems.

"I don't remember taking any daisies out of the cooler."

So much for not disturbing the man.

He didn't seem to mind the intrusion; practically pulled up the empty chair beside him for her to sit while he nestled the stem at the base of the arrangement. "Do you remember when I told you about the time I accidentally ordered ten cases of blue daisies instead of one?"

She smiled as she lowered next to him. "You said it was your first week helping your mom out at her shop and you thought you could hide the extras before she found out."

"Then you remember that she found them in the back of her minivan later that morning."

The twinkle in his eyes was as charming now as it had been the first time she'd heard the story. She could imagine a sixteen-year-old Lincoln, unruly hair falling over his face as he tried to hide a whole garden. In fact, she didn't have to imagine much beyond the scrapbook photos his mom had shared with her during their short engagement. There were less rips in his jeans now, and his hair was a few shades darker, but there was still a bit of boyish mischief behind those eyes of his.

"By the end of the day, she had us all making blue daisy bouquets to deliver to the hospital staff. I think every doctor, nurse, and candy striper received one. She didn't get mad at me for mixing up the order, even though I know it cost her." He shook his head, then rotated the vase to inspect his work. "Always putting other people first."

"That sounds like her."

"Yeah, she was pretty great. It's no wonder everyone loved my mom."

Kate looked at the smile that didn't quite reach his eyes, and her heart broke. For him. For the future they'd never had together.

"She really was the perfect mom. I know I probably shouldn't say that, but I used to envy you. I'm sure my mom was only doing her best with seven kids"—cheating on her husband and abandoning her family notwithstanding—"but even when I was younger, it felt like I was more of a babysitter than a daughter. Heaven forbid I ever needed anything from her. That would just be selfish." She hadn't meant to go there, but then it always had been easy to talk around Lincoln.

He sat back, unreadable gaze shifting from the bouquet to her. "I know you and your mom haven't been very close. But there's still time to have the kind of relationship with her you've always wanted."

Was there, though? They'd only grown more distant since her mom's second divorce. Besides her annual Christmas card and birthday phone call, there didn't seem to be much of a relationship to salvage. Even now, Dani's wedding and the big family Easter weekend before were the only times she'd seen her mom since being back on island. What would they even have to talk about? It wasn't easy with her like it had been with Lincoln's mom.

His hand found hers, warm and secure. It should've felt strange, yet the familiar gesture comforted her like a long-awaited embrace. He gave it a little squeeze, the action constricting her heart just a little bit more.

"All finished."

Kate flinched at the sudden intrusion. Her hand slipped from his as she looked at the room of expectant faces.

Right, the bouquets.

Kate tried not to sound disappointed when she smiled at the woman. "Those turned out beautifully. How about I get a picture with everyone holding their vases?" Cool air replaced the earlier warmth as she slipped from her spot beside Lincoln and reached for her camera. Back turned to the room, she quickly swiped a sleeve beneath her eyes, then turned around with a practiced smile.

"Okay, how about we form two rows at the back of the room so we can squeeze everyone in." She went into photographer mode, guiding everyone to their places while continuously aware of Lincoln's laser-focused attention. She positioned him in the center of the group, surrounded by a cloud of white flowers and female attention.

"That's right. A little more to the left. And make sure I can see your faces behind your flowers. Great. Now, everyone say 'flowers.'"

The shutter clicked right before Doris, in the front row, frowned. "You need to be in the picture as well."

"Oh, I don't know. I'm really just helping for the day."

"But you made a bouquet," insisted another.

She didn't have much chance to object before one of them tugged her into the group. "Okay, okay. But I need to set the timer first." And catch her breath. After propping the camera on a box and punching a few buttons, she grabbed her vase and slipped into place on the fringe as the indicator light blinked red.

"Oh no you don't." Lincoln reached over and pulled her closer, much to the ladies' delight. They parted like a veil until she could feel his breath tickling the hair around her forehead. Not to mention the press of his body against hers as the group squeezed back in.

It was only a photo, so why was her heart rate gaining speed with the countdown?

"Everyone say 'sweet pea!'" yelled a voice behind her.

A sprig of eucalyptus jabbed at Kate's ear, and she found herself stepping deeper into Lincoln's side. Warmth enveloped her—all-encompassing and dangerously heady. The spicy scents of sandalwood, rose, and something else she couldn't put her finger on muddled her brain.

"You're too beautiful to keep hiding." His voice was barely a whisper, one she might not have heard had he not dipped his head a little closer.

She looked up, eyes locking with his right as the camera flashed.

Some people talked about fireworks or time standing still. But there was no choir singing in the background, no shock of electricity when their hands touched. There was only the chatter of women and a sea of white flowers as everyone dispersed to their seats. Yet Kate couldn't shake the familiar feeling of this moment.

A moment that, in fact, felt a lot like coming home.

But that was crazy.

Ridiculous.

The thought alone ought to send her into another panic attack. The thought of him. Of calling this island home when it hadn't been for so long.

But it didn't.

And that alone had her heart nearly skipping a beat.

Nine

SHE WASN'T FALLING FOR LINCOLN AGAIN. AT least, that's what she told herself as she stole another glance across the green.

"Hello. Earth to Kate."

Someone tapped her on the shoulder, causing her to turn away from the small building on the other side of the tent-studded green.

Oliver was looking at her with a hiked eyebrow that said he could read her mind.

She knew he couldn't. But that infuriating half frown of his did nothing to hide his obvious objections to the amount of time she'd been spending with Lincoln.

"You look like someone dog-eared a page in one of your books." Her brisk morning walk after church had turned into a coffee run and then a visit to her brother's bookstore, where she'd found him brooding over a box of old, dusty tomes. He'd been the one to suggest the art show in the park, not her.

Whose fault was it really if she stole a glance or two while she was there?

His face went practically stony. "Don't joke. You'd be horrified too at the things I've found in books over the years: drink stains, torn pages, and don't even get me started on bookworms."

All that came to mind was curling up with a favorite book, but based on his grimace, he wasn't talking of the human variety.

She lifted her camera to take a picture of an artist with their easel. The pinks of the apple blossoms popped against the loosely painted background like many of the other pieces hanging from the displays. Maybe if she backed up a little, she could get everything in one shot. And with the trees framing the white tents, it would make a striking contrast.

One eye closed, she adjusted the viewfinder as a man stepped out from one of the tents. Although his hair was more salt than pepper, he was every bit the image of Oliver in thirty years.

"Wait, is that Dad? Did you know he was coming?" She turned in time to see her brother shrug.

"Mom didn't tell me anything when I had lunch with her yesterday. You should've come, by the way. She made those stuffed peppers you always used to like."

"Hmm." Raising her camera once more, she watched until Daniel Sullivan disappeared behind the next set of covered booths. "Maybe she invited him to the show as well."

"After the awkwardness between them at Dani's wedding? I doubt it."

Yeah, she supposed that was true. But then why did it look like he'd been walking in the exact direction of her mom's table?

"You can't avoid her forever, you know."

"Who says I'm avoiding anyone? I came with you to her art show, didn't I?"

"That remains to be seen. We haven't *actually* gone in yet." Not that he was rushing ahead either. She knew things were getting better between him and Dad, but the road to reconciliation was a marathon, not a sprint.

"There you are, Kate." A woman's voice, followed by an uneven crunch of grass behind her.

One look over Kate's shoulder, and Oliver was making a beeline toward the covered tables. When Kate finally turned, she understood why.

"Janine, hi." The woman wore another matching sweater and skirt but was hobbling toward Kate with one foot encased in a big, fat walking boot. "What happened?"

Janine was breathing heavily, as if she'd just finished arguing the merits of the pre-industrialization era. "If you must know, I was organizing the maritime-history display at the fort yesterday when I dropped one of the cannonballs on my toe. It pretty much ruined my blue suede Mary Janes. I've tried nearly every cleaner from Doug's Market, but I'm afraid the gunpowder stain is never coming out."

"I'm sorry to hear that. But how is your foot?"

"A minor stress fracture. But the doctor has me in this boot for four to six weeks. And right as the weather is starting to improve."

Compared to the weekend, today was downright balmy. The perfect weather for an art show and bike tour.

Wait. The historic tours.

Kate looked again at Janine's booted foot as her stomach tightened.

"If this happened yesterday, who led the walking tour this morning?"

Janine waved a dismissive hand in the air. "I got Nora, Seb's youngest, to cover for me. Sweet girl, once you get past the teenage attitude. It's those cell phones, I'm sure of it. When I was a kid, we learned how to talk to *real* people instead of texting each other from across the room."

She made it sound as if she were in her eighties rather than her forties.

"So does that mean she's also leading the bike tour that leaves in an hour?" Kate asked hopefully.

The woman blinked, eyes large behind her glasses. "The girl is sixteen and has homework due tomorrow. I might encourage people to take a greater interest in this island's history, but not at the detriment of one's education."

"Oh, right." Kate's ears grew warm under the woman's owlish stare. Of course school was more important than the festival. But now Janine was looking at her as if she were one of those teenagers who thought of little more than boys and texting.

"That's what I was on my way to tell you. You'll have to find someone else to cover both tours for the rest of the week. At least until next Saturday."

The whole week?

Her eyes drifted once more to Lincoln's workshop, hidden now behind the trees, as if that alone could summon him. She'd hoped to photograph the blossoms inland, which were now starting to open. Maybe even ask Lincoln if he wanted to tag along on his day off for inspiration.

This is for Dani, she reminded herself with a sigh. She'd already missed so much of her baby sister's life, growing up and then moving away. A few sacrifices was the least she could do. That was the real relationship she should be focusing on right now, anyway. In a week, Lincoln would be gone again. It had been hard enough letting him go the first time. Maybe this was God's way of protecting her heart. Keep her busy enough not to wish for more.

Janine must've said all she'd intended, because she hobbled off in the direction of the tents, leaving Kate alone with her camera. Oliver was nowhere in sight either.

"Everything all right?" a familiar deep voice asked.

Tingles washed down her arms as she turned to see Lincoln

walking toward her. The rich navy shirt made his eyes all the more intense as he tilted his head to the side. Enough for her to smell the spicy scent of . . . clove. That's what she'd smelled on him the other day during the workshop. It simultaneously reminded her of sipping vanilla chais on her parents' porch in high school and building gingerbread houses with Lincoln at his mom's house for the church Christmas party.

"All good here. Everything's okey dokey." *Okey dokey?* Yeah, she wouldn't believe herself either.

To his credit, though, he didn't laugh at her.

Much.

"Then why are you standing at the far end of an empty field and not mingling with everyone else?"

"I was taking pictures. That is part of my job, after all." Okay, so maybe it was a stretch, but could she help it if the man still made her brain go all fuzzy, even after all the water that had passed under the bridge? The seven-hundred-fifty-foot bridge, according to the Lake Huron experts.

"Then why is your camera turned off?" His lips twitched as she inspected the screen, which had indeed gone black.

The dark ends of his hair were still damp, curling above his shoulders like waves swirling into quiet tide pools. His eyes seemed clearer this morning, calm as the cloudless sky above them and just as bright. Maybe it was the clean air and time away from the city that was softening his hard edges. Giving him space to breathe.

She felt it too. Like she'd awakened from a long slumber to find that winter had faded into spring, and new life was just beyond the horizon.

When Kate smiled like that, a man could almost believe in second chances.

He couldn't remember why he'd walked over here, just that he'd do about anything to keep her smiling at him.

But then, without any effort on his part, her light dimmed.

"It's Janine."

The one from the meeting who didn't like Christmas lights? "She's not giving you any more trouble about the festival, is she?"

"In a manner of speaking . . ." She tilted her head side to side before her shoulders slumped. "Actually, no. It's not her fault, just bad timing, I suppose. I was planning on taking a trip inland today to photograph some of the apple groves, but now I have to fill in for the bike tour in less than an hour."

He'd kinda been hoping to catch her with a free moment to talk, but he should've known better than to assume. Maybe he'd read more into yesterday's workshop than she had. After all, she was only trying to make sure the festival went off without a hitch. But that didn't answer for her soft gasp when he'd tucked her into his side for the group photo, as perfect a fit as always.

He definitely hadn't imagined that.

"I like bike riding."

"What?" Her blank look did little to tame the skip in his chest. *Use your words, man.*

"I mean, if you don't mind the extra company, I'd be more than happy to tag along. I may not know all the history points, but I can certainly help wrangle a few tourists, if that's what's needed."

"Really? Are you sure you have the time?"

Knowing Kate, she was giving him an easy out in case he hadn't meant it.

Which, in fact, he very much did.

"It's my day off, remember? I'd be happy for the distraction. There are only so many flower arrangements a guy can take for one weekend. Even a florist." He gave her what he hoped was a convincing smile, then tacked on, "I've been cooped up all morning. Some fresh air sounds nice."

"And what do you call this?" Kate lifted her arms toward the blue sky.

He glanced around the expansive lawn hemmed in by flowering trees on one side and Lake Huron on the other. Yes. This was a far cry from the concrete-and-steel forests of Detroit. "You make a fair point. I suppose I meant to say I could use the activity. Besides, I hear the best way to truly see the island is on a bike." When the silence stretched on, he added, "I promise, I won't slow you down."

Could you be *any more obvious?*

But he didn't really care so long as she said yes to letting him help. Nothing could fix what had already happened between them, and he wasn't about to add to her burden with excuses about his own hardships. That was his cross to bear. But he *could* do this for her. He waited as the gears turned inside her head, observed the tiny scrunch of her nose and heard the soft hum that said she wasn't sure.

"Okay."

"Okay, as in I can help you with the tour?" He wasn't being pushy. Just looking for clarification.

"Okay, as in you're welcome to join. It's been so long since I last visited, it'll take all my concentration just to remember the history, let alone keep track of a dozen or so tourists as well. Not that they can get too lost on Jonathon Island. It's only four miles wide." She clipped the lens cap back onto her camera, which now swung loosely at her side as she checked her watch. "We only have about forty-five minutes. Why don't we head on down and I can talk you through the route on our way? Unless you need to take care of anything first. Maybe change?"

If she was comfortable riding in her jeans and nice shirt, then so was he. Besides, it would be a leisurely loop around a relatively flat island. Probably not even enough to break a sweat. "My shoes have already been baptized in mud more than once on this trip. Not much point in trying to keep them clean now."

And that's when the full force of Kate's unencumbered smile hit him the second time that morning.

"In that case, maybe we can take the scenic route. You haven't really visited Jonathon Island until you've seen its wildflowers."

His chuckle ran deep. "You mean besides the apple blossoms?"

She took a step away from the artists' tents, and he followed. "You'd be surprised by what all you might find here. We might be small, but it's a world all its own."

As he was quickly learning.

They stopped at the corner of the park for a carriage to pass, then turned toward a main street that had been plucked right out of history and dropped into the twenty-first century.

"It's like a real-life Brigadoon here."

She raised a delicate eyebrow. Not arched like the painted ones from the city, but natural and silently mocking. "You've watched *Brigadoon*?" The very thought seemed to make her chuckle. "Whatever happened to 'musicals are for teenage girls and hopeless romantics'?"

He shrugged, a playful grin spreading across his face as he skipped up to the sidewalk. "Maybe I'm secretly a hopeless romantic at heart." Bending at the waist, he held out a hand like the guys did in those shows.

"Or just hopeless," she teased, ignoring his hand.

"Would you believe me if I told you I used to watch them with my mom?"

He couldn't tell if she was smiling with delight or holding back her laughter. Kate was one of the few people he'd met who could laugh without making a single sound. It was an art form, really, when one thought about it. One he could easily spend a lifetime appreciating.

"Yes, I actually would." Her body stilled save for the steady rhythm of her steps, nearly two for every one of his. "I can imagine the two of you huddled around a bowl of kettle corn, her humming along to the songs while you humored her like always."

"That doesn't mean I liked them."

"Of course."

"But they're good memories now." The best, actually, outside of the flower shop. "If I could go back and do it over, I'd be a little less snarky and actually listen to the songs my mom was always singing. You know?" He was looking down at Kate rather than where he was walking, and nearly collided with a basket of petunias hanging from the wrought-iron lamp post.

That's when her giggles hiccuped beside him, slipping into the cracks of a heart that had stopped beating long ago.

She turned her rosy face toward him, sunlight making individual strands of her brown hair look like spun gold. As if God had knocked open the doors to heaven and shone down a spotlight for him to pay attention. But one blink, a shift in the clouds, and it was gone.

"Yeah, you're a real Gene Kelly," she shot back.

"Hey, the guy was never attacked by flowers." He swept the few fallen buds onto the street with his foot. "Maybe I should submit a complaint to the city about their flower basket heights. That, and a place this special deserves more than your run-of-the-mill petunias. I happen to know a fantastic florist as well as the director of tourism, you know."

"Interim director," she corrected. "But I can pass your suggestion along to Dani when she gets back."

"Where would be the fun in that?" His shoe bumped something soft, and then he was looking down into her upturned face.

Even without the halo, she was still the prettiest woman he'd ever met. Delicate cupid's-bow mouth, slender neck that was beginning to blush slightly from the sun, and eyes the color of a cymbidium orchid. Halfway between amber and chestnut, he'd always been drawn to the flower's understated beauty. It was beautiful because it was, not because it called attention to itself. Much like the woman standing a foot in front of him now.

If she knew the power she held over him, she could ask any number of things and he'd say yes. And not out of guilt or obligation.

But because he wanted to.

She took another step back, as did he, drawing his attention to the Island Outfitters sign painted across the glass display in front of them. "Well, this is it."

He hadn't even noticed the rows of mint-green cruiser bikes lined up out front until now.

"We'll have to make a few trips," she said, reaching for the nearest bike. "But between the two of us, we should manage it before the tour officially starts."

"Wait, we're taking *all* of these?" There had to be almost a dozen bikes here. And only two of them.

"Yep. Which means we should probably get going. I'll go and tell Blake we're ready to take them over if you want to get started."

The little bell above the door chimed as she slipped inside, leaving Lincoln alone with a heap of bikes from yesteryear and a basketful of questions.

Ten

SPENDING TIME WITH KATE WAS A LOT LIKE riding a bike. Surprisingly easy and enjoyable.

Lincoln kept to the back of the group, a river of brightly colored helmets between him and Kate, who was currently pointing at something through the trees of Lake Shore Drive.

"The white stone complex to your left is Fort Jonathon. The historical society still runs live reenactments, and you can even sign up to fire the cannon."

So *that* was the booming sound he'd kept hearing all week. He'd thought he'd accidentally left another bug bomb lying around the shop and it had gone off. But when there wasn't any smoke, he'd written it off as something happening down at the docks.

"And that building south of us across the water is Round Island's lighthouse, one of one hundred and fifty lighthouses in Michigan. Later in the tour, we'll get to see Jonathon Island's very own on the north side of the island and maybe even take a peek inside if we're lucky." They didn't stop but continued to pedal around the bend in the road.

The cool breeze kicked up as they rounded the southern tip of the island, fresh and invigorating. The town and marina slipped behind him, along with the clanging of ships' bells, clop of carriages, and bustle of Main Street. Only half a mile further, and it felt as if they were the only people on the island, save for a couple walkers on the other side of the road.

"Lake Shore Drive is the only highway in the United States without cars. It circles all eight miles of Jonathon Island, providing one-hundred-eighty-degree views of our little spot in the middle of Lake Huron."

"Why aren't there any cars?" piped up one of the teenagers, the oldest of the family of five who'd joined their group at the last minute.

"That's a great question, Mason. In the sixties, a number of locals raised concern as more cars began to populate the island, so they brought it to the town council to have them banned. It must not have taken much convincing, because the island has been car-free ever since."

Lincoln smiled. They must've been related to Janine.

"What do people do in the winter?" asked the boy's dad. "Surely you can't expect someone to ride a bike through the snow."

"Most people own golf carts and snowmobiles. Of course, they still allow some vehicles for construction and emergency access, but they need a special permit to ferry them up from the mainland."

That must've answered their questions for now. The boy rode easily between his two sisters, their parents on either side like something out of a magazine for the all-American family. They even wore matching T-shirts, if one could believe that. But the longer Lincoln stared at their yellow backs, the more something yawned inside of him begging to be filled. Not that he'd be caught dead wearing something like that. Although Kate could definitely pull off the sunny yellow if she wanted.

Lincoln squinted against the glare reflecting off the rippling water. With the afternoon sun to their backs, every tree, rock, and outcrop practically glowed.

"And this," Kate said as she stopped near a sign, "is Lover's Leap."

He followed the direction of her raised chin to a crumbling tower of rock on the other side. It didn't look like much, but with a name like Lover's Leap, it had to have an interesting story.

"What's so special about a rock?" This time, it was the boy's youngest sister who spoke up. Maybe around six or seven, she stood there frowning, face all scrunched up as she tipped her head back to see.

Unlike her flustered responses at the city council meeting, Kate's answer was relaxed as she turned to the girl with twin braids and smiled. "While it might *look* like any old rock, this one is special. It has its very own story."

"Like a fairy tale?" The girl's eyes widened. "Are there mermaids in this lake?"

No one could be immune to such cuteness. Which was why everyone, including Lincoln, smiled in wait for Kate's reply. Not that he believed there were such things as mermaids—at least, not this far north or in a lake—but he knew what it was to be met with the unexpected.

"I'm afraid it's not that kind of story, but there is a princess."

"I knew it!" the girl shouted, letting her bike tip to the ground as she jumped.

A wave of chuckles washed over the group, drawing Lincoln in closer until he was no longer standing at the back. He hadn't spent much time around kids, but it was obvious Kate had a soft spot for the little girl and her charming questions. Throw in the dimples and the way she beamed at her dad when he lifted her onto his shoulders, and even he could imagine doing the same one day.

Kate had the group eating out of the palm of her hand, despite the lack of a PowerPoint presentation. She could tell them any number of made-up facts or anecdotes of the island and they would listen.

Lincoln looked up again at the craggy limestone tower to their left as Kate began to spin its tale.

"Well, a long time ago, there was a princess. Her father, the chief, loved her very much, so he planted flowers all across the island, calling them 'spring beauty' in honor of his daughter. One day when she was strolling through the forest, she met a man who was also enjoying the pink-and-white flowers. Upon looking at each other, they fell in love and went to her father, asking to marry. Now, the chief was very wise and knew only a great warrior would be worthy of his daughter's hand. But he was swayed by her pleas and gave his blessing for a wedding at the next full moon."

They all listened in silence. But where the others were caught up in the romance of it all, he couldn't help feeling he knew this story. A family who didn't think the guy was good enough for his daughter? Yep, been there. He'd seen enough of Oliver's glares over the past weeks to know the feeling hadn't changed. It didn't matter that he'd walked away *for* Kate's own good.

"But before that day came," continued Kate, "another tribe called on their island for help. There was a war on the other side of the water, and only with their aid could the other tribe hope to survive. So the chief rounded up the men, including the one meant to marry his daughter, and they sailed north to an uncertain fate, leaving behind wives, mothers, and children.

"Every day, the princess would watch from this cliff, a bouquet of wildflowers clutched to her chest, as she waited for her beloved to return. The first frost came, wilting the last of her father's flowers. She picked what little remained and again stood watch over the eastern shore. The others told her to come down. 'It's getting cold," they said. But from the bottom of the hill, they couldn't see the small grouping of boats that appeared on the horizon.

"Clutching the flowers tighter, she rushed to the edge of the cliff, hoping to see him among the returning warriors. Instead, she saw the sorrow etched in the droop of their shoulders. Overcome by her own grief, the princess ran toward them, forgetting about the cliff. And there she fell, flowers still clutched to her chest as the last reminder of her beloved before joining him in the afterlife. The tribe mourned her loss greatly, forever preserving her memory by tending to the little pink-and-white flowers that bloomed in her spot the following spring.

"Or so the story goes . . ."

With a little shrug, Kate lifted her arms at her side as if to say that was all. Her face turned rosy under the resulting applause, especially that of the little girl who jumped right in with a bucket of questions about the princess and if the story was really true.

Lincoln let the others go ahead with their comments while he slipped again to the back of the group. The limestone outcrop towered over them, the little bunch of bright flowers at its base like a finger pointing straight at his heart.

Was that how Kate had felt when he left? Like the princess who'd waited faithfully only to be rewarded with heartache? He knew she'd been upset—hurt by his abrupt decision. He'd always figured she'd moved on though. Found her prince somewhere else, one with far fewer ghosts and more to offer than a broken home and an unpredictable future.

He wanted to look away from the flowers that resembled blood-streaked snow but couldn't.

What kind of God allowed such suffering in this world, especially at the hands of those who are supposed to love and look out for you? His own dad had let them down more times than he could count, and then he'd gone and let down his mom and Kate as well.

Like father, like son.

But no. He wasn't his dad. And if God truly was a father like his mom always used to say, then maybe there was a chance he could somehow find a way to be the kind of man who could make Kate happy.

Maybe there was a chance that *he* could be happy.

While the rest of the group took turns snapping photos of the rock and the water, Lincoln slipped out his phone and scrolled to the photo Kate had texted him yesterday after sharing it on the island's official tourism page. He'd stayed up far too late last night studying that picture and replaying the day's events.

He navigated to his social media page—the one Felicity managed at his request—and saw the immaculately curated selection of photos. The Shinola Hotel wedding, the floral chandelier. Kate had called his arrangements enchanting, but all he saw was a business. One centered around the idea of love when he really knew so little about the subject. Definitely not the kind of passion from Kate's story just now. Who was he really fooling? His twelve thousand followers or himself?

He clicked on the Add button, an odd sense of urgency driving him. Without stopping to think, he selected the photo and added a short caption about "spring beauty," then tagged Kate's personal account before posting it.

She'd probably never see it. No doubt she'd stopped following his page the moment she realized who he was. However, this wasn't about getting her back. At least, not entirely. He couldn't undo the past, but he could do whatever it took to make sure her business, and her happiness, had the best chance of succeeding.

Whatever the cost.

Even if it meant breaking his social media hiatus, which was sure to backfire on him like it always did. But for her, he was willing to take the chance.

It was a long four miles from the lighthouse to the Grand Sullivan Hotel.

That's what Kate told herself when she let the Peterson family take the lead after the stop at the Jonathon Island lighthouse. Then came the retired couple from Manitoba and the honeymooners after them.

Something bittersweet knocked against her chest as she slowed to join Lincoln at the back. Was it a bad idea? Possibly. Should she keep to the front and do her job like she'd signed up for? Undoubtedly. But then again, she also had an obligation to look out for *all* members of the biking tour. Especially the ones who'd hardly spoken a word the entire past hour.

"Shouldn't you be up front?" He wasn't smiling. Not exactly. But only a person with the emotional capacity of a teaspoon would take Lincoln at face value.

"I put the kids in charge for a bit." She wasn't falling for the grumpy exterior. He liked the Petersons as much as they all did. Especially Emily and her princess obsession. Kate may have stolen a couple of glances toward the back while telling the story, and if he wasn't watching her, he was watching the girls and their brother with a longing she'd never noticed before.

"You're probably a better tour guide." His bike drew even with hers as they cruised past cedar forests and whitecapped waves.

A gull screeched overhead, and the scent of fresh earth filled her lungs. "We all have to start somewhere. Why not here?"

"Yeah, why not here?"

She wasn't sure if he'd meant for her to hear his echoed response, but there again was that same wistful tone in his voice as she'd seen in his expression back at Lover's Leap.

"I can see Jonathon Island is a special place. And not only because of its unique history and lack of vehicles. Things feel different here. Slower. More simple. Even you seem—"

"A little crazy for stepping in to run a festival?" she suggested. Yet he didn't echo her airy chuckle.

A Victorian roofline poked through the trees, a sign they were nearing the upscale Driftwood Hills neighborhood and the Grand Sullivan. How many times as a kid had she ridden this loop between Uncle Seb's house and the golf course behind the hotel for lessons with Dad? Before he'd stepped aside and handed her off to a pro. Then came the divorce and the fire. It was great that Dani had found a way to rebuild the hotel after all these years, but Kate feared that some things weren't as easy to restore as brick and plaster.

Lincoln was right. Growing up on the island had been simple … until it wasn't.

He chuckled to himself. "I was going to say this place suits you."

"In a good way, I hope." She could only manage a quick glance over her shoulder, but his intense gaze held hers captive.

A nod, then, "Definitely."

It was only a nod, yet a pleasant tingling sensation washed up her arms. Kate hummed to herself, the vibrations in her chest mirroring the gentle rattle of the handlebars as they coasted down the slight hill.

"So, why'd you leave?" he asked once the path leveled out once more. "I think I can count the number of times you mentioned this place before now on one hand." There was no accusation in his voice, only curiosity.

It struck her that she'd almost married this man, yet there was a whole part of her life she'd never shared with him. A whirlwind romance indeed. He might've been the one to walk away, but maybe that had been the mature thing to do at the time. After all, how were two people supposed to share a life if they couldn't manage to share their pasts first?

But she was older now. And wiser, she hoped.

"Childhood homes have a way of preserving the best and worst of memories. We were starting a new life together, and I suppose I wanted a fresh start." No, that wasn't entirely true. Yes, she'd wanted another chance at happiness, but that was supposed to include her family as well as Lincoln's.

"I get that. There's a lot in my past I'd rather forget."

Was he talking about their almost-wedding? She'd be lying if she said she hadn't wondered what had really happened all those years ago. She could ask, but that seemed far too dangerous a question.

"So why come back now?" His voice carried on the same wind that whipped the ends of her hair. Free, but wild and unpredictable at the same time.

"Because I'm a glutton for punishment?" Wasn't that the truth?

The hitch in her lungs fell flat at his silence. But then, maybe he was only studying the curve in the road ahead. She definitely hadn't just made a fool of herself by bringing up the past and then brushing it under the—

"You don't have to pretend with me, Kate." Earnest. Sincere. Intentional, as with everything that Lincoln did.

And that's when it hit her. She could share anything in the world with him and not have to worry about what he'd think. He'd be leaving as soon as the festival was over, and then they'd go their separate ways. For a week, she didn't have to pretend she had her life all put together. And at the end of it all, she wouldn't have to worry about getting hurt, because there were no expectations.

No future. No repercussions.

"I guess I'm so used to doing whatever it is people expect of me. Dani wouldn't understand. She's the youngest of the family, whom everyone always doted on. Oliver would only try to analyze things which James would then try and fix. As much as I value family, I don't need another lecture."

"You definitely won't get that from me." His laugh was deep and soothing, like a balm. "Anyway, I'm pretty sure Oliver still hates me. Not that I can blame the guy."

"He doesn't hate you."

"He doesn't *not* hate me. You saw the look he gave me that first day on Main Street. I thought he was about to deck me right in front of the coffee shop."

"After you nearly knocked me to the ground."

"Saved you from that horse and buggy, I think, is what you meant."

More like turned her carefully curated world upside down. Something she'd been in desperate need of, according to her doctor. *You can't keep going like this, Kate. It's not healthy for your brain or your body to push yourself so hard all the time. You need rest. Maybe someone to talk with to figure out the real reason you feel you have to keep proving yourself to everyone.*

Raised voices ahead demanded her attention, and she looked up as Jack, the island dog, raced after the kids. He only wanted to say hello, but the loud bark startled Emily, who drove her bike right into the nearest bush.

She hated walking out mid-conversation, but she couldn't very well abandon her responsibilities either. "I need to see if she's okay, but I'd really like to continue this once the tour is over."

"Go, do your thing. I'll still be here when you're done."

And the funny thing was, she believed him.

Kate leaned into the pedals before the scene ahead of her could dissolve even further. A few minutes later, she managed to pull the tour together for the final stop at the hotel gardens before releasing them back outside the Tourism Bureau on Main Street.

She didn't ask Lincoln to help her return the bikes to the rental shop, yet he did anyway, keeping his promise until it was just the two of them back in her office. There, her clipboard sat askew on the edge of the large desk, as if reminding her of all the other festival duties she had to take care of. Yet, for the first time in a long time, she wasn't ready to rush back out there. Another minute or two of peaceful escape was all she needed before returning to reality.

"Sometimes I wish I could stay inside this office and hide from the rest of the world, you know? Hit pause for a moment and pretend that I don't have a million and one things to do right this second."

"I do that all the time." Arms loosely crossed in front of his chest, he leaned against the open door. "Problem is, you tend to miss out on a lot if you're always hiding."

"At least there'd be time to enjoy a cup of coffee in peace," she said, picking up a half-full mug from beside her open laptop.

The corner of his mouth twitched. "If this is about coffee, I'd be more than happy to get you one of those cinnamon lattes you like so much." The room felt suddenly small with his broad shoulders filling out the doorway.

Kate swallowed, losing her train of thought until he cleared his throat.

"Uh, you said something back there about bad memories. I hope . . . I mean, what I'm trying to say is . . ." He dropped his gaze to the carpet, old and dingy from years of neglect. A long exhale later, he shoved his hands into his jean pockets, clearing his throat once again. "I'm sorry for hurting you like I did. Before, I mean. If my being here in any way has brought that all back, I—"

"Lincoln."

"I want you to know I thought I was doing the right thing at the time, but now—"

"*Lincoln.*"

Storm-cloud blue rose to meet her. All these years, she'd wondered what she'd say to him should she get the chance, and now that he was about to apologize, all she could do was say his name.

No expectations. That's what she'd wanted a moment ago, right? But now he was bringing up the past, and she didn't know how to reconcile the man who'd walked out on her with the friend she so desperately needed now.

"I wasn't fishing for an apology." Was she curious? Yes. But opening that door was a whole other level of complicated she wasn't willing to deal with right now. "The past is the past. I suppose that's what I was getting at about wanting to start over." Which she was completely, one hundred percent failing at. Especially when the way he was looking at her had her fingers suddenly tingling with the need to smooth the creases from between his eyebrows.

"I meant what I said earlier. You don't have to put on a brave face for me. You're already one of the most impressive people I know. Always have been. I was stupid to let you go." Instead of retreating through the open door, he took a step closer. Tilted his head toward hers.

All sorts of bells began to clang inside her brain.

Mixed signals. Poor decisions. And how moments like this surely couldn't be good for her anxiety and racing heartbeat.

She tipped her chin up as strong, calloused fingers brushed against her hand.

"Kate, I—"

Someone gasped from the hallway.

Lincoln stepped back like he'd pricked himself on a thorn, cold air replacing his earlier warmth.

Dani stood gaping in the open doorway, a paper bag in one hand and a roller suitcase in the other. "I thought I'd drop in and surprise you," she squeaked as paper crinkled at her side. "But it appears you beat me to it."

Eleven

LINCOLN COULDN'T EXIT THE OFFICE FAST enough. Not that Kate blamed him, yet his sudden absence did little to stanch the emotions tugging at her chest.

Or the knowing look now twitching at the corners of Dani's mouth.

Dani set the paper bag on top of the filing cabinet, hints of chocolate hazelnut replacing Lincoln's woodsy scent.

Kate hated uncomfortable silences like this one. Even more so when her baby sister was looking at her like the time Noah Rampart asked her to the homecoming dance sophomore year. They'd only gone as friends, but that hadn't stopped Dani from making kissing faces at her through the front window as they drove off in his mom's golf cart.

She opened her mouth to speak, but Dani beat her to it.

"Liam wanted to head straight to the house after getting off the ferry, but I thought I'd drop by and see how you and the festival were holding up." She unwound a Tuscan-yellow scarf from around her neck, drawing out the torture with a grin. "Good thing too, by the looks of what I just walked in on."

"I was just coming in to pick up the checklist for tonight's puzzle challenge. I had to step in at the last minute to guide the historic bike tour, which set me back time-wise."

"And the handsome stranger? Was he helping you find the checklist that's sitting on the corner of the desk?"

Kate's face heated. She didn't need to think too much to imagine what it must've looked like to Dani. Not that there'd been anything to see. It wasn't like Lincoln had kissed her. And she most definitely hadn't been about to let him.

"Yes, actually. He's been a huge help the past week. And second . . ." Kate ducked her head, suddenly very interested in the old map of Jonathon Island hanging beside the open door. She couldn't look at her sister when she told her the truth.

"Lincoln's not a stranger."

Dani's expression shifted in slow motion as the words sank in. "Wait. That guy with the wild hair was Lincoln? As in the guy who dumped you right before you were supposed to get married Lincoln?"

Kate winced. Was it getting stuffy in here, or was it the eight-mile bike ride she'd recently finished? She needed air. Knowing Dani would be right on her heels, she stepped into the hall and toward the back door. Blessedly cool air washed over her as she walked outside.

"He didn't exactly dump me. It just wasn't the right timing, that's all," she said, reaching the bottom of the apartment steps. At least, that was the line she'd told people when they'd asked. It was either that or relive her worst memory a hundred times. Even if she were more open like their actress sister Ashley, falling apart wouldn't solve anything.

Dani's suitcase clunked behind them, protesting Kate's excuses as much as its owner. "What else do you call showing up late to your own rehearsal dinner and then walking out for good before the cheesecake was plated? It took you so long to get over him, even if you didn't admit as much at the time. And after all these years, what is he doing here? And why haven't you told him to shove—"

"Because you invited him," she blurted out.

Kate shut her mouth and blinked. Oh, why had she ever said anything in the first place? See? This was exactly why she usually kept things to herself. Then she wouldn't be standing outside the apartment, feeling all awkward again—only this time with a heaping of guilt for having raised her voice in public.

Surely now Dani would leave. She'd been traveling for nearly twelve hours straight and likely had no desire for Kate's histrionics.

"Your voicemails…" Dani let go of her bag and smacked a hand against her forehead. "I saw them as soon as I landed at JFK but only had time to listen to the first one. I'm so sorry, Kate. I had no idea who he was when I reached out to him about the festival. Just that he came highly recommended."

"It's okay. You couldn't have known." After all, Kate had been following him on Instagram for months and hadn't suspected.

They stood in awkward silence behind the pizza parlor, the scents of garlic knots and marinara sauce swirling around them.

Kate's stomach rumbled in response. Between the art show, the bike tour, and then Lincoln, she'd completely forgotten about lunch. And as much as she wished she could offer Dani something to eat after what must've already been a long day of travel, she hadn't had time this weekend to go to the grocery store.

That's when she remembered the bag.

"Do you know what an even better sister would do?" Kate said, trying to lighten the unexpected serious mood. "Share some of that delicious biscotti I keep smelling."

And just like that, things clicked back to normal.

"Only if you've got some decent coffee to go with it."

Kate smiled. "It's not Italian roast, but it's dark and has caffeine in it."

"Sold."

Dani led the way up the steps and made herself at home in her old apartment while Kate got to work. Exactly six minutes later, she emptied the french press between two mugs, poured in a heavy dose of cream and sugar, and plopped one of the mugs into Dani's outstretched hands. A little brown liquid sloshed over the side of Dani's cup, sending Roma bolting for the safety of the couch. After wiping up the mess with a tissue, Dani reached into the bag and pulled out two cigar-shaped cookies the size of small baguettes.

"Wow, now that's a cookie."

"Just wait till you try it. It's nothing like the brick sticks you find in America."

The pastry practically melted in her mouth. It didn't even require a dunk in her coffee, yet she washed the chocolate hazelnut confection down with a sip.

"For what it's worth"—Dani swirled a little more milk into her cup, then tapped the spoon against the rim—"I'm still sorry about all this. Just say the word and I can cancel the interview. Being on the same island with Lincoln is one thing, but having to pretend to get along and work together in close proximity is something else."

"You don't have to do that. We've already been working together on the festival, and nobody has killed anyone yet. Besides, I really need that interview." Her cheeks warmed at Dani's scrutinizing stare, and not from the coffee.

"So, what *is* going on between you two, then?"

"Nothing. Really, we're just friends."

"Whatever you say. But friends don't look at each other the way he was looking at you when I walked in."

If her face hadn't been hot before in the small office, it was now. What did Dani really know? She'd seen all but a few seconds before Lincoln had hightailed it out of there. Kate didn't even know what was happening here, so how could Dani?

"All I'm saying is be careful." Genuine concern softened her voice. "I'd hate to see you get hurt again."

Married less than a month and she was apparently now an expert on relationships. A thought about spinster older sisters crossed Kate's mind, but she shoved it down as quickly as the next bite of biscotti. Dani had a point. Maybe it wouldn't hurt to listen.

"Don't worry. I promise not to go falling in love in the next week."

Dani frowned. "That's not what I said and you know it. You could walk out that door and meet the love of your life right there on Main Street."

"I think you're remembering your own fairy-tale romance. Not everyone is lucky enough to end up working with the man they're supposed to marry."

Dani snorted. "You do know I hated everything about Liam's original plans for the hotel restoration, right? He wanted to do away completely with the turrets and the summer porch. Imagine that."

Imagine that.

But she was right. They'd had to overcome their fair share of obstacles in their relationship.

"And it wasn't Main Street," Dani said with a playful flick of her scarf. "It was the airstrip."

"Potato, potahto."

Dani's snort dissolved into a fit of giggles that had Kate laughing until her side ached.

This. This was what she'd been missing and why she'd been working so hard to make sure the festival was a success. For her business, yes. But also for Dani. For sisterhood. For all the blanket forts and late-night campouts on the back porch that seemed like a lifetime ago.

"You know, now that you and Oliver are here, we should have a family dinner at our place. Liam would love it. Being an only child, he adores the idea of having a big family." And based on her sudden blush, she wasn't only talking about the Sullivan siblings.

"To big families." Kate raised her mug in a toast, to which Dani clinked hers sheepishly in response.

Soon their conversation drifted to Italian architecture and gelato. Every picture on Dani's phone had a story, but it was the ones of both her and Liam smiling at the camera that stirred a longing inside Kate for something more.

As Tuscan villas, blue skies, and golden hills rolled across the screen, her mind drifted to thoughts of Lincoln and whether or not he still made his mom's tiramisu. A secret family recipe, she'd called it. One that might've been passed along to Kate had things gone differently.

She could almost taste the velvety mascarpone and sponge, with just enough cocoa and coffee to make one think they'd been swept up like Elijah straight to heaven. She'd be a liar if she said she hadn't thought about that tiramisu over the years, wondering if it, and the future that went with it, was still as sweet as she remembered.

I almost kissed Kate Sullivan.

A crisp, minty aroma stung Lincoln's nose as he brought the bunch of eucalyptus down onto the table.

Swack.

I almost kissed *Kate Sullivan.*

Swack.

The sharp smell took on an almost medicinal quality as a couple of the silver-dollar leaves fluttered to the shop floor. He dropped the bundle lest he accidentally strip every leaf from the otherwise hardy plant. He was way beyond the subtle fragrance he'd been going for. Even if he stopped now, he'd be bordering on chemical warfare if he put these anywhere near the arrangements for tonight.

You want to impress her, not suffocate her with fumes.

He paused. Shook his foggy head.

Them.

It was the members of the Bloomfest committee he needed to impress. Felicity had texted him that morning saying she planned to call later in the day with an update. Good news, he hoped. They were the ones who held his future in their hands, not anyone on this island. Yet Kate was pretty much the only thing he could think about these days.

Hence the dismembered foliage stinking up the workshop.

He stepped away from the carnage and toward the open window for some much-needed fresh air when he nearly collided with Dwight.

"Ope, sorry about that." Fiberglass rods and tackle jangled as the two men danced around each other, but Dwight's hearty chuckle put him instantly at ease.

"No harm done. Strong as titanium, and the gear's even better." He slapped his knee and laughed again. He'd probably used the joke a hundred times, but that didn't stop the tiny speck of moisture he swiped from his rosy cheek.

"Glad to hear it. Say, you were up and out the door pretty early this morning. Catch any fish?" One of the historic charms of the inn was its paper-thin walls, which meant he could hear whenever the door across the hall from him opened or closed. Including the six a.m. wakeup call he'd received this morning.

"Yes and no. Some days they're practically jumping out of the water. Others it's just you, a fishing pole, and some quality time with God."

"So which was it today?"

The twinkle in the man's eye seemed promising until he swung a decidedly empty cooler Lincoln's way. "I could ask the same of you."

Was it that obvious?

Lincoln fidgeted with the red-and-white container before handing it back. "I'm not really much of a fisherman. I wouldn't even know where to begin." Never had been, really. His dad had meant to teach him when he was a kid, but that would have required being sober long enough to thread a worm on a hook.

Dwight hummed to himself as if amused—or in deep thought, Lincoln wasn't sure. "They're always biting, so long as you know where to cast your line. Twenty years and I'm still learning. Maybe in another twenty, I'll have figured out their secret." Deep-set lines framed his face in a constant smile. "And looks to me the day's not over yet." The man nodded toward something in the distance and smiled.

Lincoln turned, and sure enough, Kate's chocolate-colored golf cart was puttering toward them.

"That'll be my cue." The man hiked the plastic handle into the crook of his arm, facing the harbor.

"Are you heading back out already?"

Dwight shook his head. "Nah. Fishing's great and all, but it's the people that really make a place special. If you need any more *fishing* advice, I'll be down at Martha's on Main, deep in a bowl of her famous bean soup. But I think you'll be just fine on your own." The way he peered over the top of his glasses when he said that made it clear they were no longer talking about salmon and trout.

Okay, Master Yoda. So what exactly was he supposed to do now?

By the time Kate had rumbled over the gravel path and parked outside the workshop, Dwight was long gone. Fishing analogies and all.

A few pale-pink apple blossoms clung to the dash, inspiring his next words as a wagon full of tourists rumbled past. "Looks like you're the bloom I needed to brighten my day."

Kate scrunched her face and yelled, "What?" over the loud clop of hooves.

"I said you're the—"

The horses stopped for the next point in the tour, and the sudden silence cut him off. Along with the rest of his fleeting stupidity. Had he really just tried using a pickup line on Kate?

Great. And now she was looking at him with rapt attention.

"Uh, I mean, we'd better get those blooms loaded up today while it's still bright out."

God, just take me now.

There wasn't even a cloud in the sky on this perfectly mild and downright beautiful spring day. What had Dwight said about the fish are always biting? That might be the case, but with bait like his, he'd sooner drive all his chances away with one single cast.

"Are they in here or the coolers out back?"

Lincoln blinked, then followed the direction of Kate's outstretched hand to the shop door.

"Inside. But I should probably warn you, the smell's a bit strong . . ."

She swung the door open, and her eyes widened as she seemed to hit an invisible wall. "Well, that should clear my sinuses for the next year or so." She laughed. "Remind me to stop barging into your workshop. First bug smoke, now this." She waved a hand in front of her nose. "Are we taking the wildflower arrangements or the tall ones next to the windows?"

"The wildflowers."

The others were an experiment for the festival's gala next weekend. He was still working out the design. White or colorful? Elegant and refined or bursting with texture? It hadn't come to him yet, but like with all great works of art, time would tell.

"They're small, but there are a lot of them," he said, joining her inside. Nearly two dozen bud vases sat in rows across the long table, taking up the majority of the real estate not occupied by eucalyptus and dogwood stems.

"No kidding. I still can't believe so many people signed up for the floral watercolor class tonight." She gladly accepted the cardboard box he handed her and started nesting one vase beside the next.

It took nearly three boxes to get them all tucked away and into the back of the golf cart.

"Looks like we're all ready to go." Clapping her hands together, she turned as he was setting an extra vase and floral tape into the nearest box. Her hands brushed his chest for only a second, but the warmth and the memory of the other day lasted for much longer than their awkward little dance.

"Where is it we're taking these again?" she asked, voice a little breathy as she circled around to the driver's seat.

His mouth tugged at the corner. So he wasn't imagining things. Good to know.

"Oh, that's right. The Jonathon Island Center for the Arts. Duh." She released a short, breathless chuckle. "It's not like they'd be offering painting class in the middle of Smith's Hardware."

"I wouldn't put it past them," he said, mouth slipping into a grin. "An island with horse-drawn carriages and working cannons seems capable of all sorts of surprises."

"Like starting wars over fudge?"

He didn't know what a fudge war was exactly, but did it matter? "Exactly."

Somehow, the double-wide bench seat seemed smaller than before, his shoulder brushing hers as she turned the key to start up the cart. If he hadn't known better, he'd have thought she intentionally hit the sidewalk curb to jostle them closer together, but maybe that was just what he would've done had he been the one driving.

"Thanks for helping a guy out," he said as they zipped around a corner, bringing her right elbow flush against his. Not that he minded one bit. "I could've carried these myself, but it would have taken a few more trips on foot."

"It's my pleasure." Her voice was chipper and bright. "Anything to help out with the festival. With Dani back, she doesn't need me as much, so I had the time." She stole a glance over her shoulder, their eyes meeting for a long second. "I'm glad I could be here."

With you.

It went unspoken but was understood all the same from her bashful smile.

Wow. Even at fifty percent, her smile managed to leave him speechless.

Victorian storefronts passed in a blur, along with the apple blossoms that perfumed this moment with something sweet and full of promise, and . . . pungent?

They slowed rapidly, and then the cart stopped altogether in the middle of Main Street.

Lincoln hopped out to check under the hood, then paused. Wait, did this thing even have an engine, or was it one of those battery-powered carts? He scanned the side panel, looking for some kind of release, when a bell sounded behind him. He clambered back inside the cart right as a pack of cyclists zoomed past on either side of them.

Not that Kate seemed to notice.

She tried the key once. Twice. "It won't turn over." She slumped against the seat in defeat. "Dani said the power gauge was broken, but I was positive it still had plenty of charge left."

"So much for curbside delivery," he joked. But between her shaking hands and sudden frown, it was too soon. "I'm only kidding. Hey, it could be worse. We could've capsized on one of those turns back there and lost all the boxes."

Instead of laughing with him, she groaned. "The boxes. I was supposed to help you, not create another inconvenience."

This time, he didn't hesitate to put his hand on her arm. "Kate, it's fine. Really. Like you said before, it's not a big island. How many blocks is it to the arts center anyway?"

"Three."

"Perfect. My legs could use the walk."

Kate shook her head. "You don't have to pretend to be fine. It's my mistake. I should be the one to find a solution that doesn't involve two wasted trips."

"Who says I'm pretending? We can make an afternoon of it, if you're up for it." His phone began to buzz in his pocket, but he let it ring through. If it was anything important, they'd leave a voicemail. Right now, his sole focus was Kate and making sure she stopped beating herself up over nothing.

She eyed him suspiciously over the steering wheel. "You're awfully optimistic about all this. That's normally my role."

She was right. Normally, he'd let his emotions get the better of him and ruin what could be a wonderful moment. "What can I say? Island life must be rubbing off on me. All those fresh sea breezes."

"It's a lake."

"Even better."

His phone stopped ringing, but it was Kate's hum of acknowledgment that had his ears perking up.

The Bloomfest committee might hold his professional future in their hands, but the only future he was worried about right now was the next hour or so with Kate.

Twelve

K IND? *CHECK*.

Selfless? *Check*.

Calm enough under pressure to keep her from having a full-blown panic attack?

. . . Check.

After confirming that the battery was, in fact, shot, she'd put the thing in neutral while Lincoln pushed her the entire block back to her apartment. If that wasn't already enough, he'd carried more than his fair share of the boxes back and forth between there and the arts center without a single complaint.

Not even a grumble.

Who was this man, and what had he done with the grumpy Lincoln from the past few weeks?

Kate looked up from the table with the vases and toward the front of the art center's classroom, where the instructor in her blue-and-green-stained apron was laughing at something Lincoln had said. He visibly blushed as the older woman eyed his jawline—and other chiseled angles—like he was Michelangelo's *David*.

He'd stepped in as her rescuer this morning. It was only fair she returned the favor.

"Sorry to interrupt," she said as she walked over to join them. And based on his loud exhale, he was more than happy for the intrusion. "I was just looking at the time, and it looks like we're already running a bit late. We should probably get going soon."

Lincoln's brow furrowed. "Late for what?"

She forced an out-of-character pout, hoping he'd catch on to the ruse. Ashley wasn't the only actress in the family. "You haven't forgotten about dinner with my family tonight, have you?" She hooked her arm through his and tilted her head in what she hoped was a convincing flirtation.

The muscles in his arm tensed at her touch, and he gave a sly grin. "Right, dinner." His voice took on a husky tone that muddled her thoughts.

Oh my. Had this not all been for show, her knees might have buckled under that intense gaze of his.

Kate swallowed. "I'm sorry," she said, angling toward the artist as if just remembering she was still there.

"Nonsense. Two people in love should never have to apologize."

She flinched. In love? Who said anything about love?

"I couldn't have said it better." Lincoln wrapped his arm around Kate and pulled her close enough to feel every inch of his granite-toned body beneath the T-shirt.

He was enjoying this far too much. He knew she couldn't step away unless she wanted to break character. A few harmless flirtations were one thing. They didn't have the power to shake the well-built walls around her heart. But this prolonged nearness stirred things she'd thought long buried.

With another apologetic smile to the woman, she practically dragged Lincoln from the classroom, a feat that probably looked as silly as a pony hauling a tractor uphill. His rich laughter vibrated through their still-linked arms and straight to her chest.

"I'm sure the coast is clear by now." She went to slip her arm from his, but his featherlight hand on her elbow was more than enough invitation to linger.

"Just in case she follows us out here, I think we should wait for at least another block."

She conceded his point and let him lead her down the steps. So what if it was make-believe? No person alive could fault a girl for wanting someone to wrap their arms around them and tell them it would all be all right.

"There's never a dull moment around you, Sullivan."

"I could say the same for you." His shortened strides made it easy to keep in step, even if it did make it difficult to tell what he was thinking. "You know, blowing up buildings and all . . ."

"That only happened once."

"Roping me into being your assistant for a day."

"Admit it, you had fun."

She had, actually. Far more than she'd allowed herself in a long while.

"How about, as a thank-you for all the *fun*"—she accentuated the last word—"we take the rest of the afternoon off and grab something to drink at Martha's. My treat. There's a new festival cider on tap I've been meaning to try."

That was something friends did, right? Old, platonic, and not-at-all-looking-for-a-relationship friends.

Lincoln's hesitation said otherwise.

Oh, now she'd really put her foot in it. Here she was, practically hanging off him while he was probably working out a polite way to turn her down.

"I don't drink anymore." Cool air chilled her side as he slid his arm free and rubbed the back of his neck. "I've been sober for almost five years now."

Sober? But that didn't make sense. That would imply that he'd been a heavy drinker before, and the Lincoln she remembered never had more than a couple of beers.

"Oh. I'm sorry, I didn't know."

"It's not something I usually talk about. People tend to act differently once I do, so . . ." He shrugged. Maybe that brush-off had worked for him in the past, but she knew when something was bothering him. She'd almost married him, after all. It had only taken one burned lasagna to learn that he scratched his forehead when he was lying.

"I'm not most people," she teased before thinking better of it. Then again, he hadn't looked at her the way he was now in a long, *long* time.

"Kate Sullivan, you are anything but most people." A pause, and then . . . "I wouldn't say no to an ice cream though." He was smiling down at her, a mischievous glint in those hard-to-read eyes of his.

"Well, you're in luck. I know the perfect spot."

Right across the street from Martha's on Main sat the Fudge Shop on the Corner, an even quainter food truck permanently parked beside it. The Volkswagen van had been retrofitted with a pop-up top and fold-out counter, the yellow and sparkly purple paint like a psychedelic time warp as they approached Lily's Ice Cream.

"Kate, hi! What brings you by?" Lily beamed at her from behind the counter. Lavender streaked her otherwise pale-blonde hair, matching the bold colors of her dress.

"Hey, Lily. Lincoln and I were just dropping off flowers for the art class and thought we'd stop by for a scoop." She eyed the large flavor board, trying to ignore Lily's not-so-subtle looks between the two of them. "They all sound so good. What flavor would you recommend?"

"Well, today's specials are pistachio, maple bacon, and rocky road. But we've got loads of options to choose from. The pistachio is my favorite, but we have a new festival specialty: apple pie à la mode. I can even put a little caramel sauce over the top if you want. It's a real crowd pleaser."

"Ooh, that does sound amazing." Especially if the buttery aromas coming from inside the ice-cream truck were any indication. Then again, she'd probably get a stomachache from all the sugar. "I think I'll just go with a scoop of vanilla bean though."

Amusement radiated from Lincoln's quirked eyebrow. As if that were too subtle, he practically scoffed when she asked for a cup instead of a cone.

"What's wrong with good old-fashioned vanilla ice cream?"

"Nothing, if you're eighty and watch reruns of *Leave It to Beaver*." His lips shifted into a teasing smirk. "Come on. What flavor do you really want? Sky's the limit."

Lily hovered in the window as if wondering whether or not she should go ahead and start scooping or wait.

Guilt tapped at Kate's chest over the inconvenience, but not as loudly as Lincoln's invitation. The idea of indulging in any fantasy, even if it was only ice cream, seemed so far out of reach.

However, it was only ice cream. A grown woman shouldn't get teary-eyed over a bowl of frozen cream and sugar. She changed her order to a waffle cone of apple pie with caramel sauce at the last minute as Lincoln scanned the menu once more.

"Chocolate, really?" She gaped at his brown cone as he thanked Lily. "And you were giving me a hard time."

"Hey, it's got hazelnuts in it. Besides, this is exactly what I wanted." He dug out a spoonful and held it out for her to try it.

Lily was still busy pouring caramel sauce over her cone, so she accepted the offering and closed her eyes as the velvety cream melted onto her tongue.

"It's not too late to change your mind again," he said, meeting her fluttering gaze. Who needed hot fudge sauce when a look like that could melt an entire ice-cream truck?

"Here's that second cone for ya." Before Kate could juggle the ice cream to a different hand, Lincoln was already handing over his credit card.

"Hey, this was supposed to be my treat as an apology for taking up your afternoon."

"You'll just have to get the next one, then," he said without a second's pause. "How about dinner sometime. Say, tomorrow?"

The same questions as before crept back in, but so did something akin to hope.

And then her shoulders fell.

"I'd love to, but I can't. I'm supposed to be at Dani's place for an actual family dinner tomorrow." She'd gotten the text right before leaving to pick up Lincoln and the flowers. Everyone who lived on island would be there: Dani and Liam, Oliver and Eliza, and Mom. Kate could always call back and cancel, but was that what she really wanted? A second chance with Lincoln?

Yes.

The thought came so unbidden, it nearly bowled her over.

"Another time, then?" His forehead pinched ever so slightly. "Only if it's what you want, of course." He was being *way* too understanding for someone who'd just been shot down. Not that she'd intentionally done so, but family was family. And she'd already committed to one fledgling reunion.

And that realization was the beginning of her undoing.

She nodded. "I'd like that."

He walked with her all the way back to the apartment and around back to where the cart and its dead battery waited.

Was this your plan all along, God? The golf cart, the festival . . . She could have offered the position to any of the florists on Dani's list, yet she'd chosen Lincoln before she'd even known it was him. There had to be a lesson in there somewhere about divine intervention and all that.

"It's getting late. I should probably clean up the workshop before tomorrow's class."

"Yeah, I've got lots to take care of as well." Like figuring out what in the world was happening here.

Lincoln turned to leave, but before he reached the sidewalk, she called after him. "And I don't watch reruns of *Leave It to Beaver*."

"Oh yeah?" His smile matched hers.

"Call me old-fashioned, but I prefer something with a little romance to it."

He slowed to look back, then stopped on the edge of the gravel path. "How much romance are we talking about? Something tragic like *Gone with the Wind*?"

No. She'd had enough tears. "More like between *Casablanca* and *Brigadoon*."

He ducked his head, but not before she saw a slow smile unfurl.

Lincoln wasn't going to let Kate down by being late to his next workshop.

"Hey, Felicity. I'm sorry about missing your call earlier, but I don't have much time to talk." He'd hardly gotten any sleep last night, replaying yesterday afternoon with Kate in his head. And then he'd slept through his alarm this morning. Not even Dwight's early fishing trip had woken him, and he'd slept until well after eight thirty.

Hair still wet from his shower, he zipped his jacket all the way up to ward off the unexpected chill as he stepped off the inn's front porch.

"I'll make this quick, then." Her voice seemed overly chipper. Far more so than their last conversation. "You got an email from the Bloomfest committee. Something about them trying to call yesterday but it not going through?"

"I was busy delivering flowers with Kate. I saw that they called and was going to get back to them later today."

"Well, they sent an email to the company account this morning, and they want to know if you'd be available to meet with them on Friday."

"This Friday?" He shoved his key into the lock and stepped into the frigid workspace. Man, was it cold in here. He'd have to turn up the stove to keep the flowers from freezing. "Unless they don't mind driving four hours north up I-75, I don't see how that's going to work." He couldn't very well leave. Not in the middle of the festival.

"They saw the Instagram post," she said, sidestepping his response. "Everyone loves a small-town hero. They can see you're putting in some real effort, maybe even enough to dispel the bad reviews."

He was far from a hero and she knew it. But still . . .

"They really said that?"

"Why else would they want to talk to you?"

So that was a no. But at least they hadn't entirely closed the door on him yet.

"I can't leave right before our busiest weekend, but if they're willing to do a video call, that could work." He couldn't guarantee the internet would be much better than the cell service, but it beat having no meeting at all.

"This isn't something you should do over the phone, hon. Those calls can be so cold and impersonal, and that's the opposite of what you're trying to do. If you leave after your last workshop on Thursday, you'll have enough time after a morning meeting to be back on the island that evening. Saturday morning at the latest."

He jabbed the switch on the stove, and the fan whirred to life. Hot air blew up at him as he stood, and he wrinkled his nose at the musty smell.

"Would you like me to set it up for you? They need your response by today, I'm afraid." There was a clicking noise in the background, meaning she must be at the computer, already beginning a new email.

"Seems like you've got it all planned out." As much as he didn't want to admit it, she was right. Leaving the keys on the table, he went back outside and rounded the building to where the coolers hummed out back.

Correction. One cooler hummed, the other was decidedly quiet. Had someone accidentally unplugged it? A quick check confirmed it was still plugged in, but something had definitely gnawed through the electrical cord.

"Hey Felicity, I've got to go. It appears one of my coolers went out." At least the door was closed, so hopefully none of the flowers had gotten too cold with last night's temperature drop. Not quite to freezing—otherwise the island would have lost more than a few cut flowers—but still not ideal.

He opened the lid and frowned at the row of limp peonies on top.

Okay, much less than ideal.

"I'm sorry to cut this short, but I need to run into town for some more flowers before my next workshop. Send me the details, and I'll figure out a way to make it work." He could almost guarantee the small local shop wouldn't have the same imported heirloom varietals he'd had shipped to the island. But at this point, any flowers were better than none at all.

Felicity rattled off a few more quick messages before signing off.

"Love you too. Okay, talk to you later."

The open cooler silently mocked him as he shoved his phone back into his pocket. A month ago, something like this would've set him off much like Mrs. Howard storming into his studio back home had. Yet the frustration he'd normally expect didn't come.

Instead, he laughed.

It really wasn't funny. He'd spent a small fortune selecting the perfect flowers for his upcoming class, and now half of them were no better than potpourri.

He chuckled again. Maybe he could borrow Kate's oven to make it official—a new festival souvenir for all the tourists to take home with them.

He flicked the lid back in place and angled his next steps toward the road. There wasn't much he could do about the cooler or Friday's meeting, but if he left now, he might just have enough time to save today's workshop. He could make do with roses, gerbera daisies, and baby's breath if he had to.

Like old times with Mom.

He walked the familiar trek into town, passing the bookstore, Smith's Hardware with a row of petunias fluttering on the front porch, the pizzeria and Kate's apartment above it. The golf cart was exactly where he'd left it, even if Kate was nowhere in sight. Not like she hung around the place all day waiting for him to drop by. That would be silly.

Although, the idea of having someone to come home to after a long day of work made something swell inside of him. Not hope, exactly. More a sense of rediscovering a long-lost dream.

The row of historic storefronts opened up at Ferry Street, and a sharp chill blew in off the harbor, making Lincoln pick up his pace. If he hadn't checked the weather app on his phone earlier, he'd think they were in for a late spring storm. Never mind the clear blue skies overhead.

He hurried the rest of the way to the end of the street. The local florist sat only two doors up from the ice-cream truck, the toasted scents of waffle cones and sugar following him inside. He recalled Kate saying something about the owner being off island for part of the festival, but from the Open sign on the door, they must be back already.

The first thing that struck Lincoln was how small the store was. Sunlight streamed in through the large picture windows, making the room feel more spacious than it really was. Pockets of flowers stood out in little explosions of petals and color in all directions, and he had to watch to make sure he didn't accidentally knock over a tower of seed packets on his way toward the back counter.

The ding of the little brass bell echoed like a cannon through the small space.

"I'll be with you in a minute." The disembodied voice came from a room he hadn't noticed before now. An office, perhaps? Something heavy thudded against the adjoining wall, causing the framed pictures to shudder.

"Maybe I should come back another time," he said, leaning across the counter. The voice didn't respond, and images of an elderly woman pinned beneath a pile of boxes had him reaching for the flip-up counter when a much younger woman than he'd expected rushed out.

"Sorry about that. You won't believe the morning I've had. First, my coffee maker decided to croak, and then there was a mix-up with the delivery. I've got sunflowers coming out of my ears and no place to put them. Apparently it doesn't matter that my original order was correct." She looked up from the pile of ribbons and craft paper she'd swept to the side and sighed. "But you didn't come here for me to tell you all that. What can I do for you Mr.—"

"It's just Lincoln. And no worries. Believe me, I understand rough mornings." And botched flower orders. "But since I'm here, what do you have in the way of white flowers?"

"Well, we've got roses, of course. But if you're looking for a bouquet, I'd recommend the hydrangeas instead. Far more unique."

"Sounds great. But . . . um . . . I might need a little more than a dozen stems."

"That bad, huh? What'd you do? Stand her up for an important date?"

What? How could she—

But no, she was only trying to make a sale. "It's nothing like that." Not unless the woman had a five-year timer tucked away in back. "I have a workshop for the festival in a couple of hours, and one of my coolers went out last night. The flowers I was planning to use are shot. And it's too short notice to call in a new order."

Her pleasant smile dimmed. "So *you're* the big-city florist they decided to hire for the festival." It wasn't disdain in her voice, exactly. But she was obviously far from a fan. "You don't want white."

"I don't?"

She shook her head. "White is for sympathy. This festival is a celebration, not a funeral."

Okay . . . definitely not a fan. "What color would you suggest, then? I already have some other pink—"

"No pink."

"But the apple blossoms are pink."

"Exactly." She looked at him like he was stupid. Which, come to think of it, maybe he was. "They're meant to be the stars, right? No, you need something that will make them pop, something that says 'Hello, world. Welcome to Jonathon Island' without asking for too much attention themselves."

"Sounds like you've already got an idea." One that was boxed up in her office and ready for a delivery. "How about sunflowers, then? They're simple, bright, and not at all pink or white." Didn't hurt that they were also Kate's favorites. And based on the woman's relief, he'd have more than enough for an extra bouquet.

"A wise decision." She punched a few buttons on her iPad to ring up the order, her surly attitude melting away as she rang up the bill. "Will that be all?"

He gaped at the total. Apparently small-town business didn't mean small-town prices. But then he reminded himself of Kate.

If anything, they'd make a nice surprise before the family dinner this evening, which she was obviously worried about. Not that she'd said as much, but her lips had this funny way of going all thin and tight when she was pushed outside her comfort zone. She probably didn't even realize she did it, but he enjoyed that he could still read at least some of her thoughts.

Especially if there was something he could do about them.

"You'll want to keep those inside tonight. I heard it's supposed to get pretty cold. Maybe even dip below freezing."

Lincoln tapped his credit card against the screen and frowned. "That's not what my weather app said. Are you sure?"

"Positive." She cinched a ribbon around the stems, brow furrowing as she peeked out the window behind him. "One thing you quickly learn living on an island is how to read the signs. Stick around long enough, and you might catch on as well." It sounded like a warning and an invitation all in one.

After giving her the address of the Quinns' old tack building, Lincoln thanked her for the tip and the flowers and stepped back outside.

Did it seem a few degrees colder than when he'd walked inside?

Barely a breeze stirred the baskets dangling from the streetlamps, yet the woman's warning clung to him like a Japanese beetle to a rose bush.

He fished his phone from his pocket, then pulled up the weather app and waited for it to refresh. A yellow triangle flashed near the top, and his stomach sank.

A freeze warning would mean more than a few wilted flowers in a cooler. Roses and peonies he could replace. But the apple blossoms were another matter entirely.

Too cold, and the festival would be over before he could say Great Lakes Floral Association.

Along with his reason to stay.

Thirteen

KATE SHIVERED AGAINST THE CHILL OF THE refrigerator. "I don't see it. Are you sure there's fresh basil in here?" She opened the crisper drawer but found only parsley and a rather shriveled-looking lemon she wished she could unsee.

Socks shuffled over the hardwood floor as Dani's hip bumped hers in the small galley kitchen. "Huh. I was positive I bought some. I might not be the greatest cook, but I can at least follow a grocery list."

"That's okay, hon. I still love you, even if you forgot the basil." Liam's voice carried over the sound of him chopping tomatoes, while Mom, Eliza, and Oliver sat around the white granite, topping their pizzas.

Dani's mouth puckered to the side before her face lit up. She slid behind Kate toward the sink, where a small green plant was growing in a terra-cotta pot. She plucked a few leaves of parsley from the plant and lowered her voice. "You and Lincoln seemed pretty cozy at the arts center yesterday." Luckily, the others were too busy making culinary masterpieces to hear, but not so busy that they wouldn't notice Kate strangling her younger sister in the heart of the twelve-hundred-square-foot bungalow.

She'd forgotten just how fast news traveled in a small town. Fake or not. "You know artists. Always on the hunt for a model to paint or something. It would've been cruel for me not to have rescued him."

Dani seemed skeptical. "Hmm. So getting ice cream together was purely selfless, then?"

"Of course. What else would it have been?"

Kate's thoughts slipped back to the surprise bouquet she'd found when she'd dropped by her apartment to change before dinner. Sunflowers and blue daisies. She suddenly wished Lincoln were here. Not as her plus-one, per se, but maybe then her mom would stop with all the questions.

Why aren't you seeing anyone? Have you tried online dating? Would you like me to ask around?

"My friend's son recently moved back to the island." Her mom started up again as if she could hear Kate's thoughts. "Noah. You used to go out together, didn't you?"

"We went to homecoming. Once. And only as friends. You remember, he was on the golf team with me. It would've been weird."

"Well, he's not your teammate now." Tucking her auburn hair behind her ear, her mom arranged the last of her pepperoni slices and topped her heart-shaped pizza artfully with the fresh parsley.

"That looks amazing," cooed Eliza, who sat on the other side of Oliver. Her dark, silky hair went past her shoulders, accentuating her wide smile. Kate liked her more every time she hung out with her. Even more so for the way she brought out Oliver's fun side. He deserved as much.

Kate munched silently on a breadstick cracker from her corner of the kitchen, attention divided between the oven timer and her mom's disapproval of her life decisions. At least she could make sure the pizzas didn't burn on her watch. Surely her mom couldn't find fault with that.

"Kate?"

"Hmm?" She looked up from the three minutes remaining on the timer to see her mom and everyone else in the kitchen staring at her.

Her mom held out Eliza's phone with the picture from the flower workshop, making her stomach sink. She must've been flipping through her Instagram account. Oh, why had Kate accepted the tag on that particular photo of herself and Lincoln? "So it's true. When were you going to tell me that you and Lincoln were getting so cozy? I had to hear it from Annabelle Kennedy, of all people."

Um, never? "You and I haven't really talked much lately."

"And whose fault is that?" The look she gave Kate made her feel like a little kid who'd messed up again.

Kate's chest began to tighten at her mom's harsh tone, but she stuffed it back down before it could lodge in her throat.

"Sweetie, the man breaks your heart and you invite him right back in? That's called a toxic relationship dynamic. Believe me when I say I know what I'm talking about."

Kate clamped her mouth shut before saying anything she'd later regret. But this wasn't anything like her mom's affair with her high school sweetheart, Ryan MacBride. For starters, Kate didn't have a family to break apart. And second, she still didn't know where she and Lincoln stood with each other. Friends, yes. But more?

"Speaking of reunions . . ." Dani grabbed the bottle of cabernet Eliza had brought and topped off their mom's glass. "Mom, did I see you talking with Dad at the art show on Sunday? I didn't think he was coming until the gala next Sunday."

Dani's distraction worked beautifully, causing all heads to turn toward their mom, who was . . . blushing?

"He had a meeting in Traverse City with some potential investors. They finished early, so he decided to drive up for the day."

"Why didn't he let anyone know ahead of time?" asked Dani, lowering the bottle. "Or at least drop in to say hi? I know Liam and I just got home, but we want to run a few questions by him and James about the hotel restoration before we move ahead to the next phase."

Mom wrinkled her nose as if she'd seen the same questionable lemon hiding in the fridge earlier. At Dani's questions or because of the soft lecture she hadn't gotten to finish? "That's probably my fault. I knew he was only here for a few hours after the show, but then we went out for coffee and the time just got away from us."

Kate coughed on her wine, throat burning from the acid going down the wrong way.

"Like a date?" asked Oliver. His eyebrows were slowly coming down from his hairline, but not enough to cover his disbelief.

Mom and Dad . . . back together? And here Mom was, giving Kate a lecture about spending time with Lincoln.

"It was only coffee." She waved a hand as if it had been brunch with friends.

"You could hardly stand being in the same room as him at our wedding last month," said Dani, eyes wide. "What changed?"

"If you must know, I asked him to come." A bit of color tinged their mom's pale complexion. "I'm not proud of how we handled things at the wedding, and it made me realize how uncomfortable we've probably made things for all of you kids over the years. Cheating was one of the biggest mistakes I ever made, and I've waited far too long to apologize. To him and to you." She fluttered her lashes, and Dani took her hand and gave it a reassuring squeeze. "We had a good talk. He's trying to change as well, and apologized for his part in the divorce. He's even talking about selling the Florida hotel after buying back the Grand, and retiring to spend more time here. He missed out on so much. As have I."

Kate grunted as she reached for another breadstick. The snap rang a little in her ears, along with her mom's late confession. "I might not have much experience, but burning down the Grand doesn't put him too high on the Dad of the Year charts."

The first crack appeared in her mom's otherwise poised expression, as it always had when Kate attempted to share her feelings on something. "At least he's trying this time."

The Grand's renovation was Dani's baby. Just the fact that Dad had given her the go-ahead on the project said a lot. But real, personal change? It would take more than a construction crew to tear down those walls and start over.

There was a loud knock at the front door, but Dani seemed too distracted by their mom's shocking revelation to notice.

Maybe it was a late delivery. Who else would stop by after six?

There it was again.

Kate set down her glass, then slipped from the loud kitchen and down the narrow hall in her socks. A rush of unexpectedly frigid air greeted her as she opened the front door, along with a face she hadn't expected to see until tomorrow.

"Kate." Lincoln's eyebrows dipped as he stood out in the cold. "What's wrong?"

That was supposed to be her line. Yet there he went, reading her like a garden rosebush. Limp petals, bug-eaten leaves. He saw it all and knew exactly how to fix it.

"You're cold. Here." He peeled off his jacket and draped it over her tense shoulders.

Immediately, his warmth enveloped her, and she had the strangest desire to bury herself in his arms. But as much as she felt drawn to his comforting presence, now was not the time or the place.

"Lincoln, what are you doing here?" His presence might be a welcome rescue, but it still begged the question.

His gaze flicked to the empty hallway behind her as he shoved his hands into his pockets. "I tried calling but you didn't pick up."

His large shoulders filled the small porch, and he looked suddenly uncomfortable at the muted voices drifting through the open door. He rocked on his feet before finally speaking again. "I remembered you said you were having dinner at your sister's place tonight. It didn't take too much asking around to figure out where to find you."

His shoulders rose and fell in a sheepish shrug, but only something important would have him seeking her out here.

Something was up. The same sinking sensation she'd felt earlier rushed back, followed immediately by more footsteps and the faint smell of burning pepperoni.

"Kate, you're letting all the cool air in. Whoever it is, just invite them . . . Oh." Dani stopped right behind her, the sudden silence growing more uncomfortable by the second until Lincoln cleared his throat.

"I'm sorry to interrupt, but we've got a problem."

Lincoln didn't care if Kate's sister was looking at him as if he were the big bad wolf. If they didn't get going now, she'd have a lot more than an interrupted dinner to worry about tomorrow morning when all the apple blossoms were lying wilted and frozen on the sidewalk.

"Dani, what's all this?" Kate's mom swooped in out of nowhere, frowning as she scanned him from head to toe exactly as Oliver had during their first run-in a couple of weeks ago.

Speaking of, the man himself appeared, bringing another man and a dark-haired woman Lincoln didn't recognize with him.

Lincoln swallowed the knot in his throat. He'd known what he was dropping in on, but seeing them all behind Kate with their judgmental stares was another thing entirely.

Please God, give me strength.

"I need Kate." Boy, wasn't that true? But there'd be time for personal admissions later. "And anyone else who can lend a hand."

"What's the rush?" Oliver crossed his arms over a graphic T-shirt, the raised threshold giving him an extra inch on Lincoln's six foot two. "Unless something is on fire, I think you should leave."

Something *would* be on fire if the guy kept butting in before Lincoln could explain.

"Look, I know I'm probably the last person you hoped to see tonight, but believe me when I say I have the island's best interests at heart."

Blank stares greeted him, but Kate's steady presence beside him settled his nerves enough to form a coherent sentence. "There's a freeze coming. I've checked the weather forecast, and there's no way around it. The way I see it, we're probably going to lose every last apple blossom by the end of the night unless we work together."

"What did you have in mind?" Drowning in his coat, Kate couldn't have looked more adorable if she'd tried. Everything about her was pure and selfless and so downright attractive he could hardly remember how he'd survived the past five years without her in his life.

Man, he loved this woman.

The realization struck him so hard, he nearly lost his breath. But now wasn't the time for grand declarations. Maybe he wouldn't be able to convince her family to listen to him, but he had Kate's attention, and that was what mattered most.

Kate swiped her shoes from by the door and slipped them on in record time.

"What about the pizzas? They'll burn if we leave now." No surprise, this came from her mom, who was looking between him and Kate in mild bewilderment.

"Go ahead and eat without me, but I'm going with Lincoln." Kate took her place beside him in front of her family. He didn't miss the slight tremor to her shoulders as she did so, yet she didn't back down. This Kate was so much stronger than he remembered. Far more than she gave herself credit for.

Dani swiped a coat from the hall closet and joined them. "Same here. Without the apple blossoms, there'll be no more festival."

Even Oliver seemed to understand the importance of what was happening. Finally. "I'll call Russell. I'm sure he's got some extra space heaters and blankets you can use."

Lincoln bobbed his head in thanks, and Oliver reciprocated.

Discussion over, he grabbed Kate's hand, and they and Dani booked it down the street and around the corner.

The phone tree was already hard at work by the time they reached the top of Main Street. The lights inside Smith's Hardware spilled over the Victorian porch, where a handful of people were talking animatedly.

"A freeze this late in the spring?" muttered one of the women.

"Wouldn't be the first time. Remember that snowstorm back in '99?"

Lincoln recognized Mayor Seb Jonathon's salt-and-pepper hair and broad shoulders, even beneath the puffer jacket. The man's keen eyes locked on to the three of them before he raised his hands to get everyone's attention.

"All right, people. Quiet now." The noise settled to a low din as everyone turned expectant eyes on him. "Thank you all for coming on such short notice. As you've heard, we have a freeze warning on our hands, but thanks to Lincoln here, we may still have time to save at least some of the trees."

Lincoln felt a few eyes on him, but he kept his glued to the man on the top of the stairs who was . . . looking straight at him?

"Lincoln, would you mind walking us through what needs to be done?"

If some people had been watching him before, they all were now. The sun, now low on the horizon, cast their faces in darkness. He scanned the shadowed crowd.

Was that skepticism or trust in their tight-lipped expressions? *Think man, think.*

A few more people joined them, drawing his attention to a lumpy mound of black plastic beneath the railing. Hadn't there been a row of petunias there earlier? "Does anyone have extra tarps or blankets they'd be willing to lend?"

Crickets would've cut the silence.

Come on, people. This is your island we're trying to save here.

Finally, someone raised their hand. "I've got a couple old drop cloths from when I repainted my house last fall. Will that work?"

"Good, that's perfect. Anyone else?"

The crowd had doubled in size, buoying his hopes that maybe this could work. They had the manpower, now all they needed were the supplies.

"I remember seeing a bunch of tarps at the Grand," said Dani from beside him. "Half a dozen, maybe ten. I can run and go get them right now."

"I'll drive. It'll be quicker," said Liam, who jogged up to Dani from the street. Everyone else from the house was climbing out of the golf cart he must've driven—including Kate's mom, who kept to the fringe of the crowd.

Okay, this was a good start. But with over thirty trees in the park alone, a dozen or so covers would only get them so far. What they really needed was a heat source. "Russell, do you happen to have any space heaters we can borrow from the store? Maybe some extra-long extension cords as well?"

But the man was already shaking his head. "Afraid I just sold the last heater this morning. I do have some old propane lanterns that might do the trick though. They're portable too."

"And we can use the outdoor patio heaters from our restaurants. Isn't that right, Patrick?" Martha elbowed a man with a wiry mustache, who had also been at the council meeting a couple of weeks ago.

"Should be about six or seven in total, I reckon."

"Even better. Grab what you can and we'll meet you at the park."

In a matter of minutes, everyone was busy either carrying supplies down the road or loading them into the back of golf carts. Someone even hitched a couple of horses to a wagon where five men were busy laying the larger patio heaters on their sides.

Someone else dropped an armload of what looked to be old climbing rope onto the grass, and Lincoln turned to see Noah. "I hope it's enough. I heard what was going on and remembered these old things collecting dust in my parents' basement. Thought you could use them to secure the tarps."

He might not like the guy, but he'd never been happier to see him than right now.

"Great idea. I think we're almost finished here, so we can probably start carrying things over." He shrugged a coil of rope over his shoulder as Noah did the same. Kate grabbed the last one, and together, the three of them hurried after the wagon clopping up the hill.

Lincoln didn't stop to wonder if any of this would actually work. All he knew was that if they sat around and did nothing, they'd lose all the flowers for sure.

The hiss of a lantern greeted them as they stepped onto the grass. Warmth blossomed around them and the other volunteers, who were still looking to Lincoln for direction.

"We've got the lanterns going." Russell's voice rose from the crowd. "Now what would you like us to do with the tarps?"

Lincoln wasn't good at being put on the spot. If he seemed to know what he was doing, it was only because no one else was speaking up.

Good thing for Kate and her quick thinking. She handed him one end of a blue sheet, the other still bundled to her chest. "I assume we start with one of these?"

Breathe in. And out.

Pretend it's only Kate you're talking to. Walk her through the plan.

He peeled his gaze away from the crowd and focused on her brown eyes, her soft, encouraging smile.

"We're going to cover these trees as best we can to create a pocket of warm air around the branches." *This'll work. It has to work.*

Looking at Kate, he waited for her silent nod before continuing.

"Right, now take your corner, and on the count of three, I want you to throw your end as high as you can over the tree. I'll do the same, but it'll only work if we're in sync."

She took a few steps back until the sheet was laid out between them and the nearest tree. Dressed in a garland of string lights, the pink-studded branches reached up toward the sky as if waiting to catch the sheet for them whenever they were ready.

"We go on three. One . . . two . . . three."

The corners floated up and over the crown to whoops and hollers below. Before the breeze could strip it back, Noah rushed in with a length of rope to cinch the tarp at the base of the trunk.

One down, the rest of the park to go.

The group dispersed from there, giving the same treatment to each apple tree as they went. It seemed nearly half the town had turned out to help. At some point, a fire truck even showed up, led by Chief Macintyre as they used the folding ladder to reach the taller trees around the park.

An hour later, Lincoln shook his head in disbelief and admired their handiwork. The lumpy forms looked about as out of place as he felt. A faint glow dotted the surfaces where the string lights rested against the sheets, giving them an almost eerily romantic glow.

Kate's hand slipped into his, and he gave it a reassuring squeeze. For her or himself, he wasn't entirely sure. All he knew was that it felt . . . right.

"It's going to work. I know it." She gave another squeeze. The sleeve of his jacket swallowed both their hands, creating a soft cocoon all their own.

"How can you be so confident?" he asked. "We could still lose most of the flowers if we haven't knocked them off already with the tarps."

"Then it'll make for a great story one day." Her head rested on his shoulder like it was the most natural thing in the world.

Which, maybe it was.

He'd always rolled his eyes whenever his mom used to talk about soulmates. There was no way a good and loving God would have chosen his dad—an unreliable, abusive drunk—to marry the sweetest angel that ever walked this earth.

Then again, who'd have ever thought he and Kate would be back here after everything, as if some invisible string had been pulling them together all along?

Fourteen

LIFE DIDN'T GET MUCH BETTER THAN STAND-
ing around the bonfire with a mug of hot chocolate clasped
between your hands, surrounded by family and friends.

Firefly embers floated over the beach as people took turns roast-
ing marshmallows. Liam was already on his fourth of the evening,
a brown smudge on his shirt visible as Kate snapped another photo
in the waning pink light. Dani was laughing beside him, practically
glowing from their time under the Italian sun. Even Mom looked
pleased as she swapped watercolor tips with Kate's cousin Mia.

Kate's aunt and uncle used every excuse to host at their beach-
front property. And saving the island's apple blossoms was definitely cause for celebration.

"Is there a reason you're over here and not celebrating with the
rest of them?"

She looked up, half hoping to see Lincoln emerge from the
shadows and only slightly disappointed when it was Oliver instead.

"I will in a moment. I just wanted to get a few more pictures while the light was still good."

Not a lie, exactly. But she wasn't about to tell her twin brother that she might be falling back in love with her ex-fiancé.

"And here I thought you were trying to avoid someone."

"Maybe I am, but here you still are," she teased. He rewarded her with an exaggerated eye roll before plopping down on the rock beside her.

"Chocolate?" He held out a partially unwrapped bar, which he'd likely pilfered from the s'mores kit.

For a moment, they sat watching the waves rise and fall against the rocky shore. The sun dipped below the horizon, the beam of the nearby lighthouse growing stronger from its point along the craggy coastline until it flashed past them.

"She's right, you know." His voice was loud in the silence.

"Who?"

"Dani." He looked toward the house, making it impossible for her to read his thoughts. "You and Lincoln have been spending a lot of time together lately."

"Because of the festival."

"I know." Oliver's head bobbed like a piece of driftwood caught in the current. "I also know you're not the type of person to say no."

"And what am I supposed to be saying no to? Saving the apple trees? They've been on this island longer than we've been alive. Longer than our parents have been alive." She crossed her arms over her chest, the extra-long sleeves of Lincoln's jacket getting in the way. Right, she hadn't given it back yet.

"You're too trusting, Kate. I just don't want to see you get hurt again."

"And you think the worst of people." She didn't mean for it to sound so harsh, but she wasn't the one trying to ruin this perfectly wonderful evening. Couldn't she have tonight? He could lecture her all he wanted after Lincoln left. But one look at Oliver's flat mouth and furrowed brow had her rigid shoulders softening into a faint slump.

"I'm sorry, I shouldn't have said that." This was why she usually kept her feelings stuffed down where nobody could see them. It was less messy that way. Prevented her from saying things she didn't mean and letting down those who needed her to be strong. "You've always been there for me when I needed it. I know you're just trying to look out for me."

He didn't appear upset, but sometimes it was hard to tell with Oliver.

Slowly, he nodded, and the tension between them receded. "It's obvious there's still something there between you two. Yes, Lincoln stepped up tonight in a big way—for the island and for you. I'm not saying he hasn't matured in the last few years, but does that really mean you can trust him not to leave again? After all, he lives in Detroit, and you'll eventually go back to Petoskey. I don't see any way in which this can end well for you."

Why did Oliver always have to be so logical? He wasn't wrong, but right now, she didn't want to hear statistics about failed relationships or a Psychology 101 lecture. It wasn't like she hadn't already been wrestling with the same questions all week with maddeningly little success.

She set the chocolate aside and had started to stand when Oliver's heavy sigh cut the silence.

It turned into a breathy chuckle before . . . "I'm doing a really bad job at this."

"Actually, you're doing a fantastic job at winning the Worst Brother of the Year award." Wrapping her arms around her torso, she looked toward the glowing fire but didn't move. She could match Oliver's silence as long as he liked. It wasn't like she had any other place to be at the moment. Definitely not searching out Lincoln, who she'd last seen disappearing into the house twenty minutes ago.

Something rustled in the bushes behind them. Probably a squirrel or salamander. But that wouldn't explain the faint scent of sandalwood and … cinnamon? She took a step forward, planning to investigate, but then Oliver spoke.

"I might have reservations about the guy, but"—he added before she could interrupt—"I didn't come over here to give you a lecture. I want you to be happy, Kate. Truly."

"What happened to me being too trusting?" Maybe it was a bit childish of her, but he sure had a strange way of showing he cared. A bit like Mom, yet his track record was considerably more reliable. She pulled Lincoln's jacket more snugly around her and chanced a look at her brother, surprised to see his hesitant smile.

"Can you blame me for worrying?" All of a sudden, he was a little boy again—different graphic T-shirt, hair a shade lighter, and a few less wrinkles around his eyes, but the same lopsided grin that made it impossible to stay mad at him for long. "With you being back here … it brought up old memories. It's my job as your brother to be protective."

"I know. And all I'm asking is that you give him a fair chance. He isn't the same person he was back then. Neither of us are." She took his hand and gave it a good squeeze. A gesture he returned.

"For you, Katydid, anything."

She scrunched her nose at the old nickname and laughed.

He ducked her playful fist and stood. "Just know if he so much as upsets you, I have an entire shelf at the bookstore that will tell you exactly how to hide a body without a trace."

"Remind me never to get on your bad side."

"Too late for that." He snatched her camera from the bench, looking a bit too much like the Cheshire cat. "Remember that time you kicked my soccer ball into the lake?"

Kate stuck a hand on her hip and frowned. "You never played soccer."

"Not after that day, I didn't." He took a couple steps toward the water as she squealed and ran after him.

When was the last time she'd raced across the rocky shore and splashed in the frigid water just because? Her wet socks and cold toes might protest, but her heart hadn't felt so full in years.

There had been days—years, in fact—that she'd wished she could disappear, hide from the world and her fears so it was only her and God, who'd never disappoint her. Who'd always love her no matter what she did or didn't do. For years she'd wished that she, Katherine Marie Sullivan, was worthy of love without strings.

But not today.

Today she'd felt the love of an entire island. She had Oliver, her best friend, who always had her back. And to top that all off, Lincoln was once again fast becoming the man of her dreams. Only this time, she wasn't afraid to invite him into her world, as small and imperfect as it might be.

She talked about second chances when it came to Lincoln, but maybe this was her second chance as well.

At happiness. At a family.

And at love.

There was no way he could move now. Not without one of them noticing him.

Lincoln's back ached as he crouched behind the wall of bushes between the house and the beach. His hands had already started to grow numb from the ceramic mugs he clutched, and he wouldn't be surprised to wake up with a dozen or so mosquito bites tomorrow morning.

Kate had almost seen him when his foot slipped a moment ago. If it hadn't been for Oliver distracting her, he'd have found himself in the very awkward position of having to explain why he was spying.

Not spying.

Being thoughtful.

Or at least, that had been the plan when Dani had all but shoved the two mugs to his chest and told him to go find her sister. A plan he'd been all for until he'd walked up on what seemed like a very private conversation.

One in which he seemed to be the central topic.

I'm not saying he hasn't matured in the last few years, but does that really mean you can trust him not to leave again?

It wasn't so much Oliver's judgment that had a lump forming in his throat as Kate's silence that stretched afterward. He wanted to rush out from behind the bushes and promise her this time would be different. *He* was different. He had to be. But that would only prove he'd been listening in on their conversation.

If he really wanted to prove himself to Kate, he'd need more than empty words or what amounted to stalking her when he should learn to trust instead.

Which meant walking away from his hiding place before he accidentally made an even bigger fool of himself.

He waited until Kate and Oliver were closer to the beach before backing away. He felt his way forward in the waning light, careful not to spill hot cocoa over his shirt. It wasn't until the big cedar tree at the top of the hill that he stood to his full height, the muscles between his shoulder blades protesting the change in position.

Warm light spilled through the large picture windows of the Jonathon house. A sweeping porch wrapped around the sprawling estate seated on the northern coast of the island, the beam of a lighthouse competing with the crackling bonfire. It was nice of the mayor to open up his house like this. Even more so when the s'mores kit and cocoa bar made it seem like inviting half the island over for a late-night bonfire was a regular occurrence.

He could barely make out the silhouettes seated around the blaze, laughing and having a good time. Odd how he'd been here less than a month, yet this place already felt more like home than his small studio apartment back in Detroit.

But what exactly was his place here?

Lincoln leaned against the tree's large trunk and studied the canopied branches above.

Honestly, he hadn't allowed himself to think that far ahead until now. Being with Kate felt too good to taint with worries of the future. But only a fool would keep the blinders on. Whether he wanted to realize it or not, their time together was running short. The smart thing would be to end things now before they got any more out of hand, but the thought of walking away from her a second time was like ripping open an old wound.

Any sudden movements, and he'd risk bleeding out.

"God, I could really use some direction right about now." The prayer felt foreign on his tongue, but right. Like greeting an old friend he hadn't spoken to in a long while. He didn't expect a response. It wasn't like a voice from heaven would tell him exactly what to do. He wasn't Luke Skywalker, and God wasn't some Jedi-force ghost who spoke in riddles.

Head tilted back, he could only make out a few stars through the dense foliage. Knowing the rest were there was enough, even if he couldn't see them from his vantage point.

"On clear nights like tonight, you can sometimes see the Milky Way." Kate's light soprano snuck up behind him in the shadows, and he turned to see her duck beneath a large branch. Why was she walking barefoot in such cold weather? She'd catch her death like that. And why were the ends of her pants wet?

At least she still had his jacket, a fact which warmed him far more than cocoa or a kerosene lantern ever could.

"Here, you look like you could use this." He handed her one

of the mugs, which she accepted with a chocolate-melting smile despite the chill in the air.

She took a tentative sip, cinnamon-dusted whipped cream sticking to her upper lip. It took all his restraint to keep himself from reaching out and wiping it away with his thumb, her soft, perfectly smooth skin against his like before.

"You remembered," she said with a slow smile.

He swallowed, suddenly glad for the lack of patio lights on this side of the yard. It was only hot chocolate with a few toppings. Nothing compared to her sister's sugar-bomb explosion of a drink. No. This was simple and sweet, exactly like Kate.

"When it comes to you, I remember everything."

Her eyes grew wide, and the air whooshed from his lungs. Wait, had he actually said that out loud? His face grew warm, but he didn't look away.

Neither did she.

His heartbeat was thrumming so loudly in his ears it nearly drowned out the other voices around the bonfire.

There was no way she knew that he sometimes still dreamed about her dimpled smile or the way her wavy hair had framed her face the night he'd proposed under the linden trees outside her old apartment. That same hair now fluttered against her cheek in the breeze. Demanding to be tucked behind her ear.

He didn't move a muscle as she stood with him against the base of the tree. It was a large trunk, but not so large that her arm didn't press against his. He reeled in a steadying breath.

Easy on, cowboy.

"It looks like you might've saved the festival tonight," she said between sips.

Okay, this was good. He could do small talk. "It was everyone else, really. I only sounded the alarm."

"And knew what to do. I'd bet everyone would still be in town trying to figure out what to do if you hadn't stepped up like that."

She cupped her hands around the mug, and he did the same with his.

"Would you believe me if I told you I was making it all up as I went?" He wished he could see the thoughts playing across her face right now. He'd never been the best at communication, but with Kate, he felt safe enough to share his doubts.

"But it all worked out, didn't it?" Her head rested on his shoulder as she looked out toward the sound of the waves. "Some of my happiest memories are here. I'd just finished my second year in college when I drove back up for my youngest brother Tyler's graduation. I set up the tripod with my new camera facing the water, and after we got the nice family photo, I got one more of us throwing him in the water for good luck."

"Now that's a picture I'd love to see."

"I still have a framed copy of it back at my apartment in Petoskey." Her soft laughter resonated through his chest as her hand brushed his.

For a second, he thought about taking hold of it and never letting go. It would be so easy to start over. But he'd always wonder if she had chosen the real him or only the nice, cleaned-up version of himself he'd been presenting.

"Kate?"

"Yes?"

Her face was so near his, he had to focus on the branches above her right ear to keep from losing his train of thought. Even in the darkness, he could get lost in those golden eyes of hers, looking up at him with such innocent trust.

A trust he didn't deserve.

He could sense more than see her brow furrow in the still quiet. "I owe you an explanation." And she'd better not interrupt him again, saying it wasn't true. Any more excuses and he'd never say it. This was his second chance. Not a do-over, but a shot at fixing what he'd broken. "I never meant to hurt you. I thought . . . I thought I was protecting you by ending things when I did."

"Protecting me from what?" Her voice was quiet but encouraging.

Myself. The man I thought I'd inevitably become.

"Growing up wasn't easy." There, that wasn't so difficult. He'd cracked the door open, and the rest seemed to flow from there.

"My dad was rarely around, and when he was, he'd come home drunk and in a bad mood. Mom always made excuses for him—a hard day at work or something else that wasn't true—but it only got worse. Things were quieter after the separation, but even then, Mom refused to give up on him." Something she and Kate had in common, it appeared. Kate needed to know. To go into this with her eyes open. She'd either hear him out and stay, or she'd choose to walk away from this sheltered cocoon beneath the branches.

Not that he'd blame her if she did. But it would have to be her choice.

"I wasn't much better. Acting out in my teenage years, getting into fights in school. It didn't matter to the principal that the older boys were picking on someone else. I stood up and fought back, but all that did was get me suspended for a week. Dad was livid. Smashed a bottle of Jack against the wall before he dropped me off at Mom's, even though she was recovering from another stint at the hospital."

The worst part hadn't been the yelling. It was the way his mom had looked at him, eyes filled with tears but arms wide as ever. He hadn't deserved a hug then, and he didn't deserve one now. Not Kate's slender arm, which slid between him and the rough tree trunk, nor her silent acceptance.

"We didn't see him after that, and for a long time, things were better. Good, actually. Mom's lupus seemed to be under control, and then I met you." A glimmer of happiness, but it had only been that.

"That Friday, Brady had taken me out for a celebratory drink before the rehearsal dinner, and then I was supposed to pick up Mom before meeting you there. She must've sent Dad a last-minute invitation without telling me, because he was already at the house and stumbling all over the place. I'll never forget the sound of his raised voice, of glass breaking as he went on about being invited to his son's wedding as an afterthought. I stepped between them right as his fist swung into my face. At least it wasn't Mom's, but I lost it, Kate."

His hands were shaking now. "I hardly remember hitting back, I was so angry. A neighbor must've called the cops, because they showed up not long after and took him away. But by then it was too late. How was I supposed to promise to love and protect you when I'd become the very thing I hated most about my dad? Walking away was the only thing I could think to do. I realize now that probably wasn't the right decision, but I wasn't thinking straight that night."

His breaths came uneven and shallow. He'd never shared this story with anyone besides the lawyers. Not even Felicity, though she'd learned about the night's events from his mom a few weeks later, before the trial.

"What happened? To your dad, I mean." Her voice was so quiet, he was afraid he'd imagined the gentle question.

Lincoln sniffed, let the tension ebb from his body like the receding tide as Kate's warmth gave him strength. "He got fifteen months for drunken assault. By the time he was out, Mom's health had taken a turn for the worse. He wasn't at the funeral—not that I'd expected much from him after everything—but . . ." Even a card would've been something. Anything to acknowledge the years they'd shared together, however toxic they might've been.

He couldn't bring himself to look at Kate. He didn't know what she was thinking. Didn't want to know. He couldn't bear to see the tears and know that he'd been the one to ruin whatever chance at happiness they might've had.

For the second time that night, her hand brushed his. Slender fingers entwined with his rough calluses, making his breath hitch.

Why wasn't she running? She was supposed to be angry and push him away like everyone else. Not turn more to face him. Definitely not draw his hand to her chest with an achingly sweet yet torturous smile that cut straight to his heart.

Moisture clung to her lashes, then fell to her toes like a fallen star.

Lincoln steeled himself for the worst, the agony of silence stretching between them. He studied her face, searing her delicate nose and perfectly bowed lips into memory. Any extra time with Kate, even this, was better than nothing. It would have to be.

Her hitched breath broke the silence, slicing him like a knife. This was too much. He'd only made things ten times worse by opening up. It had been selfish and unthoughtful and—

She sucked in another breath, only this time, she wasn't frowning. Those tender lips spread upward, causing the skin around her eyes to crinkle ever so slightly.

Wait, was she laughing?

"Uh, this wasn't the reaction I was expecting."

She wiped her free hand beneath her lashes and smiled up at him. "I know, but it's the funniest thing."

"I'm glad you find my pain amusing."

"No, it's just—" She tipped her head as if searching the branches for the words. "For the first time in . . . I don't know, forever . . . I'm not afraid anymore."

"Odd time for a revelation like that, don't you think?" But he couldn't help the tug at his own mouth. Some of the weight seemed to lift from his shoulders, even if he didn't fully understand why.

She shook her head with so much force, he was afraid she might tweak something. And why was she looking at him like that? As if he'd bared his heart and not his ugly soul. Her next chuckle sounded like a hiccup, the most precious hiccup that only seemed to shine a light on how different they truly were from one another.

"I choose you, Lincoln St. James. I know it doesn't make much sense, but I do. We all have messy pasts and things we'd rather forget."

"Not you. You're perfect." His head was spinning. Why else would he have grabbed her other hand for support?

"I'm far from perfect," she tossed back. "I'm indecisive, a people pleaser, and I run myself into the ground trying to live up to my mom's expectations." Her mouth quivered for only the briefest of moments. "I didn't just volunteer to help my sister out of the goodness of my heart. I was forced to take a break from work because I ended up in urgent care due to a panic attack. How's that for messed up?"

She took another step, her toes bumping against his boots in the grass. Her hair had a windswept look from running along the beach, and she looked small bundled in his oversized coat. But she couldn't have been more beautiful had she been dressed in white.

"Maybe so." His breath hitched. He lowered his head a tentative inch and stopped. "But you're perfect for me."

She rose onto her toes, and he caught her. Pulled her in close lest this was all a dream. But she was real, and here, and kissing him as if not a single moment had slipped by in the last five years.

It all crashed over him like a tidal wave, his arms clinging to her like a life preserver after a long storm. She tasted like chocolate. Like future nights cuddled by the fireplace and promises yet to come.

He'd do things differently this time. Be different.

But this.

This would never change. The way he cared for Kate, how she made him feel both vulnerable and invincible all with one single kiss. An earth-shattering, homecoming, make-a-guy-move-mountains kind of kiss.

Fifteen

ALLING BACK IN LOVE WITH LINCOLN WAS like rewatching a favorite movie.

Comfortable, reassuring . . .

And blissfully uncomplicated.

Kate wasn't going to think about the fact that the festival was almost over, or that they both had other lives to go back to eventually. Why ruin this perfectly wonderful dream with worries about the future?

Other people got their happy endings. Why not her?

Golden sunlight streamed through the open blinds, bathing the apartment in warm light. She'd awoken to Lincoln's text that the trees had survived, which was cause for celebration. Coffee and breakfast in town and then an early walk around the park.

Exactly like their first date five and a half years ago.

After tossing nearly every shirt she owned onto the bed—not that there were many options—she settled for a pale-pink top with butterfly sleeves. Never mind that she'd have to wear a jacket the moment she stepped outside. Forty-five-degree weather was not meant for cute spring outfits or open-toed flats. But this was *her* fairy tale, and no amount of late-spring frost was getting in the way.

The furnace roared to life, blowing hot air at her from the ceiling vents. Still wearing her fuzzy socks, she skipped into the living room, where Lincoln's sunflower bouquet greeted her on the coffee table. In three days, they'd do the interview with *American Wanderer*, and then she'd have it all—a reconnected family, a thriving career, and maybe . . . possibly . . .

There was a knock at the door, and she suddenly felt like a teenager again.

"Coming!"

She grabbed the nearest jacket off the hook and threw it over her mismatched shirt and pajama pants before opening the door to Lincoln's crooked smile. He'd actually shaved, making him almost unrecognizable but somehow even more handsome than last night on the beach.

"I was wondering where that had gotten to. It looks good on you."

She looked down at the hunter-green jacket and oversized arms and cringed. "Sorry about that. I didn't mean to kiss you last night and then steal your coat." Her face suddenly grew warm. "I mean, I'm not sorry about the first part. The kiss, I mean. It was great. Wonderful, even."

Wonderful? Ugh, where was a hood on this coat when she needed one?

At least Lincoln seemed to be enjoying himself at her expense. A little too much, based on his resonant chuckle. If only he could have done her the same favor and worn bunny slippers.

"I should probably go change before I say or do anything else embarrassing."

"Like invite a handsome stranger into your apartment?" he teased, stepping into the small kitchen-diner. He spotted the sunflowers right away, although it was his grin she couldn't take her eyes off.

"You're hardly a stranger," she said as she dashed around the corner to the safety of her bedroom. It took her less than a minute to change into a pair of bootcut jeans and replace the fuzzy socks with her leather flats. A fresh coat of tinted lip gloss finished the look, along with the pale-green scarf Dani had brought back for her from Italy.

Lincoln was seated at the table in front of a small pile of wilted leaves he'd plucked from the flower arrangement. He looked up when she entered, and accidentally snapped off a flower head. Not that he seemed to notice as he stared at her.

She fluffed the fabric knot at her neck, suddenly self-conscious. At least she hadn't opted for the yellow sundress. "Is it too much? It's too much."

He was speechless for only a few moments before he regained his normal rugged charm. "I think you might freeze a bit, but I don't mind loaning you my jacket a little longer." He swept the pruned clippings into his hand to toss into the trash, then leaned a casual hip against the kitchen counter.

Words left her. Kate's normally put-together and professional demeanor had been replaced by a bumbling, awkward, teenage version of herself. "O-okay."

He helped her into his coat for the second time in as many days, then held the door for her as she grabbed her purse and keys from the table. It wasn't until the door clicked behind them that she finally released her held breath.

Why was she so nervous? This was Lincoln, for crying out loud. It wasn't like they didn't know each other. After all, they'd been engaged. She knew how he took his coffee—black, two sugars— and that he hated the nickname Linc.

She also knew how difficult things had been for him the past few years and that this was as much a risk for him as it was for her.

But neither of them was the same person they'd been five years ago. They'd started over, worked hard, and knew this wasn't something to be treated lightly.

So why were her hands suddenly sweating as they walked down the narrow staircase?

She shoved them into the pockets as they stepped into the crisp morning air, puffs of fog forming in front of them. The sidewalk glittered from last night's frost, which was already beginning to melt under the blue skies.

A pile of leftover tarps lay next to the parked golf cart, another reminder that last night hadn't been a dream. Kate stepped into the damp grass to retrieve them and sucked in a quick breath as the barely-melted frost seeped into her shoes. "Wow, you weren't kidding about how cold it is."

Lincoln's chuckle caused more ice crystals to billow around his face as he took her hand and pulled her toward him, back to solid ground. If wet grass was the equivalent of an army of storm-troopers, he could be the Han Solo to her Princess Leia any day.

"Sure you don't want something a bit warmer?" he asked, lips close to her ear as they finished their little dance. "Some hardy snow boots, perhaps? Maybe those fuzzy socks I saw you in earlier?"

"Ha, ha." She tested the damp grass again but with the same result. "The tarps are going to get wet."

"I'm afraid it's a little late to prevent that, based on the icicles hanging from that top one."

She swatted playfully at his arm, to which he responded by trying to tickle her through the thick jacket.

The tension suddenly melted from her chest and stomach, replaced by the comfortable friendship that had, against all odds, bloomed over the past few weeks. Oliver would surely object. Mom didn't approve of anything Kate did. And while Dani might be in her corner, she was newly married with rose-colored glasses and couldn't be trusted for an objective opinion.

"What are you thinking about so intently?" Soft wrinkles framed Lincoln's eyes as he peered down at her. He couldn't hear her thoughts, so why did it seem like he could?

"What makes you ask that?"

"Well . . ." His gaze roamed her face as if studying one of his bouquets. "You get this faraway look in your eyes, and the left corner of your mouth hikes up like it is now."

"And when did you come to that realization?"

"Like I said before"—his voice became lower, more gravelly—"when it comes to you, Kate Sullivan, I remember everything."

Any thought that last night had been a dream vanished. Not that she'd really questioned it, but people had a way of saying one thing and meaning another when it came down to it. Her parents, friends. Even Lincoln—at least, the Lincoln she'd known before.

But not this man standing in front of her. A man who looked like he very much wanted to repeat last night's kiss right here on the edge of Main Street for all to see.

She tucked a piece of hair behind each ear and took a half step back. Baby steps. "Since you asked, I was actually wondering if Jill Kelley will have any of her famous sticky pecan rolls left."

He tilted his head in amusement, then nodded. Took her cue and responded with . . . "She wouldn't happen to be related at all to Martha or Patrick Kelley who were at the park last night?"

Kate couldn't help but smile. Maybe this could work after all.

She didn't know how or what it would look like, but there was no way a person could feel this blissfully happy if God hadn't placed those desires there for a reason. Right?

"You've got a lot to learn about small-town life on an island."

"I'm looking forward to it." The way he stared at her when he said that, his gaze holding her like a warm embrace, pushed aside the rest of her lingering doubts.

She could imagine him picking up his usual from Good Day Coffee before heading out for a leisurely day of fishing down by Sunset Cove. She'd meet up with him for a picnic on the beach, then take pictures of the sunset while he named each plant and wildflower they passed on their walk back to town. While she was dreaming, she might as well throw in a photography studio with a florist shop in back. A one-stop shop for anyone in search of happiness on their visit to the island. And a little cottage for two down by the water's edge.

"But first." He held out his arm, and she gladly slipped hers through. "Let's see about those pecan rolls."

Planning the finishing touches of the festival gala with Kate was, surprisingly, as much fun as planning a wedding—and without the added stress of opinionated mothers and threats of social-media ruin.

"How about something like this?" Kate angled her phone to show Lincoln a white tent strung with lights and what had amounted to a back-breaking amount of Italian ruscus and mums.

Literally. He'd had a crick in his neck for weeks after that wedding. Even if the photos posted online had turned out stunning.

"Unless your sister's got a canopy hidden inside that hotel of hers, I think we'd better stick to something a little less *Twilight*-inspired. There might not be any flowers left in the entire state if we import them all just for one gala."

She flicked a piece of popcorn at him, which he easily dodged.

It hadn't been easy wheeling that popcorn machine down the street, even less so with the overwhelming smell of decades-old butter stinking up the side patio of the Island House Inn.

Lincoln set aside the sketch he'd been working on. "So how did you manage to get roped into this again?"

"I volunteered." She continued to scrub at the large glass box, which looked about as old as everything else on the island. "I used to love watching the movies at the fort when I was a kid. We'd go as a family every summer. Oliver and I would sneak in a thermos of hot chocolate when Mom and Dad weren't looking. Dani and Tyler would beg for their own cups until we eventually caved, while James, Ashley, and Zachary would share their Fourth of July candy with us."

It all sounded so perfect. Simple, yes, but in a way that had him thinking about white picket fences and how an apartment in the city was no place to raise a dog . . . or a family.

He never wanted this moment to end—Kate reminiscing about her childhood while he worked on the gala arrangements. But that would mean missing his meeting with the Bloomfest selection committee tomorrow morning and probably his last chance at convincing them to take a chance on him. He still had another hour before his ferry left, which wasn't nearly enough time to make up for the lost years.

Something he fully intended to rectify when he got back tomorrow evening.

"I remember this one time"—the glass muffled her words but not the lightness in her tone—"we went to see *The Princess Bride*. I was probably a freshman in high school, so everyone was still here. We brought a picnic basket and everything, including these chocolate-covered pretzels Mom always made. We were quoting lines from the movie. Ashley knew them all by heart. Oliver and I were joking that she looked exactly like Princess Buttercup, with her blonde hair and regal posture, when Tyler scared us right as the Rodents of Unusual Size popped up on the screen. I was holding the pretzels at the time, and when I jumped, they went flying all over the blanket and into the grass. I was so afraid my parents would get mad at me, but nobody could ignore Dani's contagious laughter. I can't remember another time I've laughed so hard I actually cried."

Her face had a faraway look, as if she were picturing it. "Nobody cared about the pretzels after that. We were together, and that was all that mattered. The nine of us, all huddled together on that too-small picnic blanket, surrounded by all our closest friends."

Lincoln leaned against the porch railing, a smile tugging at his lips. He could picture a younger version of her, face glowing as much as it was now.

"Sounds like a wonderful childhood." In a blissful, uncomplicated sort of way. He caught her gaze through the glass, along with the sudden droop of her smile.

"I'm sorry, that probably sounded insensitive, didn't it? After everything you shared the other night—" She went to stand and bumped her head on the metal canister. A shower of stale popcorn rained down on her, punctuated by a sharp "Ouch!"

Lincoln was right there, pulling her away from the ancient death trap.

"There I go again, putting my foot where it doesn't belong."

"I think you mean head," he teased, hoping to keep the mood light. The last thing he wanted was another serious conversation before he left. Anything that could ruin this moment with things like logic or difficult questions. "Good thing you've got a hard noggin. Maybe I'd better check on the popcorn maker to see if you didn't break it instead." He pretended to inspect the machine, to the sound of her musical laughter.

"I'm going to choose to take that as a compliment." Her voice was light and infused with humor.

"You should. Absolutely." Only someone as stubbornly generous as Kate would've accepted his apology so willingly. Even when she had every right not to.

Smiling, Kate lowered herself onto the top step beside her festival notebook—now marked up in red since she'd lost her blue pen—and patted the wood beside her.

He didn't need a second invitation to join her.

She scooted over and drew her knees to her chest, then laid her head on his shoulder as if it were the most natural thing in the world.

A light breeze played with the pages of his discarded sketchbook, which she now picked up. "Are these your final designs for the gala?"

"It's only a few ideas. Nothing solid yet." The flowers were already locked in and sitting in the repaired refrigerator behind the studio. But the arrangements still didn't feel . . . right.

She continued to flip through the pages, pausing on the one he'd been working on up until a couple of minutes ago. "Lincoln, these are amazing."

He shifted beside her, unsure why her praise felt so difficult to receive. "They're still missing something. I don't know what yet, but it'll come to me eventually. My mom used to keep a journal with all her notes and designs. I still have it back at my studio at home. Maybe it'll spark some great ideas. If nothing else, it'll give me something to think about on the long drive." He hadn't meant to spoil this moment by bringing up the trip, but nothing in her expression changed.

In fact, she looked downright angelic sitting there on the porch, late-afternoon sun like a halo over her head. Only someone as selfless as her would accept him for exactly what he was. Past and all.

"What are you thinking about right now?" He'd taken to asking her that question the past two days since the kiss. At first, it was fear that had prompted it—fear that she'd realize what a terrible mistake she'd made and think better of it. But each time he asked, he became more comfortable with it. He wanted to hear about everything, from her childhood memories to what she ate for breakfast this morning to—

"You're pretty amazing, you know that, right?"

"Me?" Maybe she'd hit her head a little harder than he'd realized. "If anyone is amazing, it's you. The way you've given me a second chance. How you were nothing but excited for me when I told you about the meeting with the Bloomfest committee."

A meeting he was less and less inclined to go to if it meant missing a single moment like this one.

She scrunched her nose and smiled. "You found your dream and you're going for it."

"They haven't selected me yet."

"But they will. I'm sure of it." She had enough faith for both of them—the kind that made others want to believe as well. "And when you get back, we can celebrate with that dinner you talked about the other day. Six o'clock at Martha's tomorrow night?"

It would be a tight squeeze to get through the meeting and then the four-hour drive back up the state, but the thought of her waiting for him on the other side was more than enough incentive.

"I wouldn't miss it for the world."

They sat that way for another few minutes, watching the boats sail in and out of the harbor and families stroll along the lake path.

His eyes wandered over the picturesque scene and settled on a family of three down by the edge of the lawn. The man and woman walked hand in hand with a little girl between them, her bronze curls bouncing with each step. All at once, the couple lifted their arms, and the girl squealed as she soared into the air before landing gently back on her feet. Lincoln watched them until they disappeared down the path, but the girl's happy giggles still carried on the breeze.

It took all his willpower to stand when the time reached 5:45. Another fifteen minutes and he'd miss his ferry. Something which sounded far too tempting when Kate smiled up at him, showing those dimples of hers. Especially when she rose on tiptoes, her peony-pink lips meeting his. He pulled her closer without hesitation, dislodging the unruly curl that had a mind of its own.

"I'll be back before tomorrow evening, I promise." They had so much to talk about, and hopefully, they'd get the chance for many more conversations to come. They'd figure something out. They had to. Why else would God have brought them back together?

"Text me when you get there, okay?"

"How about I call instead?" Hearing her voice had a way of soothing his worries, something he could use before tomorrow's meeting.

"I'd like that."

She walked with him the short distance to the dock and waited as he boarded the boat.

He held her smile in his memory long after he'd lost sight of her across the waves and begun the four-hour drive south into the city. He could still picture her wind-tossed hair as he pulled into the covered garage and ascended the concrete steps to his third-floor apartment.

He should feel tired at ten o'clock in the evening, but he was wide awake with thoughts of Kate, the island, and that family of three skipping down the lane.

Lincoln's keys grew heavy in his palm as he neared the top step. For all the planning and bending over backward to get here, he hadn't spent much time thinking about what things would look like if he did make the cut. Bloomfest was meant to launch a career in Detroit. Not on a remote island in the middle of Lake Huron.

He stopped and stared out the glass windows at the city below.

Would Kate be happy living here? She seemed so much happier and more at peace on the island. The old doubts threatened to resurface, but he shoved them down as he opened the door to his floor.

God will make a way.

He was sure of it.

His phone dinged an incoming message, and he smiled as Kate's image popped up on the screen. He hadn't had someone check in on him in a long time, and it felt nice knowing she was thinking of him. He pulled up her contact information and was about to call when he turned the corner and looked up to see a man waiting outside his apartment. Salt and pepper streaked his tousled hair, and he wore a Detroit Red Wings T-shirt beneath a heavy rain jacket.

Lots of people supported the local hockey team, but Lincoln only knew one person who had a different patch for each time they'd won the Stanley Cup. Thankfully, they'd had a stellar record in the nineties, but he'd never forget his dad's reaction when they'd lost to the Colorado Avalanche. That was the first drinking binge he could remember.

Lincoln's stomach clenched as he froze two doors down.

But it was too late. The man lifted his head, familiar blue-gray eyes locking with his. The same eyes that had filled Lincoln with guilt the day the police carried him away.

"Hey, son. It's been a long time."

Sixteen

LINCOLN CLOSED HIS EYES AND PRAYED IT was some kind of trick. A side effect of the four-hour drive he'd just completed. But when he opened them, the man was still standing beside the door to his apartment, as disheveled and unapologetic as he remembered.

"Dad. What are you doing here?" His grip tightened around the handle of his duffel bag—anything to hold on to lest he do something he'd later regret.

He shouldn't be here. Five years without a word, and he thought he could show up unannounced on his floor?

His dad's only response was a slight shrug, both hands shoved into his pockets.

Lincoln forced his hand to relax, blood pulsing back into his white knuckles. *He's not worth it.* Fighting the man wouldn't solve his issues. He'd already tried that and lived to reap the consequences.

"Do you need money? Because if that's what you came here

for, you're out of luck." There was no way he was fueling another alcohol binge. "I don't owe you anything."

The hunch of his father's shoulders made him appear older and smaller than Lincoln remembered, once dark-brown hair now patched with gray. "Can't a dad drop by and check on his son?"

"Not like this. You should've called."

"And let you ignore me again?"

Lincoln clenched his jaw. Had he known the alternative, he would've endured an uncomfortable phone call. But he hadn't, and here he was.

The man released a heavy sigh and ran a hand through his thinning hair. A few pieces stuck out at an odd angle, but he didn't seem to notice. Or care. Come to think of it, his eyes did look a little red. Had he already been drinking? "I'm sorry, that wasn't fair of me."

"Fair? *Fair?*" Lincoln tried to keep his voice low enough not to startle the other tenants that shared this hallway, but his dad wasn't making it easy on him. "Fair would've been you seeking help years ago, not taking your anger out on Mom and me. You never should've come back. Maybe then we could've at least moved on."

It all came rushing back—the broken promises, the missed graduation, the hospital visits. It had only ever been him and Felicity in the waiting room as they ran test after test. It had been Lincoln who'd taken care of Mom between school and work when she came home.

His hands ached for something to do—anything to keep them occupied besides balling them into fists.

"Mom's already gone. Not that you care. You weren't even at the funeral." He was done making excuses, done looking for the good his mom had seen.

Like Kate saw in him.

The air left his lungs like a gut punch. He dropped his bag onto the geometric carpet as if it had bit him, the shock racing like a bolt of electricity straight to his heart.

I'm nothing like him. I'd never do to Kate what he did to Mom.

So why was his chest pounding with the urge to prove those accusations right here in this hallway?

"I grieved in my own way," his dad shot back. For a moment, Lincoln thought the man might actually apologize—for walking away, for the drinking, for all of it—but the old spark snuffed out whatever else he might have said. "Wouldn't expect you to understand that though. How long did you wait before taking over your mother's business? Three months? Four?"

If his dad was looking for any kind of reconciliation, he'd shattered that possibility.

"You don't get to accuse me of anything. You walked out on this family when it suited you and have only caused more trouble. I did what I had to do after she was gone, no thanks to you. Everything I did was to preserve her memory." To hold on to the good ones lest the others drown them out. "I'm sorry you went to prison. Really, I am. But I'm done making excuses for you, done blaming myself all these years when it wasn't my guilt to carry."

The fight seemed to drain from his dad, accentuating the wrinkles around his face—deeper now than they had been five years ago. He released a long breath, eyes closing a few seconds before finally meeting Lincoln's cautious gaze. "You did what you had to do. And I—I forgive you."

Wait. "*You* forgive me?"

The muscle in Lincoln's temple throbbed as he bit down his response. He had grappled for years with the guilt and shame his father had caused, trying to make sense of it all. And now he showed up offering forgiveness? Lincoln wasn't the one who'd yelled at Mom when he walked through the door after a couple of drinks with Brady. He wasn't the one who'd split his son's lip or given him a black eye.

But Lincoln *had* been the one to end things with Kate and walk away just the same.

"I couldn't see it, but I was completely out of control," his dad continued. Face pinched, he rocked forward on his feet. And back. "That time in prison changed my life. Saved it, in fact. I've been clean for four and a half years."

"That's great. But that still doesn't change the past."

"I'll admit I was angry. Angry at the world, at myself, and definitely at God." His dad took a tentative step down the hall, then suddenly stopped. Looked at the wall sconce, the apartment number beside the door. Anywhere but Lincoln. "That wasn't how my life was supposed to turn out, ripped from my family and left to rot in a cell. But that's where God found me, in a dingy prison chapel with a hipster chaplain and a paperback Bible. I can't tell you how many times I've wanted to talk to you since. To tell you all this." For the first time, his dad's voice cracked. His eyebrows pinched in a pained expression—for Lincoln's sake or his own, Lincoln wasn't sure—before rising to meet his. "Son."

Son? He was really trying to go there? "You gave up the right to call me that a long time ago."

His dad extended his hand toward Lincoln, who flinched.

Took a step back.

It was too much. His dad being here, talking about Mom and God and being a changed man. It was all just way too much to take in at once.

Lincoln scooped up his bag, unsure where to turn. "I, um, I need to go." He'd pictured this moment a thousand times, and never once had it involved him walking away. This was his chance to lay it all bare and be done with it. But the wounds were too deep. Too fresh, even after all this time.

It was as if he were watching himself from a distance as he hurried down the corridor and pushed through the door to the stairwell. He made it to the safety of his car before the emotions began to spill over, shaky hands moving the steering wheel by instinct as he drove the two miles along darkened streets to his studio. He needed a distraction, anything to keep him from turning around and driving back to the apartment.

Lights off, the cavernous space engulfed him as the door clicked shut behind him. His duffel bag thumped against the concrete floor, the sound loud and thunderous and fitting.

The bottom desk drawer stuck when he tried to yank it open. *Of course.* Felicity was always getting on him about fixing up the place—something he could finally agree with as he fought the ancient wooden beast. It took a few good jiggles to get it open, and when he did, the contents sloshed forward in a jumble.

Something like glass clinked against the panel, and he pulled out an old bottle of whiskey he didn't remember putting there. A second of doubt was all it took for him to chuck it into the trash before turning back to the drawer.

It had to be in here somewhere. If anything good came from not listening to Felicity, it was that he hadn't had time to clean the thing out in years. Mom's journal had to still be in here. He remembered tossing it in along with the probate paperwork and—

Something sharp jabbed his finger. He yanked his hand away to find a smear of blood on his fingertip. "Oh, for the love of . . ." He stormed his way to the sink, where he plunged his hand beneath cold water. The bandages and disinfectant were in the cabinet below as usual, and he made quick time taping himself back together before returning to his office.

This time, he reached in slowly, feeling past the papers until rough wood snagged on the fabric Band-Aid. Curious, he pulled out the rectangular frame, and his breath hitched at the photo.

His mom was smiling back at him from outside the shop, standing beside a teenage version of himself. She was holding a bundle of blue daisies to her chest after having slipped one behind her ear. She'd been laughing when Felicity snapped the picture—about what, he couldn't remember. But he could almost hear it echo back to him within the deafening silence of the empty studio.

He plucked the pieces of broken glass from the frame, taking extra care not to scratch the image. A fresh red stain blossomed in the upper corner, dark and permanent. Kneeling on the cold concrete, he tried to blot away the blemish but only managed to smear it more.

"I'm sorry, Mom."

It was what St. James men did, it seemed. Apologized after breaking things beyond repair. It didn't matter how many chances they got, how many times they were forgiven. They'd always mess up.

He'd always mess up.

He'd seen the way his dad had taken advantage of his mom's gracious kindness. How he'd taken every second, third, tenth chance and found a way to throw it back in her face. Even if he was right this time and had changed, it was too late for her. His dad's salvation had come at too great a cost, one Lincoln wasn't sure he was willing to accept.

"Love is patient. Love is kind . . . It always protects, always trusts, always hopes . . ."

His mom's voice came unbidden, a bittersweet memory that reminded him just how far he'd fallen. "I'm sorry I couldn't protect you, Mom." From his dad, from the illness that had eventually taken her from him.

"God, You call yourself a father, but I don't know what that's supposed to mean. Fathers are supposed to look out for their family and tell their sons what to do. I could really use some help right now." Or better yet, an organized spreadsheet telling him exactly what to do about his dad, the business, and his growing feelings for Kate. Feelings that, until this moment, had seemed full of hope and not this churning dread in the pit of his stomach.

Another text from Kate dinged on his phone, but he couldn't bring himself to look at it. Not now.

He removed the picture from its frame and clutched it to his chest as he sank into the couch against the far wall and closed his eyes. He couldn't go back to his apartment. Not while *he* could still be there.

He sank deeper into the cushion, the leather like a gentle hug he couldn't pull himself from as his body grew heavy with fatigue. The heater clicked on above him, the loud hum like a white-noise machine for his spinning thoughts. Maybe he could stay here a little while longer. Close his eyes for an hour or two.

His breathing grew deep and steady, and he slipped deeper into another memory. Or maybe it was a dream. One where he'd never walked away from Kate, his mom hadn't gotten sick, and this overwhelming sense of guilt was only a long-forgotten nightmare.

Kate tried not to worry.

If she kept her phone buried at the bottom of her purse, maybe she'd forget about the three unanswered text messages to Lincoln or her worried call that had gone straight to voicemail this morning.

Kate tossed another look toward the water through the large ballroom windows and scanned the empty horizon. The legend of Lover's Leap drifted in uninvited, and she shooed it away. "He'll be back," she whispered to herself. "He promised."

Abandoning the neat rows of silverware in front of her, she reached for her bag and dug out her phone for the seventh time that morning.

"Would you stop looking at that thing?" murmured Dani over the sound of clinking silverware. The forks, knives, and spoons had all arrived in one box, which the two of them had spent the better part of the past half hour organizing. "His phone is probably dead."

"Yeah, or maybe the ferry sprang a leak and he couldn't call even if he wanted."

But if that were the case, everyone would have been talking about it when she'd stopped at Good Day Coffee for an extra-large cinnamon latte on her way here.

No. That wasn't the reason her chest had felt tight all morning. She'd tossed and turned all night until her alarm went off at six thirty, waking her from a nightmare where she'd been holding a bouquet of wilted wedding flowers.

"What are you two girls talking about?" Their mom placed another white tablecloth on top of the freshly ironed stack and looked up. Kate shouldn't have been surprised to see her here this morning. After all, she was more a resident of the island than Kate herself.

"Nothing. Just wondering when Oliver is supposed to get here with the place cards from the printers." It was no secret how her mom felt about Lincoln. She'd made her opinions very clear at dinner. His silence now would only fuel her opinions. "Something about there being a mix-up with the cardstock."

Her mom sighed and tucked a piece of auburn hair behind her ear. "I told him I would have been glad to do them myself."

"But he's the one with the connection," Dani jumped in as she moved on to the serving utensils. With a menu of mostly finger foods, who'd have thought they'd need so many spoons? "Besides, we need your artistic eye to help with the decorations. I can't wait to see what you do with the place settings."

"Which reminds me," she said, laying out the next crisp bundle of fabric. "Have you gotten the candles I ordered for the gala yet?"

"Right here." Dani kicked a box beneath the table, which hardly budged with the weight. "All that's missing now, besides the food and music, is the flower arrangements. I hope Lincoln gets back in time to finish them."

Dani popped her head up from the pile of silverware and cringed apologetically at Kate, but it was too late.

"Back? Where did he go?" Mom squinted toward Kate, who could've flicked her sister on the arm for all the help she was this morning.

Thanks a lot, Dani.

"He had an important meeting off island, but he's supposed to be on the last ferry this afternoon." At least, that had been the plan. Mom didn't need to know about the unanswered messages or the nightmare.

"Hmm. Well, he better be. He's already broken one of my daughters' hearts. We don't need him upgrading to an entire town now, do we?"

Ouch. "That's not fair."

"But I'm not wrong."

How was it that Mom was nothing but encouraging toward Dani but could make Kate feel at fault with one look?

"We've put so much into this festival. I'm still surprised you trusted the man to hire him. Hasn't he done enough for this family?" This last bit she said to Kate. As if Lincoln's past actions were an indictment against Kate's judgment.

Then again, her track record wasn't so stellar either. Failed engagement, mandatory medical leave, hiring her ex . . . Maybe her mom had a point.

Her mom's face softened a degree when Kate didn't respond, more filled with pity than comfort. "I know people can change, honey. I'm proof of that. And it amazes me that your heart is still open and so willing to forgive him after all he put you through. I just don't want to see you get hurt like that again if he hasn't." She raised a hand, motioning toward the original pink-and-white-striped wallpaper and custom crown molding.

The entire island served to prove her mom's point. Kate liked to think things had changed around here over the years, but they hadn't. There were the same horses pulling carriages down the streets instead of cars, the same legends that had lost their mystery years ago, and the same terrible cell reception that must be to blame for Lincoln's sudden radio silence.

"People aren't like towns, Mom. They're complex and thoughtful and make you laugh until you cry." The good kind of tears, not like the moisture stinging her eyes at present. She blinked before anyone could see it and swallowed down the painful lump forming in her throat.

"This place has stood the test of time. Sure, it might be a bit old and outdated, but you know what you're getting with a classic Victorian house. That's more than you can say for most people." Anyone else would hear the soft lilt to her mom's tone and think it was some kind of encouragement.

But Kate knew from experience how the softest of rebukes could cut the deepest. Like a flicker of light over an undeveloped negative. It only took a second to distort the image, but the effect was permanent.

As much as she wanted to believe things between Lincoln and her had changed, she was still the same little girl trying to earn her mom's approval. Wanting to be loved for more than her failures or successes—simply for who she was. It was the island, she'd told herself. But that wasn't true. She'd been trying to prove herself all along—winning the state golf championships in high school, graduating with honors from Michigan State, building a successful business . . .

That was, if she even had a business left to go back to. When was the last time she'd called Gabby to check in? And she hadn't so much as taken a photo for the festival all day.

Kate reached into the box and pulled out something with three tines. Salad fork or fish fork? Were they even having salad at the gala? And why did there have to be so many types of forks in the first place?

She tossed it back. "I think I'm going to go check on Oliver and see what's taking him so long with those place cards." She swiped her bag and sweater from the table and slipped through the large double doors before either Mom or Dani could stop her. Not that they would. They were too focused on getting ready for Sunday evening's event to see the storm brewing inside.

Outside, on the hotel's long summer porch, she drew in a long breath, held it for four seconds before releasing for another count of four. Why couldn't Dr. Weston's calming techniques actually work when she needed them to? She already had the sound of nearby water and a nice floral fragrance to breathe in from the hotel gardens. Short of tracking down the nearest dog to play with, she was running out of things to try.

Stuffing down a wave of shakiness, she pulled out her phone and sent off another text.

Kate

How did the meeting go?

She sucked in a breath as three dots appeared at the bottom of the screen—she'd actually caught him this time—followed by Lincoln's short reply.

Lincoln

Fine. Just tired. I'll tell you about it later.

This was good, right? At least he was communicating with her. But that did little to calm the tremor in her gut.

Kate

If you want to talk about it, I'd love to listen.

She hit send and waited a whole two minutes without a response. He was probably driving. No reason to worry.

A bit shaky from the coffee, she tried and failed to zip her purse shut. Her phone clattered to the porch, and she scrambled to retrieve it before it could slide over the edge into the flower beds. She stood a little too quickly, the sudden head rush clouding her vision for a few seconds as her heart rate sped up. *Not now.* Not that any time was good for a panic attack, but surely there was a better place than here with her mom on the other side of the doors.

Start by focusing on five things you can see. Dr. Weston's voice prompted her to look up instead of at her blank, dark screen.

Five things. Okay, there was the yellow awning above the doorway, the green porch, a basket of red petunias, a forgotten nail left by the construction crews, and the month-old coffee stain she'd been unable to completely remove from her sweater.

Kate picked up the nail and listened to the swoosh of the water, the light breeze through the lilac bushes, faint chatter inside, and a lawn mower in the distance. The nail felt cool to her skin, the wooden floorboards solid beneath her feet, and her heavy purse dug into her shoulder the longer she stood here doing this silly grounding exercise. Speaking of lilacs, their fragrant, fruity scent wafted over the porch, mingled with the lingering aroma of her latte.

"And one taste." Rummaging around in her purse, she unearthed a pack of mint gum, the refreshing explosion of flavor like an alarm clock to her senses.

She maybe felt a teensy, tiny bit better. Even if her chest still felt as if a boulder were sitting directly on it. She was only a few steps away from the stairs when a shrill voice caught up to her.

"Kate, there you are." Martha's staccato footsteps clicked up the footpath, cutting off her escape. Apron still tied around her ample waist, she looked as if she'd come straight from the restaurant. "Do you think it's too much to have apples in the main dish as well as the appetizers and dessert? My son Isaac thinks it'll overwhelm the menu, but it's not like I can put apple blossoms into the beurre blanc sauce now, can I?"

"No, of course not." Although it might make for a memorable dish. If that was all Martha needed, she wouldn't mind if Kate—

"When you have a minute, can you stop by the restaurant and sample things? I'm afraid we need a third party's opinion."

"Sure. Whatever you need." Anything to get her home faster to her lavender candles and journal. They might only mask the symptoms, but she was not about to have a full-blown panic attack on the hotel steps.

"Wonderful!" Martha clapped with satisfaction. "I'll let you know when the pies come out of the oven."

Her short steps continued past through the open front doors, leaving Kate finally alone to manage her escape. Only, her feet didn't seem to hear what her brain was trying to tell them.

Lincoln wasn't here to talk her through things or distract her, like when the golf cart had died on them last week. If only he'd text her back. She could redirect her attention to him and his meeting instead of focusing on the shortness of her breath or how her arms had suddenly gone tingly all over.

The apartment might as well be a few miles away. There was no way she'd manage to get there without melting down in the middle of Main Street first. Abandoning her breathing techniques, Kate fidgeted with the strap of her purse until she spied the old gazebo across the lawn. Secluded, private, and far enough removed from the hotel that no one would be able to hear her meltdown if it came to that.

God, please don't let it come to that.

She hurried across the grass, her shoes damp with moisture by the time she passed the outdoor firepit with its ring of chairs and ducked into the building's shadows.

She sat there for what felt like an hour until the vise grip slowly gave. Her shoulders relaxed, and the knot in her stomach eventually unfurled, leaving her more exhausted than this morning. But while her body no longer felt like it was under attack, little else had actually changed.

Her mom could still make her feel smaller than a golf ball with her pointed comments. The gala to-do list was still a mile long. Lincoln was gone and unresponsive, a fact that had her more worried than she'd like to admit. And while she might have managed to get things under control this time without a visit to urgent care, she was no closer to getting better than before she'd left her job and Petoskey to come back home.

Home was supposed to feel safe, a place where one could sink into open arms and fill their soul with happy memories and unconditional love. But no matter what she did or how hard she worked, it never felt like enough.

She'd never be enough. Her. Plain old Kate. Even her name sounded boring and unimpressive. Not special or unique like Dani or Oliver or Eliza.

It had always been difficult trying to live up to her cousin Ariel, the country star, or Zachary, who could make a five-star meal out of practically anything you gave him. Oliver and James with their perfect GPAs, and Dani, who was single-handedly reviving an entire island with her grand plans.

And then there was Kate, the wallflower of the Sullivan family. The neurotic flower with the lopsided petals, which everyone put up with because she made a good herbal tea or something. The kind that was healthy for you, not the kind that tasted pleasant or gave you an energy boost.

Lincoln deserved something exotic like hibiscus, or fun like tangerine orange zinger. Something a person would enjoy drinking every day for the rest of their lives.

Which, if experience had taught her anything, she was neither.

But oh, how she wished she could be.

Seventeen

L INCOLN HAD HARDLY SAID A WORD SINCE the moment Felicity had shown up at the studio that morning, one of her husband's old suits over one arm and a large thermos of coffee in the other.

With the meeting over, he loosened the tie from around his neck and tossed it on top of the discarded jacket in the back seat. "You didn't have to drive me, you know. I would've been fine on my own."

"I think you meant to say 'Thank you for dragging me out of my office this morning before I missed my meeting.'"

"Thank you, Felicity." He wouldn't have forgotten, but the freshly pressed suit was an improvement over the button-down and jeans he'd packed. All of his suits—both of them—were currently hanging in his closet back home and hadn't seen an iron in three years. "How did you know where I was?"

"I had a feeling when you didn't pick up my call the second time. You always go to the studio when you need to think." She slowed to a stop as the light went red, tossed an apologetic look over her right shoulder. "Tom called and told me what happened."

Wait. "Dad called you?" He wasn't ready to go there. Not yet. Something which she seemed to understand, based on her simple nod.

She hummed as the classical station switched over to a piece from *Brigadoon*. A car honked behind them as the stoplight turned green, yet she seemed in no hurry to get back to the studio.

Suited him just fine. Normally, the old musical number would put him in a good mood, but all he could think about was Kate and how much he wished he'd never left Jonathon Island. But it wasn't some enchanted Scottish town from the eighteenth century. And she wasn't a two-hundred-year-old lass. They'd both still be there when he got back.

Right?

"So? What did they say? Whatever decision they made, know I'll always be here for you. It's what I promised your mom a long time ago."

He'd only been half paying attention to the maze of streets before he peeled his gaze from the window. He could see his mom in the gentleness of Felicity's smile. The constant support and encouragement, even when he was such a bear to be around most of the time.

He drew in a grounding breath and then . . . "They accepted my application. We're in the showcase."

"That's wonderful!" She was smiling so large a traffic camera could pick it up. Which it very well might if she drove any faster through the next yellow light.

He might not be as excited as her, but her response was enough. It would have to be. If she was happy, so was he.

"That *is* good news, isn't it?" she asked, tone growing slightly suspicious as she studied him through a few stolen glances.

"Yes, of course. It's what we've been working for all these years.

Preserving Mom's legacy." He fidgeted with the edge of the manila folder they'd given him—contracts to sign and such. "It's just—"

"Yes?"

There was no way he could tell her he was rethinking the whole thing. She'd already done so much to get him to where he was today. Anything short of accepting the offer would be an insult to her and his mom's memory. "Nothing."

"Does this *nothing* have to do with Kate Sullivan?"

His gaze snapped up to meet hers. "How did you—"

"I'm not blind," she said with a knowing smile. "I saw that picture you shared of the two of you."

"Plus a dozen other women."

"Mmm. But you weren't looking at them the way you were at her."

It all sounded so simple when she said it. "I think there might be something between Kate and me, and I'd like to give us another shot. But I also want what's best for her, and . . . I'm not sure that's me. She deserves someone who'll be there for her through it all, not some long-distance relationship that may or may not work out in the long run. If I take this job, it would revive the business. I'd be stuck here in Detroit indefinitely."

"Doing what you love, but without the woman you love beside you."

He nodded. "Exactly. I know it's not the same as Dad, but he was always choosing things over Mom and me."

"He's trying to reconnect and make up for lost time."

"Even if that's true, he's a few years too late."

"God's timing is rarely ours," she said matter-of-factly. "Look at you and Kate."

"That's hardly the same." For one, she was a saint, which he was not. And second, there probably wasn't even a "him and Kate" after all the calls and texts he'd left unanswered.

"Maybe, but do you think things would have worked out had the two of you gotten married five years ago?"

What kind of question was that? He wouldn't have had to go through everything with his mom by himself. Wouldn't have been left to pick up the pieces when she was gone. He opened his mouth to say as much, but stopped. The past few years had been torture, but they'd shaped and built him as well. Kate, too, based on the strong woman he'd fallen for all over again.

Lincoln huffed. He hated it when Felicity was right.

After parking outside the shop, she dug around in her purse and pulled out a worn hardback notebook. "Here, I figured you could probably use this." Pressed leaves and loose paper stuck out from the binding, and the pages seemed a bit more yellowed than he remembered.

"Where'd you find this?" He'd gone through every drawer in that infuriating desk and come up empty. Even though he explicitly remembered putting his mom's journal in there before they'd renovated the studio workspace a few years back.

"After last year's string of burglaries, I decided to put it with the rest of the important documents for safekeeping."

She held it out to him and, hands shaking, he lifted the front cover. Rose and the scent of lilies perfumed the air, taking him right back to his mom's bedside and those open arms.

"Your mom kept more than notes in there. I never read it, but I remember her telling me about it. She said it was her love letter. I'm not exactly sure what she meant by that, but I have a feeling you will. And who knows? It might even give you some clarity about what to do next."

They sat in her parked car while he turned to the first page, her silent presence the comfort he needed to start reading.

He paused every so often to read his mom's notes about propagating succulents or which flowers were best for a wedding. Peonies, in her opinion. The brittle page crinkled as he flipped it over, and something fluttered to the floor. Lincoln bent in the cramped space for what he expected would be another pressed flower, but froze right before picking up a photo instead.

The same as the one he'd broken the picture frame on last night.

Only, this one had writing on the back.

His bandaged thumb ached as he held it there, torn between wanting another second of his mom's voice, yet unsure if he had it in him not to fall apart all over again.

"I remember that day." Felicity's voice had gone soft. "We had a lot of laughs, didn't we?"

"Yeah, we sure did." He swallowed past the sudden lump in his throat. Flipped the image over. Saw a few short lines written in blue ink.

He read it once. Twice.

THIS IS MY HAPPY PLACE. RIGHT HERE WITH FRIENDS AND FAMILY. BUT ESPECIALLY MY LINCOLN. I ASKED GOD FOR A MIRACLE, AND HE GAVE ME YOU. YOU'RE THE BLUE DAISY OF MY HEART. EVERY DAY WITHOUT FAIL.

He turned to the next page and found another photo, this one of him covered in dirt the day he'd tried to plant a fruit tree in the backyard. Cherry, if he remembered correctly. Followed by another note.

And another.

Soon, the entire dashboard was covered with pictures and letters. Some were short and funny, while others made his eyes sting. He flipped to the last entry, another photo with a single pressed daisy next to it.

He stared at the familiar faces, searching his brain for any memory of himself and his parents going camping. He could only have been about four or five in the photo, but his dad had him on his shoulders and they were smiling. He didn't remember taking the picture, but they all looked so happy. Especially Mom.

Felicity leaned over the center console and touched the corner. Smiled. "She always loved that one."

All the other pictures, Lincoln could understand, but, "Why this one?"

"You tell me." She smiled, the kind that made her look as if she were in on some grand cosmic joke. One he was starting to feel a part of as well.

"I suppose she always believed Dad would get his life together. That we'd be the same happy family as in this picture."

"Maybe you still can."

But that was insane, right? Over twenty years of waiting, and look what good it had done for her. She'd died holding on to a hope that'd never happened. Without her, what chance could he and his dad possibly have?

But then, there were the missed phone calls. His dad showing up out of the blue at his apartment.

"Felicity?" His throat had suddenly gone tight.

"Hmm?"

Never in a million years had he expected to ask the question that lingered on his tongue. But the door to his old life was bursting at the hinges. He could either choose to open it with caution or wait for it to explode later.

"Do you know where my dad is staying?"

It was after two when he rolled up to an old motel that had been refurbished into an apartment complex a few miles outside the city. He'd have called Kate to explain everything from the past two days had his phone not died a few exits back.

Lincoln checked his watch and frowned at the time. If he left now, he could still make the last ferry to Jonathon Island and meet Kate like they'd planned. He'd taken only enough time to repack his bag and switch cars before following Felicity's directions on his way out of town. A quick stop, enough to say hi, and that would be it. But the longer he sat there staring at the Vacancy sign out front, the more he realized this needed to be more than a drive-by reunion.

He could almost imagine his mom beside him, smiling like she had in that photograph. Felicity would say that was God's presence walking beside him. And he'd believe her. Could feel the burden lifting as he opened the driver's-side door, lowered his foot to the pavement, and walked up the azalea-lined path.

The place was small, but his mom would've loved the gardens. Someone obviously cared for them enough to clean out the winter debris and plant bouquets of tulips, grape hyacinth, and Easter lilies in their place. Just like at her old house. *A hope for new beginnings*, she'd always called them.

Lincoln checked the piece of paper Felicity had given him but didn't see an apartment number. He could knock on every door and ask for Thomas St. James, but who knew how long he'd been living here? And the man he remembered wasn't exactly the neighborly type.

The snip of pruning shears floated from around back. He followed the manicured path to the right, where a wall of lilac bushes wrapped around the building. Their fruity scent filled his lungs, along with the fresh boxwood trimmings littering the grass.

An older gentleman stood hunched over a wild-looking hedge, his back to Lincoln as he shaped it into submission.

Lincoln knew better than to interrupt a man on a mission, much more so when he held a pair of sharp shears. He waited at a distance as the man continued to shape the bush, softening a corner here, removing a dead branch there.

Five minutes in, the man removed his hat to wipe his forehead, revealing an all-too-familiar head of salt-and-pepper hair that had Lincoln's breath catching in his chest.

Lincoln took a step forward. Then another and paused. He should have called ahead of time. Given some warning instead of dropping in unannounced. But the man was already turning, looking up.

"Lincoln?" His wide gaze dropped to his dirt-stained clothing, added to by his hands rubbing against his sides.

Was he as nervous as Lincoln?

Neither said a word. What did one say after so many years? So much history?

Other than . . .

"Hi, Dad."

Lincoln had stood her up.

After a half hour of waiting, it was clear he wasn't going to make their date. The table for two felt overly large at the back of Martha's, even more so when Martha kept sending Kate sympathetic looks from behind the bar.

Just a couple more minutes.

Tourists filled the dark booths to her left, while locals took the remaining tables and spaces at the long bar. Seated next to the back corner booth, she could hear the din of the kitchen every time the door swung open as one of the waiters carried out burgers and bowls of cheddar ale soup. Or came by with a jug of water to refill her glass . . . again.

"Excuse me, but are you using this chair?"

Kate looked up from her menu at a woman with silver-streaked hair and a friendly smile. Behind her, the waitstaff was rearranging two tables to accommodate her rather large family. Ten of them, in fact. Six rather energetic kids, a man who must've been her husband, and maybe a grandparent or two in the mix.

Kate was about to tell her that she was expecting someone, but that was probably a lie. One glance at the vacant space behind the bar gave her the time to make up her mind.

"Take both. I was about to head out anyway." Kate set her neatly folded napkin beside her empty water glass and stood.

"Are you sure?" the woman asked. Her forehead pinched, even though she was already sliding one of the chairs over to their cramped seating arrangement.

"Positive. I hope you and your family have a lovely evening." With a forced smile, she hiked her purse over her shoulder and made for the door. The brass bell jingled a farewell as she left the noise, and her disappointment, behind her.

The rhythmic clip-clop of a horse's hooves could be heard in the distance, but she didn't mind the walk. A pleasant evening like tonight—music spilling out of open windows and the sun casting a gentle golden glow over the harbor—required nothing more than a light jacket.

The line about perfect first dates from *Miss Congeniality* came to mind. But it wasn't April 25, nor had this been a perfect first date. Or even a date, for that matter. That required at least two committed adults. And seeing as how the ferry had already come and gone forty-five minutes ago, it appeared she was on her own.

Like always.

She stopped at Parker Fish & Chips on her way home and grabbed an order to go, the warm aroma of fried batter following her all the way up the steps and into her empty apartment. Well…not entirely empty. Lincoln's flowers welcomed her home, along with the few books she'd bought from Oliver yesterday. The retail therapy had done its job, and she was already a third of the way into the Christopher R. Moore book he'd convinced her to purchase.

"It's not your typical spy novel," he'd assured her.

She might be a romance reader at heart, but she had to admit the thrilling plot line had held her captive well past midnight. Who needed an unreliable real-life boyfriend when they had international spy Jonah Steele to keep them company?

Grabbing her dinner and book, she eased onto the sofa and slipped right into last night's scene. Twenty pages later, and halfway through her fries, she was intercepting a German secret code alongside Jonah when a loud knock yanked her back to reality.

"Coming!" Kate threw her blanket over the take-out bag and smoothed a hand over her hair. Maybe Lincoln was back after all, which meant . . .

Oh no.

Could he have gone to the restaurant after she'd left and thought she'd forgotten? And now he was at her door, probably full of questions and doubts and—

"Dani? What are you doing here?"

Her sister stood in the doorway, blonde hair piled in a knot above her head and wobbling to the side as she handed over two pints of Ben and Jerry's Phish Food. "Liam invited the guys over for game night, so I decided we'd have our own girls' night like when we were kids." She invited herself into her old apartment and shed her knit sweater over the top of one of the dining room chairs.

"The *guys*?"

"Yeah. Oliver, Cody, Declan, Hunter, and Asher. You know. The usual suspects. I think Noah might even be joining them for a bit as well." Dani had paused in front of the sink with two empty glasses and now stared at Kate. "Hot date tonight?"

Kate barely glanced at her navy dress before throwing a sweater back over it. Dani didn't need to know about her botched plans for this evening. It would only serve to prove her earlier warnings correct. "If you mean one of Oliver's fictional characters, you know it. What about you? I thought you were supposed to be leading the travel journaling class this evening."

Dani filled the glasses with a sparkling lemonade she'd withdrawn from her bag and slid one across the counter toward Kate. "Mom volunteered to help out. She had so much fun with the art show in the park, I figured she'd get more out of it than me. Plus, she's a way better artist."

Dani moved on to the ice cream and plunged a large spoon into each pint.

"There's no way you expect me to eat all that in one sitting."

"Who said anything about finishing them?" She licked a swirl of chocolate and caramel from her spoon and grinned. "Whatever we don't eat, we can save for next time. What are you doing next Friday? I have it on good authority Liam plans to turn this into a weekly event."

Next Friday? Kate swallowed her mouthful of chocolate marshmallow fluff and chased it with a gulp of lemonade. Next Friday, the festival would be long over, meaning she'd probably be back in Petoskey and at her regular job. A job that would no doubt flourish once tomorrow's interview with the journalist was published. But that did little to calm the tense knot forming in her gut.

"Speaking of the guys, where's Lincoln?" Dani asked as she plopped onto the couch. The take-out bag crinkled under the blanket beside her, but she didn't seem to notice. "Liam thought about inviting him tonight, but when he called the Island House Inn, they said he was already out."

"Your guess is as good as mine." Kate dug out a large scoop of ice cream and shoved it into her mouth before she said anything else she might later regret. But she did regret the volume of ice cream the moment the roof of her mouth began to freeze. Oooohhh, why hadn't she thought that one through? "Don't worry, I'm fine."

"Yeah, you're clearly 'fine.'" Dani bent her fingers in air quotes around the last word.

Sticking her tongue to the roof of her mouth, Kate counted down from ten as her mouth began to thaw. Enough of those and maybe she'd forget the sting of walking out of Martha's by herself. How many brain freezes did it take to replicate selective amnesia?

"Do you want to talk about it?" Gone was the teasing humor in Dani's voice, replaced by something that almost made Kate's eyes water.

Almost.

"Yes? No . . . I don't know." Despite last time, she shoved down another mouthful of cream and sugar as if that alone could keep the tears at bay. It didn't. And soon she was falling apart next to her baby sister, unlike the mature older sibling she was supposed to be.

The first thing she realized: Ice cream was meant for teary conversations. People didn't slap the label *salty and sweet* on things for no reason. And second, Dani was a really good listener.

"So he just didn't show? What did he say when you called him about it?"

"I didn't. Call, I mean." At least, not again. She wanted to shrink into the cushions at Dani's slack-mouthed stare. "But don't worry. I still plan to do the interview tomorrow, with or without him. It's what this festival and the island need. Just because my romantic life is in the gutter doesn't mean I can't follow through with my promises." She could at least hold on to that fact, a redeeming quality that proved to the world that she wasn't a complete failure.

At the risk of witnessing the stars removed from her sister's eyes, she looked up from her ice cream to see Dani place hers on the coffee table and turn to fully face her.

"Kate, I couldn't care less about whether you do the interview or not."

"You . . . don't?" Since when did she not care about driving up the island's tourism industry?

"I mean, yes, it would be a nice plug for the island. But the real reason I set it up was because of you."

"Me?" Now Kate was really confused. "Why would you—"

"Oliver told me about your panic attack and the medical leave.

Don't blame him though," she rushed to add before Kate could sputter a response. "I practically wrestled it out of him when you didn't run back to your place after the wedding like everyone else. Then you volunteered to help with the festival, and . . . I don't know. I figured maybe it would be good for you somehow. I never meant for it to be stressful. And I'm sorry if it has been. I've always looked up to you, and not because you taught me how to ride a bike or stepped in at the drop of a hat to help with the festival. I love you because you're my big sister. I probably haven't said that enough, which is totally on me, but that doesn't make it any less true." A pause, then—"I know Mom feels the same way."

For years, Kate had longed to hear those words, but now that they were out in the open, it was like she didn't know what to do with them. Could it be that easy? One reassuring touch of Dani's hand on her arm told her it was.

"And I might be wrong about Lincoln, but I'm pretty sure he loves you too."

Moisture blurred Kate's vision a second time. As much as she wanted that to be true, she'd learned that it wasn't up to her to make someone love her.

Still, she could hope.

"You saw the kiss, then?" she asked.

Dani's eyes lit with surprise, then quickly settled into a knowing grin. "We're totally going to come back to the fact that he kissed you and you didn't tell me about it until now, but come to think of it, that actually explains quite a lot."

"Oh, shush." Kate grabbed a pillow and swatted it against Dani, who returned fire with the wadded blanket beside her. A shower of french fries exploded over them, sending both of them into a fit of laughter.

Dani recovered first, pinning Kate with a half-amused, half-serious expression. "Honestly, though. What kind of guy sticks around to work with his ex—in close proximity, I might add—then saves the island's apple blossoms?"

"It's his career on the line too. And the other stuff…" Helping her with the bike tour, bringing her favorite flowers … "He was being a good friend?"

"Good friend my right eye." Dani snorted.

As did Kate. "You sound just like Dad when you say that." The snort too.

For as much as Dani had referred to *old times*, Kate couldn't remember laughing or crying this much with any of her siblings in a very long time. As kids, the seven-year age gap had always put some distance between the two of them. Sure, she'd loved Dani growing up, but always more in a big-sister sort of way. Not as the friend she was starting to become.

"Look." Dani hugged the pillow against her chest, her face growing slightly more serious. "I know this doesn't solve everything, and you can totally turn it down and it won't hurt my feelings. But I was thinking … the hotel will need a good photographer once it's finished, for all those weddings and family reunions I expect. If you're at all interested, I think you'd be great for the position. I can even put in a good word with the owner."

"You mean Dad?" joked Kate. But Dani was bouncing on her seat too much to care.

"If you stayed, we could have all the girls' nights we want. Oh, and family dinners with Oliver and Mom as well."

The more plans Dani made, the more Kate wanted to be part of it all. Even with her parents. Maybe Lincoln was right. There was still time for her to have the kind of relationship she wanted with her mom. Maybe staying here could be that start.

Setting down her ice cream, she stood right as Dani was beginning to list off all the festivals she had planned for the summer and fall, and reached for her knit sweater and keys by the front door. "I say we've got a gala to prepare for."

"Is that a yes?" Dani asked, scrambling to join her as she placed their unfinished pints back in the freezer.

"It's an *I'll think about it*." But there was actually very little to think about. She'd have to talk with Gabby, see if she'd be interested in taking over the business on a more permanent basis. But from the promising email reports she'd been receiving, the young woman would be just fine.

Even if Kate didn't have a future with Lincoln, that didn't make this place any less home. Although, if she were being truly honest with herself, she was still holding out for a miracle on that front.

God, You never promised the whole love and marriage thing. And I'm okay with that, if it's Your plan for my life. Or at least, I will be. You brought me back to my family, which is something I'll forever thank You for. But for what it's worth, I'd still really like to fall in love.

And for it to stick this time.

Eighteen

THE LAST TIME LINCOLN REMEMBERED EATING blueberry pancakes with whipped cream, he'd been seven.

He had the distinct memory of his mom humming in front of the stove as she danced barefoot around the kitchen. Dad had joined her, slipping in from behind to her squeals of delight as he spun her in a circle.

Yeah, dancing. That's what these pancakes reminded him of.

Cleaning off the rest of his plate, Lincoln chased the syrupy goodness with a swig of dark roast. Golden sunlight seeped through the windows into the small apartment, where the remnants of last night's conversation sat in the sink. Talking with his dad had been good. Beyond good, in fact. So much so that he'd ended up sleeping on the pull-out couch and woken to the comforting scent of another wonderful childhood memory.

"How much time before you need to leave?" His dad sipped his own drink, the same number of spoonfuls of sugar as Lincoln's. Another thing he'd forgotten over the years.

"It's seven right now, so probably in another half hour?" It would be tight, but if he drove a little faster this time, he should be able to make the eleven-thirty ferry. He'd already missed their date. An unforgivable offense that had probably sealed his fate, but every time he'd been about to call, his mind went blank.

Hey, Kate. Sorry I missed the boat. I ran into my dad and we started talking . . .

Yeah, it sounded as lame out loud as it did in his head. Especially when it had been so much more than talking. It had been healing. The deep kind that stung at times but meant things were being washed away, giving them a fighting chance to start over and heal correctly.

Like with his dad, this was a conversation that needed to be in person. And hopefully before their meeting with the journalist from *American Wanderer* today at noon.

Before Lincoln could make himself useful, his dad stacked their empty plates and carried them to the sink.

"Mom would've loved Jonathon Island. The small town, the flowers, the people . . . all of it." He'd told his dad everything about the past month, from the bad review to the selection committee putting him on probation and then the festival. Even Kate. How running into her after all this time had been the second chance he hadn't known he needed.

"From what I've heard, it sounds like she's not the only one." Even with his dad facing the sink, Lincoln could hear the hint of teasing humor in the words. Tentative at first, like yesterday's conversation, but then it grew to a deep, familiar belly laugh. "I might be off base here, but it sounds to me that you've made more of a life for yourself there in a few weeks than the past few years in the city." He scrubbed at the pieces of baked-on batter clinging to the fry pan, then plunged it under the hot water before drying it with a floral tea towel. Lilies, to be precise.

"Yeah, I suppose I have." A sense of peace had been gradually settling over him since he'd left that meeting yesterday, growing stronger with every mile he put between him and the city. "I think you'd like it too."

He wasn't sure why he'd said that, exactly. Or why his voice had curled up at the end as if it were a question and invitation all rolled into one.

His dad seemed equally stumped, from the way he let the water keep running even though the dishes were all clean. He finally dropped his hand over the handle and turned, eyebrows pinched. The wrinkles ran deeper than Lincoln remembered, and not solely from age.

"You think so?"

"I really do."

An entire conversation passed between them in the quiet lull that came next.

Instinct told Lincoln to pull back, to stop this train altogether before it left the station, but they'd never get anywhere if he kept making the same decisions. Kept pushing people away. The way forward was not in the past. It was trusting that God was the one ultimately in control and that He'd brought Lincoln to this place and at this time for a reason.

"Would you . . . like to come with me?" The question felt as silly as his rehearsed excuses to Kate, but not when his dad swiped a rough finger beneath his eye.

Nodded ever so slowly.

"I'd like that. Very much."

"You would?"

Another chuckle, louder and more free this time. "And get more time to catch up with my only son? What father wouldn't say yes?"

Lincoln released a breath he hadn't realized he'd been holding, along with another chink of the wall he'd built around himself all those years ago.

It took a while, but we're getting there, Mom. I'm just sorry you're not here to see this. But maybe she was, in a sense. He wasn't entirely sure what heaven looked like, but he liked to think she was smiling down on them. Yes, she'd have loved the island, but not as much as this right here. And he knew for a fact she already loved Kate.

"We'd better get a move on if we're going to catch that ferry." His dad marched over to the coat closet and tugged out a tattered old suitcase. The same one he'd packed before walking out all those years ago, only this time, Lincoln was coming with.

It took only a matter of minutes for Lincoln to toss in his toothbrush and lace up his shoes. He spent the rest of the time wiping crumbs and syrup drips from the kitchen table until his dad rolled his rather stuffed bag to the front door.

"What?" He shrugged. "We're nearly driving to Canada. Who knows what kind of layers I'll need?" He reached for a coat and hat hanging from a nearby hook and led the way to Lincoln's car "You drive, I'll navigate. Sound good?" His dad was already circling to the passenger-side door and reaching for the seat belt above his shoulder.

Okay, so not everything had changed. His dad could still be a bit stubborn and opinionated, but so was Lincoln. A realization that had him shaking his head as he closed the back hatch and joined his dad in the car.

The early-morning start might have saved them some time had half the state not decided to take a weekend vacation away from the city.

"The map is yellow all the way from Gaylord to Trowbridge," said his dad, peering at his phone through a pair of readers. "It might have something to do with this restaurant week in Petoskey I saw advertised a few billboards back, but whatever it is, it's got us gridlocked."

They'd already been on the road for over three hours, and it was still another hour to the ferry stop. Lincoln checked the time on the dash and groaned. 10:40. Even without this traffic, they'd be lucky to make the 11:30 departure.

"I think I need to call Kate and let her know I'm not going to make it." He hated the thought of letting her down again, but what choice did he have? Crawling to another stop, he grabbed his phone from the cup holder and was about to punch in her number when his dad stopped him.

"Hold on a second. I might've found us a shortcut." Squinting, he pinched his fingers to zoom in. Frowned again. Nodded. "Yes, if we take that next exit," he said, pointing at a sign a few cars ahead, "we can take the old highway for a bit and catch back up to our route near Indian River."

Lincoln studied the wall of vehicles in front of them and sighed. They'd already been stuck in this for well over twenty minutes, and there was no telling how much longer they'd be delayed. At least the other way kept them moving toward their destination.

"Okay, let's do it." If Lincoln was going to save things with Kate, he could use all the help he could get.

By the end of the next song on the radio, they'd peeled off the highway and were taking another left onto the frontage road. They were cruising at fifty, weaving through farmland and forest for forty minutes until eventually merging back onto the highway at Indian River and Burt Lake. Another twenty minutes and they were pulling into the marina parking lot.

"Go ahead and check us in. I'll take care of the bags."

Lincoln didn't need to be told twice. Leaving his dad with the car, he took off down the path toward the ticket counter.

"I need to change a ticket and purchase a second for the eleven-thirty ferry to Jonathon Island." Lincoln was going to be on that boat if it killed him. He'd already kept her waiting long enough. The next sixteen minutes crossing Lake Huron couldn't go fast enough.

"The eleven thirty, you said?" The teenager behind the counter smacked away on a piece of gum, moving with the swiftness of tree sap as she typed something into the computer.

He didn't like the way she was looking through the little porthole window behind her. Nor the distant peal of a horn.

"Looks like you just missed it." At least she had the decency to offer an apologetic frown. "Would you like me to book you for the noon trip?"

Lincoln blinked. The urgency of the last four hours crashed to a halt a stone's throw away from where he needed to be. The interview started at twelve. He couldn't be there and crossing the lake at the same time.

Footsteps echoed up the dock, barely registering as Lincoln ran through his options. A man in a navy baseball cap ducked inside the ticket booth, a few tufts of sandy-blond hair curling at the back as he grabbed a fresh stack of yellow pamphlets.

Wait . . .

"Noah?"

The man turned and smiled. "Hey, man. How's it going?" He reached through the window for a hearty handshake as Miss Bubblegum practically swooned at him. "We missed you at game night yesterday. Oliver and Liam creamed us three to one. We could've used your help."

The man's friendliness caught him off guard, distracting him momentarily from his mission. "What were you playing? Texas Hold'em? Five Card Draw?"

Noah shook his head. "Naw. Risk."

"The board game?"

"Hey, it's a classic for a reason," he said with a boyish shrug. "Just because it was created in the fifties doesn't mean it can't still make a grown man cry."

Much like the pace of this current conversation.

Noah glanced at the ticket screen, then back up, the innocent smile slipping. "Cutting it close, I see. Isn't that interview supposed to be starting—"

"About now, yeah. Which is why I really need to be on that ferry," he said as his dad finally joined him with the luggage. "Both of us."

For a moment, all Lincoln's concerns about Noah seeing Kate as more than a friend resurfaced. Had his first impression of the guy been right? One press of a button, and he could have them booked for either the noon crossing or one that would ensure he'd miss the interview and Kate entirely.

Lincoln lifted up a silent prayer that the journalist would still be there when he eventually arrived.

Noah looked between the two of them for a breath—was that a moment of hesitation?—before he tapped something into the computer. Printed off a sheet of paper which Lincoln couldn't read through the window. "Two tickets for the twelve o'clock ferry to Jonathon Island." He handed over the sheet and smiled. "And I'll make sure to tell the captain we won't be taking the scenic route this time."

Kate watched from the dock as crew members moved a ramp into position for the newly arrived ferry. Despite the herbal tea she'd downed that morning, she couldn't help bouncing on her toes as the line of people marched along the boat ramp.

Where was Lincoln? The journalist from *American Wanderer* would be here any minute, and Lincoln was still nowhere in sight.

"Relax, sis. You've got this." Dani didn't need to be here, but her presence meant more to Kate than the blueberry muffin Dani had bought for her on the walk over here. "You know this town better than anyone."

Kate quit fidgeting with the ruffled trim of her dress and sent her sister a grateful smile. "Except for you. You should really be doing this interview, not me. After all, it's your festival."

"That *you* single-handedly managed while I was slacking off in Italy."

"I'd hardly call going on your honeymoon *slacking*. Badly timed, maybe. But you only get married once." The phrase might not be true for Kate or her parents, but Dani and Liam had what it took to last a lifetime. She knew it.

"Ooh, is that her?" Dani asked, moving Kate's attention to a smartly dressed woman in her forties. The sleek handbag on her arm could certainly contain a notepad and camera, if not the names of New York's top designers.

Kate smoothed her hands down the front of her dress and was taking a few steps forward when an older gentleman drew up beside the woman. From the way he kissed her cheek, they were definitely together.

"Well, that could've been awkward."

"Kate Sullivan?"

She whirred around to see a woman in green pants and a bright-pink shirt standing at the bottom of the ramp. She had to be close to Kate's age, thirties, yet with a Gen-Z confidence Kate could only dream of.

"*You're* Evelyn Avery?" She tried not to sound so surprised. She'd expected . . . Well, it didn't really matter what she'd been looking for, other than she was really blowing it at first impressions so far.

"You can call me Lyn." She tilted her head and smiled, as if catching people off guard was a daily hazard of the job.

"And I'm Dani Sullivan. We're so glad you could make it."

The journalist shook both their hands, far too formal a greeting for her overall friendly vibe. Her very presence seemed to say *Relax, we're all friends here.*

"So, this is Jonathon Island." Her face took on a faraway look as she scanned the sailboats floating in the harbor. "I've heard a lot about this place from my boss. Says it's absolutely magical."

"We like to think it still is," Dani chimed in.

Kate shot her sister a look to *be cool*, at which Dani just shrugged.

Not that Lyn seemed to mind, from her amused chuckle. "That's precisely what I'm hoping readers will realize. Shall we begin?"

Kate glanced at her notes and the detailed map of how it was supposed to go. She and Lincoln had planned everything. First, they'd hire a carriage. Then Kate would talk about the island's history, like during the bike tour, while he pointed out the many unique flowers found only on the island. Then they'd go by the Grand and talk about the restoration. She'd then highlight tonight's concert along with tomorrow's parade and main gala, then finish the interview at the park, where the apple blossoms could speak for themselves.

Only problem—Lincoln wasn't here. She hadn't had time to talk with the Quinns about a carriage. And Lyn's abundant energy indicated she was more a woman of action who'd prefer walking to a leisurely ride.

"There's a beautiful view of the blossoms from Blueberry Hill, but maybe you'd like to see Main Street first?"

Gold hoop earrings swayed as Lyn shook her head. "This is your interview. I'm only here to help you tell the story you want."

Right. A story.

Lowering her notes, Kate surveyed the busy dock and historic buildings lining the harbor. She saw families strolling along the boardwalk while fishermen angled their lines into the clear lake waters that practically glittered under the noon sun. If a picture said a thousand words, it wouldn't be enough to capture what she felt for this island.

Lyn tapped her phone to start recording and gave them a thumbs-up. "So, Kate. Tell me a little about the festival. I understand this is its first year running in some time, but its history goes back quite a bit further, isn't that right?"

Kate peeled her attention from the horizon, wrestling to put away thoughts of Lincoln and his concerning absence.

"Uh, yes. The apple trees on the island date back to the first settlements in the eighteen hundreds. People planted all sorts of things, from fruit trees to the lilacs and other flowers you'll see if you head down any street in town. While the earliest records of an apple harvest celebration date back to the twenties, the first official spring festival started in '71 to bridge the gap created by the Fudge Wars."

"Fudge wars? Now that sounds exciting."

Dani nudged Kate with her elbow and smiled. *Keep going, you're doing great.*

"What small town wouldn't be complete without some quirky history, right?"

"This is exactly the sort of thing readers love."

Putting the lake behind them, Kate started toward Main Street as Lyn snapped a few pictures of the harbor and the shops. Baskets of pink and purple petunias hung from metal lamp posts, perfuming the air along with hints of ice cream and waffle cones from down the block.

"It was more of a professional dispute between friends, but enough to cause a rift in the town and threaten tourism. So naturally, the town council decided to throw a festival, forcing everyone to work together." Something which sounded oddly familiar now that she said it out loud.

"Fascinating. I had no idea the festival had such peacekeeping roots."

"Still does," whispered Dani to Kate.

Eyes narrowing, she turned to warn her sister off any more teasing, but her attention snagged on a man with broad shoulders and too-long hair, hurrying up the street.

Lincoln?

An unexpected weight lifted from her shoulders even as she wrapped her arms tightly around her middle.

His long legs ate up the distance, slowing only enough for him to grab the suitcase of another man, who was struggling to keep up. Kate couldn't place the older gentleman at this distance, but something about his appearance seemed familiar. The questions from the past couple of days ping-ponged inside her head as a horse-drawn carriage rolled past, but were silenced the moment Lincoln's eyes locked on hers from the middle of the street.

"Kate, I'm so sorry I'm late." He set down the bags and then pulled her in for an unexpected, yet not wholly unwanted, hug. "I promise I'll explain everything later," he whispered into her ear, the warmth of his breath making her stomach do a little flip before he stepped back with a smile toward Dani and Lyn. "Sorry for the intrusion. My dad and I got held up on the way here, but I hope we didn't miss too much."

His dad? She'd never met the man, but she could see the family resemblance in build. Yet it was his eyes that were the same, the exact shade of piercing gray-blue that Lincoln was looking at her with for silent direction.

Three seconds. That's all the time it took for her to reorient the conversation.

"Lincoln, this is Lyn Avery, the journalist who's interviewing us. And this is Lincoln, my . . ." Her *what*, exactly? Ex-fiancé turned reluctant coworker and potential new boyfriend? That was, if he hadn't changed his mind during his absence. "Partner." A cursory glance revealed his nod of relief, which had her arms relaxing at her sides. "Most of this festival wouldn't have been possible without his help."

"It was a team effort," he jumped in to add. "But one only made possible by Kate's patience and determination to see the best in everything." In *everyone*, his unwavering gaze seemed to say.

She did not want to collapse into a puddle on Main Street a second time. But if he kept looking at her like that, she very well might. "Right, where were we?"

Dani did very little to hide her snort, but thankfully, Lyn was a professional.

"I believe you were about to tell me what kinds of activities have been part of this year's schedule."

Right. The festival.

Kate launched into the rehearsed list she'd prepared, starting with the vintage bicycle rally and the different tour options to experience the island and its history. She then moved on to the art show in the park and Fort Jonathon with all of its activities—outdoor movies on the hill, live reenactments.

"Of course, there's been the flower arrangements with our own celebrity florist Lincoln St. James." She smiled at a blushing Lincoln. "Which visitors can participate in before signing up for a chance to fire one of the cannons at the fort on the other side of the park."

"Sounds like quite the event. Now I wish I'd had time to come out earlier and experience it all for myself."

"There's still the parade tomorrow morning and then the gala Sunday evening." And now that Lincoln was back, it would really be something to remember. *Stop it. You can think about Lincoln later, Kate.* Only, it was nearly impossible with him towering beside her as they crossed Blueberry Boulevard into the park. "I know you probably have other work to get back to, but it really isn't something to be missed."

"Which is exactly what I told my editor when I booked a room at the Island House Inn." Lyn tapped her phone to end the recording and slipped it back into her compact travel bag. "Well, I think this just about covers everything I need. I can't wait to share this special place with our readers."

"It's been our pleasure," Dani replied, cupping her hands together excitedly. "If there's anything else you need, please reach out. Or find one of us at the parade tomorrow."

"I just might take you up on that." A broad smile stretched across her face. "Oh, and I realize the main draw of the piece is the island, but I'd love to give both your businesses the shout-out they deserve. I already have details about Lily & Stone," she said to Lincoln, "and you're in Petoskey, right, Kate?"

Dani's encouraging presence could do nothing to stem the flutter in Kate's stomach, given the way Lincoln was watching her with unrelenting focus. What would he think of her news? Would that create more or less obstacles between them?

"Actually, I'm in a bit of a transition period at the moment. Gabby will be taking over that business while I set up something new here." She'd prepared herself for his look of surprise, not the gentle tilt of his mouth and nod of encouragement.

"The island will be lucky to have you." Lincoln didn't even pause to scratch his forehead, which told her everything she needed to know.

Kate felt the warmth blossom up her cheeks at his tempered yet genuine compliment. "As I am to have them."

Lyn's gaze flicked between the two of them. "You both seem equally driven by your work. And congratulations on being selected for Bloomfest," she said to Lincoln, who stiffened slightly at the mention of it. Not enough to be obvious except to Kate. "I saw they announced the lineup on their website earlier this morning. You must be proud."

"More than words can say." Lincoln's dad spoke up for the first time, yet it wasn't him Kate couldn't take her eyes off.

The quick blink and tilt of Lincoln's head only made her want to know more about what had happened in the two days he'd been gone. From what he'd recently told her, his dad being here was nothing short of a miracle. For Lincoln's sake, she really hoped it worked out for them. He deserved a family who loved him, another chance to have the kind of dad he'd wanted but hadn't had for all these years.

It was a good thing, them reconnecting. Only, it left her wondering more than ever where she fit into this new life of his.

Nineteen

WAS IT STRANGE TO MISS SOMEONE WHEN they were only a few yards away?

The journalist had left a couple of minutes ago to take some pictures of the trees, many of which glittered in the shade, with their garlands of string lights someone must've left on overnight. Kate, perhaps?

"Dad, why don't you head on over to the inn without me? I'll catch up with you in a bit."

"Take your time, son. I'm not going anywhere." His knowing look was anything but subtle. Same with the smirk he sent as he hoisted the duffel bag over one shoulder.

"Leave my bag. I can carry it."

His dad stubbornly shook his head. "Last thing you need is another burden weighing you down." He pretended to collapse under its weight, earning a dry chuckle in return. "In all seriousness though, whatever it is, I'm sure you two can work it out. But you've got to talk to her first."

"What do you think I'm trying to do?" Ever since he'd hurried off the boat and spotted her in that pink dress, he'd wanted to run to her. Tell her everything that had happened in the past two days. How he was sorry for being late and not returning her calls but had picked up the phone more times than he could count. How he'd been offered a spot in the Bloomfest showcase but couldn't imagine being so far away from her. And how he'd been giving it a lot of thought during the four-hour drive back, wondering what it would be like to move away from the city and call a small island town home.

But between his dad, Dani, and the journalist, it'd had to wait.

"Looks like now's your chance." A smile, followed by a nod toward the park bench. Grabbing both bags, his dad turned and said something about it being an island, and how lost could he get?

But there were far more than trails for a man to get lost on here.

Lincoln shoved his hands into his pockets, then thought better of it, even if they did feel like awkward tree limbs hanging limp by his sides.

"Hi." After all that, the single-syllable greeting was the best he could come up with?

"Hi back."

Say something. Compliment her hair or tell her what a great job she did with the interview.

"So . . . you're moving to the island, huh?" *Yeah, real smooth.*

"I'm really considering it. It feels like home. More so than Petoskey ever has." She tucked a piece of hair behind her ear, then moved her hands back to the leather strap of her purse. "That's great about the showcase, by the way. Your work deserves to be seen by people who will really appreciate it."

"You believe that?"

"Of course I do. It's *enchanting*, remember?" A slight smile played across her rosy lips. She was trying to encourage him, but the only person he wanted to impress was standing right in front of him.

"Mind if we sit?" He motioned to the bench and then lowered beside her. Her subtle perfume was nearly enough to make him forget his train of thought.

Enough. Focus.

"I'm sorry for not calling—"

"I hoped you'd be here—"

Her airy laughter eased the tension as they spoke in unison.

"Please, you first." Lincoln's explanation could wait. He'd already done enough talking in the past and made a mess of things. The least he could do now was listen.

The bench shook slightly with her bouncing knee, then went suddenly still as she clasped her hands over it. "Sorry, I'm not very good at this."

At distracting him senseless? "You seem to be doing just fine from where I'm sitting." Now it was his turn to smile. Whatever it was, he was ready to hear it. And hopefully, if she was willing, they could work through it together.

Chewing on her bottom lip, she reached into her purse and withdrew a creased envelope, his name in blue ink across the back.

"You wrote me a letter?"

"Several, actually." Her face flushed to match the apple blossoms above her.

It took nearly all his restraint not to reach out and pull her to him and kiss her senseless. Tell her things he'd never dreamed of saying again until recently. But then he looked again at the envelope and frowned. "You knew I was going to come back, right? You didn't have to write it down." Did she still think so little of him?

He tried to hand it back to her, only for her to hold up her hands.

Stubborn, beautiful woman.

"Humor me?" She was impossible to say no to in that pink dress of hers, curls dancing around her face with the lake breeze.

Shaking his head, he did as told. The paper felt stiff, but so did his fingers as he fumbled with the seal. What was the thing secured with? Superglue? And there was definitely something small and round at the bottom. He managed to tear only a small corner of the flap when it finally popped open. Releasing a breath, he slid out the page until he could read the date written in the same blue ink in the upper right-hand corner.

Lincoln frowned. "This is from five years ago." He looked at Kate, who was intently studying the blades of spring grass at her feet. Ice snaked through his chest, making his throat grow tight. He dipped the envelope over and a sparkly engagement ring tumbled into his palm.

"I thought—" Her voice cracked, reedy and thin, and ricocheted through him like cannon fire. "I really thought I could move on like you did after you left, but I was a mess back then."

"Kate." He wanted to say something, but she shook her head, indicating she wasn't finished. His heart was already beginning to crack. What else could she have to say? If this was her way of letting him down gently, he didn't want to hear it.

Chin ducked, she took a steadying breath for them both and continued. "A friend suggested I write you a letter. Not to send, of course, but for me to process everything I wanted to say to you that night but couldn't." Her eyes tentatively met his. "At first, it felt weird, pouring my heart into a letter I'd never send. But with each one, I felt . . . lighter. More . . . me. If that makes sense."

He gulped. Why would she be giving him this now if not to end things between them on her own terms? "I never should've left the island for that meeting."

Her hand on his made him grow still, and he could barely think for the soft press of her skin against his. He focused on the isolated warmth, the way she didn't pull back.

"We both had a lot to learn and growing up to do, and we rushed into things too quickly back then. I don't want to make the same mistake this time."

"This time?" A spring thaw inched up his arm and to his chest as she gave him the tiniest of smiles.

"Just read the letter."

But no matter how sweetly she looked up at him, he couldn't bring himself to do so. The Kate from five years ago had been hurt, humiliated, and abandoned. By *him*, no less. She was justified in whatever she'd written in this letter, but he didn't know if he could stomach reading it.

"Don't worry. I burned the other letters." Her hand dropped away from his with a nervous laugh.

The upward pinch of her eyebrows prompted him to unfold the page. He took his time ungluing his gaze from hers, clinging to that promise of hope as he began to read.

> Dear Lincoln,
>
> I know I should be angry at you for walking away like you did. Everyone else has told me as much. And while I appreciate their support, it does nothing to fill the hole inside of my heart.

Oh, Kate.

The page dimpled under his thumb as he willed the racing of his heart to slow so he could keep reading.

I miss your friendship. The way you made me laugh at your stupid jokes and how you always smelled like the flowers in your mom's shop. You're an angel for all you do for her, and I felt so special knowing I'd one day get to marry you. I miss that too. All the plans we had, the dreams. And yes, even the arguments over which dishware to add to the registry. I never should have let you talk me into the ugly stoneware set you picked out, even though they were as indestructible as the box advertised. (I'd know, because I tried.)

Maybe that's where we went wrong. Not over silly dishes and towels, but in not trusting each other enough to share our deepest thoughts and fears. I was so caught up in our happiness that I was too afraid to say or do anything that might risk losing it. But it happened anyway, and I can't help but wonder if things might've been different if we hadn't been so scared.

So this is me standing up to fear and saying exactly what I feel.

<u>I still love you.</u>

Lincoln sucked in a breath at the underlined words. He looked up, but Kate was gone. He spun on the bench to scan the park, but no sign of her pink dress. He wanted to race after her and tell her they'd make it work this time, but where would he check first?

Stifling a groan, he forced his attention back to her letter.

> *It's crazy and stupid, and I'm sure my family would think I'm insane if I ever said it out loud. But despite everything, I can't turn off these feelings.*

"You and me both."

> *I'm sure if we were ever to see each other again, I'd trip over my own tongue, which makes writing it all down that much easier, knowing no one will ever read this, ~~least of all you.~~ except for you.*

The last three words were written in a different color ink—red—just like the underlined confession a few sentences earlier, as if written in later.

Lincoln drew in a steadying breath.

Then another.

He stood abruptly, heart hammering against his chest with the possibility—no, the realization—that they still had a chance. But oh, why did Kate have to give him this letter and then leave? If he'd known she'd walk off while he was reading, he'd have shoved it in his pocket for later. But then he wouldn't have known what was inside. Or how she'd felt.

Still felt, if he understood the letter correctly.

A fact which fueled his long strides as he ate up the distance between the park and her apartment. But he only got as far as the road before grinding to a halt. As much as he needed to talk with

Kate, he also had a gala to prepare for. He'd always been an idiot when it came to words, but flowers he knew. Lucky for him, they had a language all their own, and if tended to properly, could say all sorts of things like *I'm sorry* or *I missed you* or . . .

I still love you too.

Giving back the ring was what one was supposed to do after calling off a wedding. Telling her ex-fiancé that she still loved him? Probably not.

Even though Kate did.

She'd proceeded to wait an embarrassingly long amount of time tying bows in the conference room, hoping he'd find her as soon as he'd finished reading the letter to tell her the same.

But he hadn't.

Not that she'd asked him to. But she *had* told him she loved him, which had to count for something. Or at least, she thought the letter said as much . . .

Now she was wondering if she'd been too subtle or somehow messed up what had seemed like a perfectly flawless plan this morning when she'd stuffed the old envelope into her purse before the interview. Kate tossed the empty ribbon spool toward the trash, only for it to ricochet off the box of candles instead.

"Whoa. Are you decorating the Grand or the Great Hall at Hogwarts?" Oliver grabbed a white taper candle from the nearest box and smirked. Today's graphic top said *Read books, not shirts.* The irony of it almost made her laugh.

Almost.

She shrugged. "Mom wanted candles."

"So you raided the Beast's castle for Lumière and his friends."

Oh, where was that empty spool when she needed it?

He peeked into the nearest box and grinned. "I don't think I've ever seen this much white. Not even at Dani's wedding. I usually don't question Mom's artistic choices, but she might've gone a little overboard this time."

"Well, the gala is all about the flowers. This way, they'll stand out." She hadn't gotten to do the whole big white wedding thing with her mom before. Maybe this was her mom's way of making up for that. Not that working with her lately had been easy, but all things had to start somewhere.

"These are going between the floral centerpieces, yeah?"

Kate nodded. Not that she knew what those centerpieces, or any of the other arrangements, would look like, but yes.

After a third try, the white ribbon in her hands looked more like an injured butterfly than an elegant bow. No wonder she was running through ribbon like film at an engagement shoot. "Lincoln's working on them right now so they'll be ready for tomorrow." At least, that's what she'd been telling herself as she sat there tying satin bows for the past hour.

Without a word, Oliver got to work separating out groups of seven for each table. Sure, he might've arranged them like a fleet of stormtroopers marching in pods from the Death Star, but at least he didn't hum "The Imperial March" while he was at it.

"As much as I appreciate the help, don't feel like you have to stay."

As far as nonverbal responses went, the subtle eyebrow tilt gave away very little, until he said, "I'm the reason Lincoln left."

Kate blinked at him, trying to figure out how he'd gotten from centerpieces to that. "Thank you for always standing up for me, but you don't have to do that."

"Do what?"

"Make up something just for me to feel better."

"I'm not making it up." His scowl deepened but quickly melted with a sigh. "The night of your rehearsal dinner, I ran into Lincoln as he was parking his car. I hadn't planned on saying anything about him being late to his own rehearsal dinner, but then I saw the bruise and the way he was staggering as if he'd been drinking, and I lost it."

"Oliver, what did you say?"

"A lot of things I wish I could take back. Namely that he wasn't good enough for you, which I realize now was entirely out of line."

Kate fumbled halfway through tying the second-to-last bow and set it aside, trying to piece together what he was saying. Was that why Lincoln hadn't come looking for her this time after reading her letter? But no, Oliver was talking about years ago. Lincoln's current distance had nothing to do with her brother.

"Are you mad?" Her brother looked exactly like he had after he'd accidentally broken her model of the solar system in the third grade. He'd even offered to stay home and help her rebuild it rather than go to the adventure park with his friends. His concern had touched her as much back then as it did now.

"About what? That my brother cares so much about my happiness that he'd stand up for me?" It didn't matter who he'd spoken to or what he had or hadn't said. "I feel like the luckiest sister in the world." To have two people in as many days tell her how much they valued and cared for her. And not because of what she did but because of who she was. Much like her heavenly Father had always loved her. She'd always known that truth, but little things like this made it feel all the more real.

Oliver wasn't a natural hugger, which was a shame—not that that stopped her from dropping her ribbon and wrapping her arms tightly around him. His hug made her feel safe and cherished and loved unconditionally. Almost as much as when Lincoln pulled her close. It struck her how different the two men were, one quiet and bookish and the other protective and a bit rough around the edges. But together they were two of her favorite humans.

Finally releasing him, she stepped back and beamed up at his sappy grin.

"I've missed having you around, Katydid. It hasn't been the same here without you."

Katydid. Just hearing the childhood nickname made her heart feel full. "I'm glad you feel that way, because you might be seeing a lot more of me in the future."

"Oh?" He held down the cardboard flaps with his free hand for her to tape them in place. "You thinking about visiting again already?"

"Something like that."

His raised eyebrow would've been comical even without her barely contained excitement. Maybe she'd expected too much from Lincoln earlier, but she knew her brother would be happy for her. "Dani offered me a job."

Okay. So maybe the other eyebrow rose to match its twin. But that didn't mean he wasn't celebrating on the inside, right? "You already have a job. Isn't that what this whole festival thing was about? The publicity for your business?"

"A little excitement would be appreciated. I am moving across the state to be closer to family, after all. That means you too, Ollie." She knocked her box against his, and like magic, his face relaxed.

"I'm sorry, you're right. Let me try this again." He stilled as if he were an actor preparing for a new scene before he broke into a boyish grin. "You're staying on Jonathon Island? That's fantastic!"

Her laughter tumbled out at his overly animated—yet genuine—response. "I'm glad you think so. But maybe a little less 'clown at a kid's party' when I tell Mom, okay?" She was nervous enough as it was for that conversation. There was no reason to think her mom wouldn't also be happy about the decision, but it would take time to shake off all of Kate's old doubts when it came to her mom.

In a very un-Oliver fashion, he raised his hand and placed it over his chest. "Scout's honor."

"Since when were you ever a Boy Scout?" They may not have

been joined at the hip as kids, but she would have remembered something like that.

"Never. But I've read enough books."

"Wilderness survival books?" Just the thought of him trekking through the forest with a tent and sleeping bag was enough to brighten her day. A thought he obviously did not share, based on his scoff.

"Better. Only the greatest trilogy ever written."

Kate shook her head. "If you say *Lord of the Rings*, I'll—"

"Do what?" Sliding the final box on top of his, he swung toward the open door with steps large enough to easily outpace her next ribbon toss. "Last one to the hotel is a katydid, Katydid."

There were worse fates a sister could endure.

A few paces behind him, she stepped into the hallway and paused. She'd left her camera in Dani's office. "You head on over, I'll just be a second."

She didn't wait for his distant reply before setting down her box and changing course. A few moments and she was there. She didn't remember closing the door, but when she stepped inside, it was the white envelope propped against her camera that stole her attention.

Her first thought was Lincoln, but he'd have had to walk right past the conference room on his way to the office. Surely she'd have seen him. So why was she looking at a glossy photo of the two of them and not the man himself?

Kate turned the picture over—the one from their first workshop together—to a few short lines scribbled on the back.

EVERY BLOOM IS A GIFT OF THE HEART, AND YOURS IS THE MOST BEAUTIFUL I'VE EVER KNOWN. I KNOW IT'S NOT A FIELD FULL OF SUNFLOWERS, BUT I'D BE THE LUCKIEST MAN IF YOU'D LET ME TAKE YOU TO THE GALA TOMORROW NIGHT.

Only Lincoln would compare a person to a flower and make her eyes sting in doing so.

She swiped a finger along her lower lashes and breathed in rose petals and lilac blossoms . . . and books.

Oliver.

She didn't know how, but Lincoln must've talked him into delivering this. Was that what he'd been trying to say with all that talk about apologies and being wrong?

Clutching the photograph to her chest, she turned to leave and tripped over the box of candles outside the conference room. At least the crunch hadn't been her camera. A few squashed bows weren't the end of the world. Even if her big toe throbbed along with her thudding heartbeat. It was so loud, she thought she could even hear it echoing within the narrow hallway.

The pounding thuds softened to a rhythmic swish of footsteps over carpet.

"Don't worry, Ollie. The only thing I hurt is my pride. And maybe a couple candles, but nothing I can't fix before Mom finds out." That was the last thing on her mind. And if she was correct, her brother would understand when she handed him her box and went in search of a certain florist with a penchant for flowery language.

"I think I can spare a few candles, just so long as my daughter remains in one piece."

Breath hitching, Kate pushed the hair from her face to see a pair of painted leather ankle boots, the colorful brushstrokes not unlike the watercolors hanging in Oliver's bookshop.

She scrambled the rest of the way to her feet as her mom's helping hand did more to steady her wobbly legs. The hand dropped away, but the warmth lingered long after.

"Would you like some help?" Her mom's voice was soft—tentative, even.

Kate opened her mouth to turn down the offer, but something stopped her. A quiet voice that seemed to say *It's time to let go.*

Snippets of last night's conversation with Dani drifted in unbidden but tinged with hope.

Sure, she made a lot of mistakes. But she hasn't had it easy. I wasn't able to realize it until last year, but the distance between us was just as much my doing as it was hers. Dani had shoved a large spoonful of ice cream into her mouth and thoughtfully swallowed as Kate had sat there processing.

Dani wasn't wrong. Kate could have easily picked up the phone or visited. But imagined conversations of how her mom would pick apart her less-than-perfect life had always kept that door firmly closed. *She's our mom. Isn't she supposed to be the one to reach out first? The one to love us unconditionally?*

I don't think she ever stopped.

She had a funny way of showing it, then.

I'm not saying she's completely innocent, but what would it look like for you to invite her in? After all, God loves us even when we fail to measure up to His standards. Which, to be honest, is all of the time. But oftentimes, He waits for us to come to Him when we're finally ready. And doesn't that make His love feel all the more wonderful?

Kate had tried to swipe away her tear before Dani saw it, but her sister had pulled her in for a couch side-hug instead.

Neither seemed to know how to break the silence until her mom finally said, "I talked to Dani this morning."

Ah. Kate's shoulders deflated a degree, but at least they were talking. "So she told you Lincoln's back, then?"

Her mom nodded. "Among other things." Instead of the predictable lecture Kate expected, her mom's barely trembling lips pressed together, followed by a very uncharacteristic crack in her voice. "I never meant to make you feel like you weren't good enough, Kate. It breaks my heart even more that I didn't tell you enough how much I love you. How proud I am of you."

Kate's mouth dropped open. She should've been mad at Dani for telling Mom about last night's conversation, yet all she could focus on was the moisture shimmering in her mom's eyes and the reverberation of her last words in her chest.

"You—you are?"

Her mom sucked in a small breath before managing a tearful smile. Another nod. "More than you can imagine." She cleared her throat. "Dani also told me you're staying on the island?" The last few words tipped up as if in question. "Maybe once you're settled, we can grab breakfast together and catch up? I want to hear all about the festival, your photography, and especially Lincoln. From what Dani tells me, he really has changed for the better."

A lump lodged in Kate's throat at both her mom's request and the blossoming hope about the future. The tension in her chest relaxed as a wave of peace draped over her.

"I'd love to."

Twenty

PARADES HAD NEVER BEEN LINCOLN'S THING. All those people and the noise. Not to mention the pellets of candy one had to dodge while navigating backpacks, strollers, and the occasional noisemaker aimed right at his ear as he swam upstream.

But Kate liked parades.

She'd call them *festive* or *enchanting* and insist on overseeing every float, carriage, and crown. Never mind that it should be *her* wearing said crown. Not some teenage girl with a cotton-candy dress and mask of professional-level makeup. Kate's beauty ran so much deeper than her chestnut eyes and milky complexion. She was kind and patient. Easy to love when she let her guard down. Even easier to be around, whether they were talking flowers, circumnavigating the island, or simply working together in companionable silence. She saw something in him he hadn't recognized in years, and after yesterday, he was fairly certain she had a heart of gold.

"Excuse me. Pardon me." He doubted the family of four heard him over the volume of the marching band, trombones sliding up the scales with aplomb. A cymbal crashed a half measure too early, overpowering the grand crescendo and the poorly timed cannon fire from across the bay.

Not that the cheering crowds seemed to mind.

Up ahead, a brush of light-brown hair wavered beneath a maritime-themed sign, which had him picking up his pace—or as much as a hundred people crammed into one town block would allow. The snare drums marched by at that moment, echoing in his chest as trumpets blared out the melody to "Sweet Caroline."

"There you are. I was beginning to think you weren't coming."

"And miss this?" Lincoln gave Oliver a wry smile. He eyed the man's T-shirt, which read *I woke up like this* with a large bug on the front. "Nice shirt, by the way."

"Thanks." His normally placid expression brightened. "I'd make a Kafka joke, but honestly, I'd just make a big stink bug out of it."

Wow. Just . . . wow.

His girlfriend—Eliza?—rolled her eyes, but the shake of her head and wide spread of her mouth said she loved the guy enough to overlook his choice in fashion and humor.

"Have you seen Kate?"

A shake of the head. "Not since she disappeared with Mom and Dani this morning." He practically had to shout over the two bass drums that marched past. "I could try calling her if you'd like?"

"No, that's okay."

He'd reread her text at least a dozen times, finally convincing himself that she had indeed agreed to be his date to the gala tonight. Not that he wouldn't feel a little more reassured to see her between now and then. Hence, he'd braved her brother's invitation to come watch the parade this morning.

"Oh, here comes the Apple Blossom Queen," squealed Eliza.

Sure enough, a white float sailed down Main Street, pulled by two large draft horses that could give the Budweiser Clydesdales a run for their money. Someone had anchored a series of arched rods to the back of a cart, forming what looked like a pumpkin-shaped cage surrounding an elevated throne that, in this case, appeared to be a chair bolted to the wood.

Lincoln's jaw sagged at the elaborate contraption. It was like something straight from a fairy tale.

"Kate was up there one year, you know."

"She was?" If there was one thing he knew about her, it was how much she avoided the spotlight.

Oliver nodded, an amused look sliding over his face. "It's a popular vote, but generally it goes to the student who has contributed the most time to the community. Church fundraisers, Christmas-box wrapping, that sort of thing."

Now *that*, he could believe.

"I like to think she enjoyed it." Eliza was grinning even wider than he'd known was possible. "She doesn't say as much, but underneath all that altruism, I think she's a little lonely. Always saying yes to people is a hard place to exist, especially when they take it for granted."

Said the spunky girl hooked on Oliver's arm.

Lincoln hiked an eyebrow. "You got all that after only a few interactions with her?"

"A girl's gotta be shown some love every once in a while." She tipped her head back to accept Oliver's chaste kiss and blushed.

Lincoln's chest actually ached. He'd plant a field of sunflowers if that's what it took to have Kate look at him with half as much adoration. God willing, he wouldn't mess things up this time. But in order to do that, he'd have to find her first.

The island's only fire engine rolled past, it and the entire fire brigade bringing up the rear of the parade as its lights flashed a silent disco.

"You gonna join us for a bit?" Oliver tilted his head toward the flow of movement. People were already gathering their things and heading toward the park, where a bluegrass band plucked away. "Maybe we'll find the others there."

Lincoln had always wondered what it would be like to have a sibling. He'd have liked a brother, someone to talk to and shoot hoops with when their parents were busy working. Oliver didn't strike him as the basketball-playing kind of guy, but he *was* loyal and protective of those he loved. Something Lincoln could respect.

And for whatever reason, Oliver seemed to be welcoming him into that inner circle.

"Maybe later. I still have a few last-minute things to take care of before tonight."

Yesterday evening may have given him enough time to put together a brand new floral scheme for the gala, but there was still the matter of transporting everything from his studio to the hotel. The Quinns had been kind enough to let him borrow one of their larger flatbed wagons, and his dad had volunteered to help. Any longer here and he'd be late.

Which meant finding Kate would have to wait.

Kate felt as if she'd fallen down a wishing well and ended up in Oz or Wonderland or some other magical place resembling her mom's closet.

"Take your pick." Her mom straightened a crooked hangar while sipping the black coffee Dani had brought her a few minutes ago from the cottage kitchen. "I apologize for the small selection of evening dresses, but I really didn't think I'd have much use for them when I moved back to the island."

Her mom's use of the word *small* made Kate wonder just how much clothing she actually owned. Obviously, there was still a lot she didn't know about her mom, but she was looking forward to many future brunch dates and conversations to remedy that.

Dani went straight for the strapless pink midi dress. She paired it with a chunky-knit sweater and a pair of beige strappy sandals she'd probably borrowed from Lily or their cousin Mia. She'd managed to slick her blonde hair into a fashionable chignon, while Kate's untamed waves refused to stay put, despite the cloud of hairspray she'd nearly choked on earlier.

"Thanks, Mom. You're the best." Dani disappeared into the bathroom to try the dress on, leaving Kate and her mom to the somewhat awkward silence that followed.

"Do you still have the red dress?" Kate's memory of it was a bit fuzzy, but she recalled thinking her mom looked like a princess in the beaded halter top. Dad had surprised her with a fancy date for their anniversary. Dani had been a baby, and Kate couldn't have been more than seven or eight at the time. Likely, it had been one of the many that had been sacrificed due to limited closet space. But if ever there was a night she wanted to feel like a—

"You mean this one?"

She hadn't even noticed her mom set down her coffee or slip into the walk-in closet, but then there it was. As elegant and glittery and red as ever.

Oh, was it red. And bold. And entirely different from anything she'd normally ever wear.

"It's perfect." Her mom's glowing smile matched the one Kate felt on her own face. She didn't say it, but those two words conveyed more than years of dreaming ever could. "Would you like to try it on?"

It was then Kate realized she'd been staring. Nodding, she held out her arms as her mom draped the delicate fabric over them. She had the strangest sense that this was about so much more than a dress. Maybe it was all those years of photographing mothers and daughters on their wedding days—witnessing dresses passed down like blessings—that had her eyes watering.

Whatever it was, it was catching.

"You'll ruin your mascara," said her mom, who wiped a finger beneath her eye. Kate couldn't remember the last time she'd seen her mom cry, and it seeped into the cracks of her parched heart.

"That's what tissues are for." A great deal of them, if this was any indication of how the evening would go. Thankfully, she still had another few minutes before Lincoln was supposed to pick her up. Not that he hadn't seen her cry before, but black streaks of makeup and puffy eyes were not how she wanted to remember tonight.

The silky fabric slid over her shoulders and hips like a dream. There wasn't a mirror inside the closet, but she didn't need one to know she'd found the right dress.

Dani's tiny gasp had Kate spinning in the doorway as the doorbell chimed.

"I'll get that. It's probably Liam. He's always running early." Mom whisked out of the room, leaving the two sisters to finish getting ready.

Kate felt her face heat at her sister's raised eyebrows and open mouth.

"Is it too much? I know red's not usually my color, and I'm afraid my hair refuses to cooperate, even with all those pins and hairspray you used on it."

"Kate, stop."

And she did. Lowering her hand from the crunchy curls, she numbly let Dani guide her toward the full-length mirror in the hallway and felt her own breath hitch at her reflection. Where she'd expected to see a lion's mane of frizz, a few delicate wisps framed her face and the rosy lip gloss Dani had insisted on letting her borrow. And the dress. It hugged her in all the right places, accentuating her curves in a way no pair of jeans ever could.

Forget fairy godmothers. Her mom and sister had the magic

touch. The woman staring back at her was anything but plain and boring, but neither was she a stranger. She was still the same girl who liked cinnamon lattes and swooned over romances and—unapologetically—still had a soft spot for Han Solo. Yet she felt different. Stronger. More . . . herself.

"You look absolutely—"

"Stunning," interrupted a male voice behind her.

Her gaze spun to where Lincoln stood in a navy suit that would put *The Bachelor* to shame. His broad shoulders filled the doorway, making her feel small yet oddly safe in his presence.

She blushed under his approving gaze as his sparkling eyes met hers. "Or should I say, *enchanting*?"

Forget Han Solo. Lincoln St. James could be her real-life hero any day.

"Was that the doorbell again?" asked Dani.

Kate hadn't heard a thing, but that didn't stop her sister from slipping down the hall and around the corner with a look of amusement plastered to her face.

His low rumble of laughter was pure magic as he kept his laser-focused attention solely on Kate. "That was subtle."

"Dani's as subtle as a cannon."

"I'd say it runs in the family." His blue-gray eyes looked like Lake Huron after a storm, flecks of silver glinting through clouds beginning to thin. He'd shaved, revealing dimples she'd nearly forgotten about and the tiny scar along his chin from where he'd fallen into a sand trap on their fifth date years ago. Despite his protests, she'd insisted they go to urgent care, where he'd received three stitches and a kiss for his heroism.

"Can we talk about that letter of yours?" He stood there watching her, obvious self-restraint rippling through his body like caged electricity. He was giving her space, she knew that. There were still so many things they had to discuss, but for once, she wished he'd lower his guard and pull her close. Instead, he stepped back and bumped into the wall behind him. "I really want to kiss you right now."

"Would that be such a bad thing?" The memory of his touch was enough to send goosebumps up her bare arms.

He shook his head but remained where he was standing. "No, it wouldn't. Except I'd probably never stop, which would make it a lot more difficult to remember the speech I rehearsed on the way over here."

The similarity between this conversation and the one in the parking lot before their rehearsal dinner wasn't lost on her, but where last time he'd been grasping for stability, the Lincoln in front of her was all masculine control and steadfast confidence. His calm presence gave her the strength to remain at arm's length, even if the hallway seemed to shrink with him in it.

"First"—he broke the connection long enough to withdraw a small bouquet from behind his back—"I want you to have this."

His fingers stilled as they touched hers. She breathed in his scent along with lilac, the heady combination making it incredibly difficult to respect his earlier request for distance.

How long was he going to make her wait? And how come he didn't look as if his heart was beating a mile a minute like hers? "You wanted to say something?"

"Uh, right." Thumb tracing circles over hers, he used his other hand to point at a purple hyacinth.

He wasn't going to make this easy on her, it appeared.

"This flower says 'I'm sorry, please forgive me.'"

"Lincoln, of course I forgive you."

"And this one"—he moved to the small yellow sunflower as if he hadn't heard her—"says 'I've always admired you and promise to be loyal.'"

Oh. *Oh.*

"The lilac represents our past. It was bold and passionate, and even though the blossoms only last for a short while, its scent lingers for a lifetime. Which is where the white veronicas come in, representing how I've never stopped caring for you and never will." He raised her hand to his lips like a knight pledging allegiance to a princess.

She tried to wipe away her rogue tear when he looked up, but his thumb caught it instead.

Kate could barely breathe. "And the pink one in the center?"

His mouth curved up on one side. "That one's my favorite."

"And why's that?" She leaned her head back to study his face, which was only a few inches from hers. Had he closed the distance or her?

"The pink peony symbolizes a lasting love. The kind that never fades. The kind that's willing to do whatever it takes to make things work, no matter how problematic they may seem."

Another tear fell, and now he was cupping her face with his hand.

"Kate Sullivan, you're the most beautiful woman I've ever known. And I'm not just saying that because I love you."

And drat if another tear didn't escape. So much for her mascara making it through this evening unscathed.

And then he kissed her. Sweet at first. Tender. Her breath filled the space for a second when he pulled back. But then her hands slid up his chest, crushing the flowers between them as his kiss became something else entirely. Deeper, hungrier. She responded with everything she had in her until the flowers fell altogether, wrapping them in their sweet perfume.

A throat clearing nearby yanked her from her bliss.

"Sorry to interrupt," said Dani, grinning from ear to ear. Her arm was looped through Liam's, and he only looked a shade more apologetic than his wife. "There'll be plenty of time for that later, but some of us are going to be late if we don't hurry."

Kate had never seen Lincoln blush so hard, but then again, her face probably wasn't much better. His kisses should be criminal for how fast her heart was thrumming inside her chest. And to think she'd gone a whole five years without.

A mistake she didn't plan on repeating ever again.

"Not before I get a picture." Her mom's heels clacked over the wood, phone clutched in her hand.

"Mom, it's not like this is prom," Dani complained on her way to the stone fireplace decorated with family photos and a tiny vase of blue flowers.

"Oh, I almost forgot." Kate quickly reached across the mantel and slipped a single blue daisy from the bunch. The idea now seemed silly compared to Lincoln's thoughtful gift, but if his bouquet could say all that, she hoped he understood her small gesture.

"What's this for?"

Kate shrugged, her doubts quickly melting under his laser-focused gaze. "I didn't want anything to be missing tonight. Your mom will always be a part of you, and I'm so glad I got to meet her when I did." She swallowed past the lump in her throat, blinked back more unexpected tears. "I know she'd be so proud of the man you've become." Taking his jacket for a second time, she pinned the small flower to the lapel.

"You're pretty amazing, you know that, right?" His hand slid over hers, holding it against his heart. A heart that was, incidentally, beating as fast as hers. "I've spoken with my dad, and he's agreed. We could both use a fresh start. I hope you don't mind if I stick around for a little longer. I heard the journalist say over the phone that Jonathon Island is going to be the next Martha's Vineyard. So the way I see it, you'll need a good florist to keep all those tourists happy."

Kate wouldn't have been able to contain her smile even if she'd wanted to. Which she didn't. Not in the slightest.

"But Jonathon Island already has a florist," she teased despite the giggle that slipped out. Which maybe wasn't a bad thing, because Lincoln flashed her a knee-melting roguish grin.

"Are you saying you don't need me?"

"Not at all. Just pointing out a fact." Like how the sky was indeed blue and the best stories always had a happy ending.

"As it so happens," he continued, "Dani recently told me that Holly has been thinking about stepping back from the big events. Something about preferring to work with the customers one-on-one."

Her chest grew even lighter. "She did, did she?"

"And while we're stating facts . . ." He leaned a little closer, tilted his head just so. "Have I told you how much I love you?"

"You may have mentioned it once or twice."

She rose on her toes, pressing a lingering kiss to his lips that was over too soon. Because they had an audience. Because they were going to be late to the gala. But mostly because she needed him to know . . .

"I love you too."

So much so that it had scared her at first. But that was before God had torn down her walls to build something so much better and more beautiful than she could ever imagine.

Something flashed, and Kate spun to see her mom lowering her phone with a grin. "I think that's the perfect picture to commemorate the evening."

"An evening that'll be starting without us in a matter of minutes," chimed in Dani with an even bigger smile.

Lincoln gave Kate's hand a squeeze. "I'm ready if you are."

And boy, was she ready. For the gala. Their future together . . .

All of it.

Epilogue

One Month Later

LINCOLN CHECKED HIS WATCH AND PICKED up the pace. Kate's ferry was due any minute, and he'd promised to meet her at the dock when she got there.

The paperwork had taken a bit longer than he'd planned, and Holly's Flowers had been all out of sunflowers, which was why he was now jogging down Lake Shore Drive with dirt under his fingernails and a pink-and-white bud bouncing in his shirt pocket.

Hopefully not too much though. If he was going to be slapped with a fine for picking a wildflower, it better be fully intact when he handed it over.

A refreshing breeze licked off the clear blue lake, cooling his arms and neck beneath the blazing June sunshine. A handful of kites dotted the cloudless sky, not unlike the number of cyclists and walkers he had to dodge as he rounded the southern cape.

"Whoa. Where's the fire, son?"

He nearly clotheslined himself on a fishing pole that swung from his dad's tackle box, and ran right into a cup of coffee instead.

"Better that than my fish and chips." Dwight chuckled beside Lincoln's dad as he readjusted his glasses. "You on your way to see our Kate?"

Our Kate.

He loved the sound of it.

With how little time it had taken for her to slip back into his heart, it was no wonder everyone who met her fell instantly in love. Even his own dad, who should've been on his side of things, acted more like Lincoln was the outsider in the equation. *Don't you go breaking that girl's heart, now. Or else I might have to unaccept your invitation for Christmas and stay at her place instead.*

On the pull-out couch? You'll throw your back out. You do know I'll have a perfectly good guest bedroom set up and ready by then.

He'd harrumphed and grinned. *I guess you'll just have to hold on to her, then. For my back's sake.*

Not to worry. He'd already learned the hard way what a mistake letting her go was. And this time, he planned to do things right and take their time.

"Well, what are you standing around talking to us for?" This from his dad, who slapped him heartily on the shoulder. "Go and get her."

Lincoln didn't need to be told twice.

The ferry was pulling into the dock when he skidded to a stop beside the railing. Water splashed beneath the wooden slats, counting down the seconds before a man in uniform lowered a ramp from the upper deck. Yellow pamphlets whipping against the breeze, he stood and waved when he spotted Lincoln.

Lincoln returned Noah's friendly greeting as his gaze dropped to the sea of tourists. His height gave him an advantage, and soon, he spotted Kate's bronze ponytail. The moment she saw him was like a lightbulb illuminating a dark room, those dimples of hers visible even through a sea of tourists.

He snatched the second suitcase from her the moment she reached the bottom of the ramp, and guided her to a quieter corner overlooking the harbor, where he could kiss her without so many witnesses.

A sigh escaped her lips. "I missed you."

"Not as much as I missed you." In her absence, he'd gone fishing with his dad and Dwight twice and joined the guys for game night—and lost every single game of Risk because he hadn't been able to concentrate.

A dusting of freckles cascaded over her sun-kissed shoulders, dancing as she laughed. "I was only gone four days."

"Which is exactly four days too many." He gave in and stole another kiss, which she gladly obliged. "How was your trip?"

"Hmm?"

God help him. The next few months were going to be pure, delightful torture.

She opened her eyes and swept them toward the harbor, but not before her face took on a beautiful shade of pink. "Right, Petoskey. It was good."

And she thought he was difficult to pull information out of. Then again, he liked the idea of his kisses rendering her speechless.

"How about your friend Gabby? Does she seem to be handling the transition okay?"

"She's incredible. Running a business is a lot to take on, but she's determined to make a go of it. Plus she's really talented. Anyone would be lucky to hire her to photograph their wedding."

Good to know.

"That's wonderful. I'm sure your friend is good at what she does, but you're the best."

"You're just saying that because you're my boyfriend."

"And proud of it."

There she went, blushing all over again. He had half a mind to skip the detour he'd planned and go straight back to her place for some much-needed reconnecting. But then that would ruin the surprise and everyone's hard work.

He reached into his shirt pocket and withdrew the first clue.

Raised eyebrows, a tiny gasp, and . . . "Lincoln, you didn't." But that didn't stop her from accepting the single bud like it was a piece of china. The pink-and-white star-shaped flower was only a little worse for wear but just as beautiful as the day they'd visited Lover's Leap. "You know you're not supposed to pick them, right? If anyone catches you, they could give you a fifty-dollar fine."

He shrugged. "I like living on the edge. Besides, they were already at the end of their season."

"I don't think Janine at the historical society would see it that way."

"Good thing it's not *her* I'm trying to impress, then."

Her laughter was like a drink of cool water on a hot summer's day. Something which they could both enjoy, but first things first.

Grabbing her other bag, he stacked it on top of the suitcase and wheeled them around to face the shore, where he'd left the carriage. "After you, m'lady." After all, she was everything a princess ought to be. Kind, generous, beautiful inside and out. It was high time she knew it as well.

He hooked his arm through hers and again drank from that spring fountain as another giggle slipped out.

"Where are we off to in such a hurry?"

"You'll see."

The fudge shop and ice-cream truck slipped by on their right, and soon they were clopping up the hotel's empty curved drive.

"What are we doing here? I figured you were taking me to see your new place."

"You know about that?"

A mischievous grin tugged at her mouth. "Dani texted me. As

did your dad, Oliver, and my cousin Mia, who I think sold you the house."

Another thing about small-town life he'd have to get used to: Nothing stayed a secret for long. Which made the fact that she was now squinting with curious confusion, glancing between him and the hotel, a flat-out miracle.

Lincoln led Kate through the open front doors, past a ladder and drop cloth where the painters had been working on the crown molding, and all the way to the new concierge desk. The fresh coat of paint practically gleamed from the sunshine streaming through the large wall of windows overlooking the water, but not as much as Kate.

"I can hardly believe the progress they've made here. It's stunning."

"Yeah, it's something special. Although, it's still missing something." He released her hand long enough to slip behind the desk, heart pounding as he picked up the new sign he'd worked on with Dani over the weekend and hung it from the brass hook on the wall. A list of services filled the placard, complete with *Kate Sullivan Photography* at the top.

A tiny gasp escaped her lips. "When did you do this?"

"I told you, four days is a long time."

Her gaze shifted from the placard to him as he rejoined her, moisture gathering at the corners of her growing smile.

"The hotel management—"

"Meaning Liam, Dani, and my brother James," she teased. Boy, was she cute when she was happy.

He shook his head and chuckled. "Will you let me finish?"

"Sorry. Please continue." She was the model of poise and restraint, save for the sparkle behind her amber eyes.

"As I was saying, the hotel management wants to feature your services as part of their elite packages." He slid a second piece of paper from his back pocket and handed her the list of names.

"You're already booked solid for the rest of the summer. Anniversary photos, family portraits. If you're up for it."

Kate stared at him, mouth agape. "But . . . how?"

He tucked a wayward curl behind her ear, still surprised at the outpouring of love he'd witnessed on this island in the past two months. Both from its people and, more specifically, the woman standing in front of him. "I'm not the only one who believes in you, Kate. This is your family, and they love you. I love you."

As if she needed more convincing, he pulled her close and pressed a gentle kiss to her forehead. Then her nose. And then to her salty cheek. But these were happy tears, ones he could spend a lifetime tasting if she smiled as radiantly at him then as she was now.

"You're something else, Lincoln Thomas St. James."

"So I've been told."

"And humble too," she added with a chuckle that resonated through him like church bells.

"The humblest."

She gave him a playful swat before tugging him down for a proper kiss.

And man, was it a kiss.

He'd made a lot of mistakes in his life, but loving Kate wasn't one of them. Not then. Not now. And he had a pretty good sense, as she looked up at him with that dimple-framed smile, that he'd never stop loving this woman for as long as they both lived.

Bonus Epilogue

Thank you for reading *Find Me in the Blooms*. We hope you loved this story. Find out what happens next for Kate and Lincoln with a Bonus Epilogue, a special gift, available only to our newsletter subscribers.

This Bonus Epilogue will not be released on any retailer platform, so scan the QR code to get your free gift. You acknowledge you are becoming a Sunrise Publishing and Alyssa Schwarz subscriber. Unsubscribe from any newsletter at any time.

Thank You

Thank you so much for reading *Find Me in the Blooms*. We hope you enjoyed the story. If you did, would you be willing to do us a favor and leave a review? It doesn't have to be long—just a few words to help other readers know what they're getting. (But no spoilers! We don't want to wreck the fun!) Thank you again for reading!

We'd love to hear from you—not only about this story, but about any characters or stories you'd like to read in the future.

Contact us at www.sunrisepublishing.com/contact.

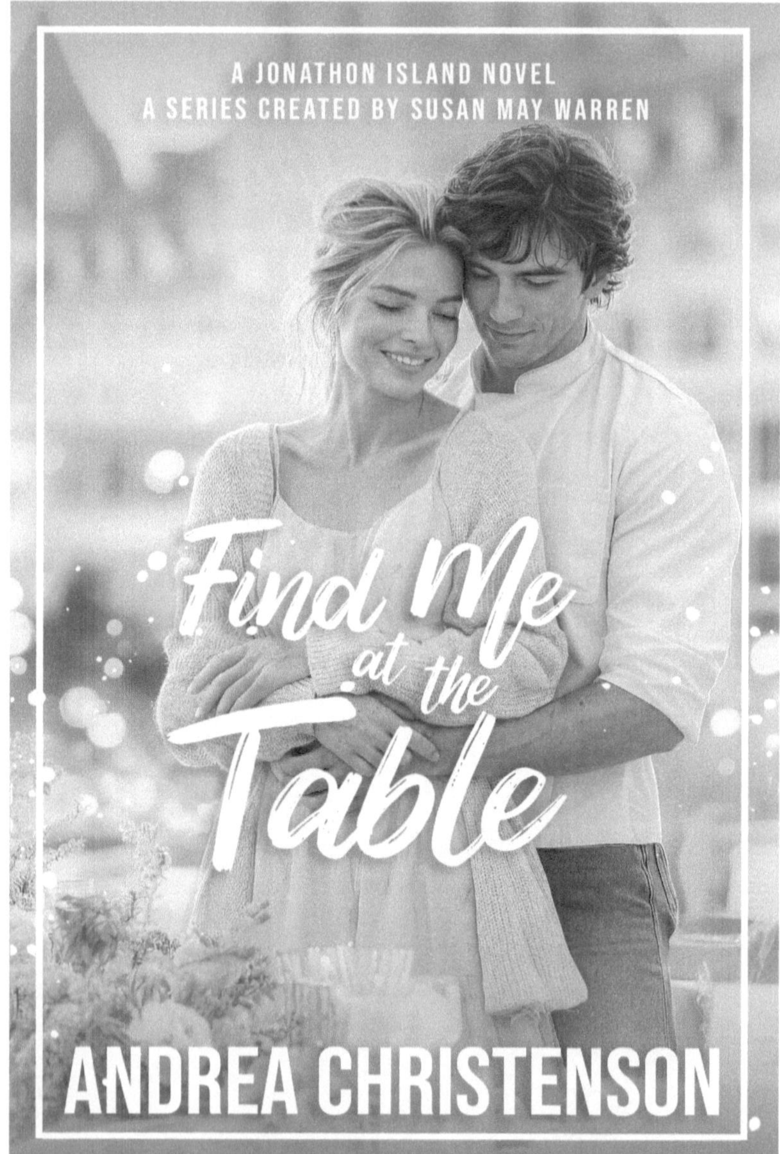
A JONATHON ISLAND NOVEL
A SERIES CREATED BY SUSAN MAY WARREN
Find Me
at the
Table
ANDREA CHRISTENSON

She ruined his career with one review. Now they have to cook together.

A food critic who can't cook. A chef who can't let go. One cooking competition that changes everything.

Ava Harper writes restaurant reviews that can make or break careers—but she's hiding a secret that would destroy her own. The daughter of celebrity chefs never learned to cook. When her editor forces her to compete in Jonathon Island's Flavor Fest, she's not just out of her depth. She's partnered with Zach Sullivan, the chef whose restaurant her review accidentally ruined.

This should be a disaster.

Zach has nursed his grudge for years. He's blamed Ava for every setback, every failure, every sleepless night. Now he's stuck in a dead-end job under a tyrannical chef, and his only shot at redemption means working alongside the woman he's spent years resenting.

The problem? She's nothing like he expected.

Between burnt garlic bread, sabotaged flour, and the watchful eyes of celebrity judges, Zach and Ava discover that the truth behind that fateful review isn't what either of them believed. As old wounds finally come to light, they'll have to decide: Is forgiveness worth the risk? And is love the recipe they've both been missing?

One

ODAY MARKED THE BEGINNING OF AVA HARPer's new start. If Judson Wright was in a good mood, that is.

She walked through the newsroom toward her boss's office. Using her right hand, she gave a swift tug to the bottom of the black blazer she wore over her slim, dark blue jeans. In her left arm, she clutched a file folder tight. Her life was in that folder.

Or, at least, the life she wanted.

The clacking of computer keys and the voices of her coworkers drifted over the tops of the chest-high cubicles laid out around the room. Along the gray exterior walls hung selected front pages from the *Chicago Herald* depicting significant events her newspaper had covered over the years. A scent of burnt coffee hung in the air. She tuned it all out as she rehearsed the speech she would give to Judson in a moment.

At thirty-five years old, Ava knew that if she wasn't focused, she'd forget her whole agenda. Today wasn't a day for distraction. Because, after searching for years—*years*—for a break, she'd finally made a workable plan. She just needed Judson to see it that way too.

"Knock, knock." She paused outside her boss's open door. The small room held a desk, a couple of chairs, and a loveseat. Judson didn't have anything on his faded gray walls, but a framed picture of his grandkids sat on the corner of his desk. What he lacked in decor, he made up for in mess. Piles of papers and news clippings, and other detritus—was that a wrapper from the sub shop down the street?—lay everywhere.

"Ava, come on in." Judson half rose from his chair before plopping down again. His Albert Einstein hairstyle was especially on point today. And he wore the condiments of what looked like a hamburger on his white button-down. Many people made the mistake of underestimating Judson based on his appearance. Her first week on the job, Ava learned the truth. He had the sharpest newspaper mind of anyone she'd ever met. He ran the metro section of the paper with an iron fist and a sharp tongue. Her columns reviewing local eateries and giving cooking advice always came back from him bleeding red in edits. Yeah. Intimidating. "Shut the door."

Okay. Good start. Judson only shut the door for important meetings.

She glanced at the chairs in front of his desk. Piled as high with papers and other items as the rest of the space. Near the couch along the far wall—also covered with random stuff—a folding chair rested in its closed position. She grabbed it and opened it. It sank a good three inches as she sat. Great. Not exactly a position of power, but maybe that would be in her favor.

"Sorry, that chair has a broken seat." Judson ran a hand over his head, but it did nothing to lessen the impact of his wiry gray hair.

"No problem." She straightened her back.

"Sherry tells me you have a pitch for me." Judson's bulldog of a personal assistant took her job as bouncer seriously. Ava had had to beg and plead for this meeting. Sherry had finally caved after Ava brought her a slice of cheesecake from Studio 67, a restaurant where she'd been sent on assignment. She'd given the restaurant a great review in her column, Ava Harper Chows Down.

"I do." She pulled the top sheet out of her folder and handed it over. It was a printout from the Visit Us page of the Jonathon Island website. Judson glanced at it before setting it down on top of his desk. He folded his hands over his stomach and leaned back in his chair. "I know the *Chicago Herald* usually only covers local news, but I had a great idea for expanding our readership."

Judson nodded. "I'm listening."

Gulp. "Lately, our sales have been declining. Well, every newspaper is seeing declining readership. In exit polls, people have stated that they can find out these kinds of news items from anywhere."

"I'm well aware of the declining sales. I just had my ninetieth meeting about that this year, and it's only the beginning of May." He laughed, but there was little humor.

"Right. Of course. So, what if we gave the readers something different?" She took a deep breath. "What if I take my column on the road? I could work remotely, reviewing restaurants that are not just in the greater Chicago area. I could do other pieces too. Food-centered still, but like on food festivals, maybe food factories or something too. Do you remember the Food Network show *Unwrapped*? It could be *Unwrapped* meets *Diners, Drive-Ins, and Dives*. Except I could review lots of places. Right now it's the beginning of May. Food festival season is just starting. I could get a jump on it." Her heart thumped. Could he hear it on the other side of the desk?

Judson's gaze sharpened. "I take it you're thinking of Jonathon Island?"

"I am. Jonathon Island in Michigan is having a food festival, Flavor Fest, in a few weeks, the first part of June. I thought that could be a trial run." She pictured the quaint village of Jonathon Island she remembered from her one and only trip there but pushed it aside. She'd stumbled across the contest advertisement while clicking around the town website and dreaming of living there. *Concentrate, Ava. No distractions.* "There will be two weekends of cooking contests with other activities in between. Cooking classes, demonstrations . . . even a fudge-tasting event. I could review the restaurants on the island as well as the contests themselves. Maybe do a few feature pieces on the chefs. I could get two weeks' worth of content from that event." She bit back the next sentence on her lips. Better to let Judson mull it over first.

"I know about Jonathon Island. My family has traveled there many times. Not lately, of course." Judson unfolded his hands and drummed them on his desk. "I don't know. Sounds expensive. The last time I brought the kids and grandkids there it cost almost as much as taking the family to Disney World."

She handed him another paper. "I've sketched out a budget and projected expenses. Their rates are low right now while the town is trying to garner new interest from tourists." She pointed at the bottom line. "But even if we weren't getting a sweet deal on lodging, I think we could reach a broader audience with these articles, and they'll pay for themselves. We could do hard copies first, then upload them onto our food blog. I've also outlined a couple other places I could replicate this experience."

"I like where you're going with this." Judson picked up a pen and marked a few spots on the paper. "Tell you what—I have to run this past the editorial team, but I like where your head is at. Let's consider Jonathon Island a trial run." He pointed the end of the pen at her. "If you can produce at least fourteen good articles and they garner some good traction, we'll consider letting you go remote full-time."

She stood, her insides feeling like they were filled with rising helium balloons. "Thank you, sir. I won't let you down."

"You never have." Judson turned his attention to something else on his desk.

Ava put the chair back where she'd found it. Her hand was on the cool doorknob when Judson spoke again.

"I see there's a charity competition here. Get signed up to cook for that. It's good press for the newspaper, plus it will give you an inside scoop." He stabbed a finger at the paper.

A few balloons popped and her stomach sank.

Judson went on. "The daughter of celebrity chefs Leah and Aaron Harper will make quite a splash. I bet you've been cooking since you were a toddler."

Now her heart was somewhere near her knees, which were in danger of giving out. "Actually, um—"

"I know you don't like to talk about your parents in your column, that's fine. But this is for charity." Judson waved a hand in the air. "And if you win, you can donate it to the *Herald*'s charity, Reading Is for Everyone."

Open your mouth, Ava. Tell him you can't cook. But the words stuck in her throat.

"I'll let you know what the board says, but in my mind, this charity competition seals the deal. Consider yourself signed up for all of it."

Gulp. Writing fourteen articles in ten days, no problem. Cooking anything more than a frozen dinner? Very much a problem.

She pushed the thought away. Time enough to deal with it later.

Sure, the job wasn't secure yet, but Ava felt a hundred pounds lighter after having her pitch over with. She beelined for the corner desk where she could see the top of her friend Emily's curly brunette head.

"I think he's going to go for it." She pitched her voice low, but Emily squealed.

"Ava, that's great!" Petite and always in a skirt or a dress, Emily Knox was the unlikely sports reporter for the *Herald*. The two had become friends after Judson sent them both on the same assignment, Emily to check out the Chicago Dogs, a local baseball team, and Ava to report on the food offerings at their park. Today, Emily wore a cream sweater over a calico sundress that brought out the blue of her eyes. "We're way past the minor leagues now. If it doesn't work out, you can always join me on the sports beat."

"Nah. I love my job, you know that." Ava shifted the folder in her hands.

"True. I don't think I've ever known someone to love writing about food as much as you do. Though sometimes I suspect you're in it for the free meals." Emily raised her right eyebrow.

Ava grinned at her. "You caught me. When someone can't cook, it helps to have a job where they're required to feed you." Except. Her heart seized. "One of the catches for this Jonathon Island assignment is Judson requiring me to sign up for a charity cooking competition." She grimaced. Would Judson really make her go through with it?

"Why are you making that face? It sounds like fun."

"You know I can't compete in a cook-off. Everyone will find out my secret." If her readers knew she couldn't cook, they would laugh her out of publication. Ava Harper Chows Down was peppered with cooking tips each week. Tips she didn't fully know how to utilize but had gleaned from the chefs she interviewed for her column.

Emily squinted. "How do you know you can't cook if you never even try?"

"The one time I tried, it was a disaster." She still woke up in a cold sweat sometimes, the fire alarm blaring from her nightmares.

"I'm sure it wasn't that bad."

"I mean, nobody died, and I didn't burn the house down, but the way my mom reacted, you would have thought I'd . . . Anyway, I decided cooking wasn't—" On Emily's computer screen, Ava spotted two familiar faces. Her gut clenched. "Emily, why are my parents on your computer?"

Emily fumbled with her mouse, and her screensaver came up. "I'm catching up on past seasons of *Life Afloat* over my lunch hour. I'm sorry. I should have asked you first."

Ava waved at the air. "No. It's fine. Are you on season three?"

"Yes." Emily's face became animated. "I love that they're on the same ship this time. You can really tell how much they love each other."

Ava stopped the automatic eye roll her eyeballs did whenever someone gushed about her famous chef parents, Leah and Aaron Harper. They'd been chefs on private yachts since long before she was born, and now they were regularly featured on the reality television show *Life Afloat*. An upstairs/downstairs-style TV program giving glimpses into the überrich lives of those who could afford luxury yachts and the staff that crewed them.

She didn't have the energy for them today. "Yep. Season three is a favorite for lots of people. Wait until you hit episode ten." Yeah, even though they never had time for her, she still made time to watch every episode. Really, sometimes it was the only way she could see them. Her parents were decidedly on the downstairs portion of the show, but the TV producers—and audience—loved them, so they were featured often, no matter which boat they were crewing.

"Did they really meet on a yacht?"

"Yep. Mom was the cook and Dad was a deckhand. She taught him everything she knew, and then they learned a bunch of stuff together. It's pretty rare they end up on a boat together now. Not too many yacht owners are looking for two highly trained chefs."

"Two chefs for parents, and yet you don't cook."

"Enough already." Ava waved off her words. "They gave me a love for good food and a talent for critiquing it—that's why I love my job so much—just not a talent for creating it myself." Her heart twisted.

"Hey, you know what you could do? Take a class at Escargot." Emily pushed a curl off her forehead.

"That French restaurant?" She'd heard good things about it but had never tried it out.

"That's the one. They give lessons there on Monday nights, when the restaurant is closed to the public." Emily tapped a few keys on her keyboard. "Yep. They have some the next few Mondays. I know they cater to beginners—my friend Michelle works there. I went to one of the classes for a girls' night out. I got some very helpful hints from the chef." Emily clicked around the website. "I just sent you the link to the sign-up."

"Thanks. I'll look into it." The band across her chest loosened a notch. "Enough chat for now. I'd better finish that article about Mainstreet Eatery. Maybe this will be the one to wow the editors into giving me everything I've ever wanted." A forever home where she could put down roots, plus the chance to chase the foodie stories she really wanted to tell? Yeah, she'd do anything for that opportunity.

There were times Zachary Sullivan knew he had the best job on earth. He whipped some horseradish into the hard-boiled yolk in front of him before spooning tiny dabs of the filling back into the quail eggs. Then he nested the filled eggs next to a prosciutto on rye open-faced sandwich. His take on open-faced ham sandwiches and deviled eggs. Needed some color. He added a sprig of watercress to one of the eggs and took a step back to see the big picture.

Like Picasso on a plate.

He'd dreamed up the food in the empty kitchen after closing time at Escargot. In the two years he'd been cooking at the French restaurant, he'd learned that the owner preferred leftovers to be eaten, not thrown out. It was fun to play around with the ingredients, trying out new recipes and flexing his creative muscles. Something that he never got to do when Chef Louie was around.

The kitchen at Escargot was quiet now. A hint of garlic, brown butter, and the lemon cleaner they used hung in the air. The surfaces of the workstations lined up in the middle of the room gleamed. Along the back wall, the top-of-the-line grills, oven, and deep fryer stood ready for service the next day. Someday he would run a kitchen like this.

He snapped a photo of his dish and texted it to his sister Dani.

Zach

Here's the elevated "church potluck food" you challenged me to make.

She probably wouldn't get the photo until morning, but he couldn't wait to prove he'd met the goal.

His phone chimed with an incoming text:

Dani

Looks great! A real winner. Wish I could do a taste test. I'll have to think of a harder task next time.

Zach

Are you still awake? It's midnight.

Dani

Can't sleep. Working on food festival details.

His sister was the tourism director for Jonathon Island, a small community in the middle of Lake Huron in Michigan. This year she had devised a full plate of festivals to welcome much-needed tourists to the island. Jonathon Island barely made it through the pandemic and the economic downturn. It didn't help that their main hotel, the Grand Sullivan, had nearly burned to the ground ten years before. Now that the hotel was being rebuilt, the town had begun a revitalization effort, and tourism was finally beginning to pick up again.

———————————— Zach

Good luck. Not that you need it.
The book festival and the Apple
Blossom Festival were successes.
I'm sure this one will be too.

As he tucked his phone into his back pocket, it started ringing.

"I think I'm in over my head." Dani's whispered voice came over the line.

"Really? You sounded so confident at your wedding." Zach massaged his forehead but couldn't stop the smile. Zach had recently catered Dani's wedding on Jonathon Island. The first time he'd been back there in many, many years.

Dani sighed. "Yeah, well, four weeks later and I'm not so confident."

"Why are we whispering?"

"Liam is asleep, and I don't want to worry him with this."

"But you'll worry me?" He transferred the call to his earbuds and stuck them in his ears, then began handwashing the bowls and measuring spoons he'd used to make the dinner. Chef Louie prized a clean kitchen. One of the few things they agreed on.

"You were already awake. Besides, I need your help."

"Sure. What can I do?"

"Come home for the festival."

"What? No." He'd already done that once this year, thank you very much. He had the scars to prove it. *You Sullivans think you're better than the rest of us.* Some cranky old man, one of the hotel groundskeepers, had grumped at him at Dani's wedding. *If it weren't for you, Jonathon Island would never have lost so many tourists.* And sure, the man's words meant little, except they confirmed all of Zach's darkest fears. He wasn't accepted and neither was his family. After all, it was his family that was responsible for the island's greatest tragedy.

"I just think I could use your moral support. I need this to go well. It'll set the tone for the whole summer. Plus, you could enter some of the contests." A rustle came from the other end of the phone. "Hold on, I'm going to move to the front porch."

"And what, compete against Martha Kelley? Or maybe Patrick? They'd love that. A Sullivan as competition." The Kelley family owned and operated most of the food places on Jonathon Island. Sure, Patrick was a good guy, but Martha gave Zach a sour look every time she saw him.

"Martha isn't competing, as far as I know. Besides, I have some others coming too. Val Anderson and Alicia Baird."

Huh. She'd pulled some good local chef talent. "Okay, fine. You have some heavy hitters."

"Please come. Did I tell you that Paul Hawkeye and Anne Green have agreed to be celebrity judges?" Her front door squeaked, and then a gentle thud echoed.

"You're kidding." The two television chefs seemed way out of Jonathon Island's league.

"Nope. Just got the confirmation today. They both loved the idea of being at a small-town festival."

"You know I wanted to work for Paul. It's one of the reasons I moved to LA after Seattle." He wiped a stray spot of egg filling off the plate in front of him. "Too bad I could never get a face-to-face with him."

"I thought that might get your attention. I'll ask again, please say you'll come."

"I'll think about it. I might not be able to get the time off since I was just over there for your wedding." He wandered over to the shared calendar hanging on the wall. "What are the dates again?"

"The first two weekends in June. Thanks, big brother. You're the best."

No one had requested that week off as far as he could tell. "I haven't promised anything yet."

"When have you ever said no to me?" Dani's smile came through the line loud and clear.

He laughed and hung up. Dani had a point—he had a hard time saying no to his family.

Jamie Randall, his six-foot-seven coworker who looked more like a Marine than a line cook, with his broad chest and close-cut blond hair, wandered over. He'd been working at Escargot when Zach first started. Unlike Zach, Jamie didn't care to move up in the ranks of the kitchen. He snagged one of the deviled eggs Zach had rejected. "Is this your new recipe?"

"Yep." Zach crossed his arms and leaned back on the counter. "I added a little horseradish and tarragon as well as mustard to the cooked yolks."

"Can I try it?" Jamie didn't wait for him to answer before popping the whole thing in his mouth. "Delicious. This should be on the menu."

"Ha. You're funny. Chef Louie would never go for it."

"Why are you wasting your talents here, man?" Jamie popped another quail egg in his mouth and chased it with a bite of ham. Suddenly, the big man snapped to attention. He gestured with his chin toward the kitchen door.

Zach turned in time to see two men enter. Marcel Boivin, the slight, silver-haired owner of Escargot and a head shorter than his companion, gesticulated widely as he walked and talked. The man next to him was the head chef of Escargot, Chef Louie Andrews.

"I just think we need a few new items on our menu," Marcel said, his French accent heavy tonight. "Ah! Hello, gentlemen." The old man clasped his hands together and nodded at Zach and Jamie. "Another excellent service tonight. Be sure to say merci beaucoup to the rest of the team." He advanced a step, leaving Chef Louie by the door, silent and glowering. Chef Louie, his chef's whites pristine and his brown hair gelled tight to his scalp, had sent the rest of the staff home after the kitchen had been scrubbed clean.

"Mr. Boivin, Chef." Zach nodded back. "I thought you'd gone home for the night."

"Chef and I had some business to discuss. What is this?" Marcel waved a hand toward Zach's elevated potluck food.

Zach stepped around the table, a lame attempt to block the food. "Nothing, sir."

"Nonsense. It looks good." Marcel selected an egg and ate it. His eyes widened. "This is fantastique. Chef Louie, you are a genius."

Wait a minute.

Louie's face cleared. "Uh, thank you."

"This is what I mean. New menu items. Chef Louie, why did you let me prattle on about it when you'd already prepared some things for me to taste?" Marcel ate one of the prosciutto on rye sandwiches. "Non. This one is pas bon. Not good. I don't know what you were thinking here. But I like that quail oeuf, I mean egg. Put it on the hors d'oeuvres menu."

Marcel breezed out, leaving Louie, Zach, and Jamie staring at each other.

Louie crossed his arms, eyes flashing. "You have been trying to undermine me ever since you stepped foot in this restaurant." Louie's French accent was not as thick as Marcel's, but it still cut through the air. "What were you trying to pull, having these things plated up?"

"I didn't even know he was going to be here tonight." But Zach's words didn't faze Louie.

"Since you feel you can upstage me, maybe you should teach the next Make-It-Monday series." Louie's hand flicked the air. "If this happens again, you're gone."

Zach sighed. "Yes, Chef."

Louie spun on his heel and stalked out.

"Chef Louie really has it in for you." Jamie carried the empty dishes to the sink.

"My first night here some big shot complimented my cooking, and Louie was offended. He's made it miserable ever since."

"Dude. What are you doing staying here and taking his mistreatment?" Jamie ran water over the plate. "Make-It-Mondays are like his idea of punishment. He only assigns them to someone on his hit list. Those classes are brutal."

A room full of people who didn't know how to cook coming in and thinking they could master it in a night? Yeah, the classes could be difficult, but he'd done them before. Shouldn't be a big deal this time either. The hardest part was being in front of all those people. "It's fine. I'm paying my dues."

"It's really not fine. He just totally stole the credit for your dish. And what dues? You've been a chef for a long time."

"His kitchen, his recipes. We all signed on to that when we came." He raised a shoulder. "And I've only been here less than two years. I'm still the new guy."

"It's not right, man. He's not doing it because you're the new guy." Jamie shook his head. "But whatever. It's your life." The big man patted him on the shoulder. "I'm taking off. See you tomorrow for another round of non-crime and punishment."

Except, maybe Jamie had a point. With Chef Louie in charge, his job was a dead-end.

He thumbed a text to Dani.

Zach

____

Fine. I'll come to Flavor Fest. Sign
me up for the contest.

Because maybe he could wow Paul or Anne and land himself a new position.

He needed to get out of this job.

Acknowledgments

To the amazing team at Sunrise Publishing—Lisa Jordan, Susan May Warren, Katie Donovan, Essie Shull, Rel Mollet, Sarah Erredge, and all the other Jonathon Island authors. It has been such an honor and joy getting to work with these amazing and uplifting women.

To everyone at My Book Therapy—thank you for being a place of encouragement that inspires us all to write great stories that draw us and readers closer to God.

I'd like to specifically thank Lisa Jordan. She makes writing a pure joy, even when I get those pages-long editorial letters and edits (which we all do, lol). I know it is her way of showing her love and care by wanting to make every story shine as much as humanly possible. I know that if I get stuck in a story or need a listening ear for me to brainstorm ideas, she's always there to help me through it. This story wouldn't be what it is without you. Thank you so much for believing in me and inviting me into the Sunrise team.

A special thank-you to my parents for always encouraging me. And especially to my mom for reeling me back in when the writer's block and existential questions hit and for helping me celebrate all the victories (from a completed manuscript to getting half a page written) along the way.

And to readers (that's YOU!), thank you so much. Your support means everything, and I pray this story reminds you how much you are loved by friends, family, and ultimately our heavenly Father.

Alyssa Schwarz is a Colorado native who attended the Colorado School of Mines, got her masters in Geological Engineering, and promptly became a watercolor artist and author (as one does). She loves writing heartfelt romances with happy endings, a bit of mystery, faith, humor, and second chances. When she's not writing, you can find her cooking, quilting, painting, or doing any number of crafty activities.

Visit her website to learn more and receive a free novella when you subscribe to her newsletter: www.authoralyssaschwarz.com

Created by New York Times bestselling author

RACHEL HAUCK

Welcome

Home to Hearts Bend

for sweet stories of romance,
faith, and happy endings.

YOU MAY ALSO LIKE...

When Noah Hebert inherits the struggling Blue Pirogue Inn, he must solve a puzzle left by his grandfather to save it from his family's nemesis, Isaac Bergeron. Teaming up with Elisa Bergeron, the café manager and his rival, they must navigate family feuds—and unexpected sparks—while racing against time.

Where I Found You by Besty St. Amant

Grace Howell leaves her life as a ballerina and returns to Heritage, Michigan, to heal. Teaching dance is just a temporary gig, until she finds herself unexpectedly charmed by small-town life and her growing attachment to Seth Warner, a man from her past with a troubled history of his own.

You're the Reason by Tari Faris

Dani Sullivan is determined to revive Jonathon Island's fading charm and reunite her fractured family. Her plan? Reopen the Grand Sullivan Hotel. But without the funds to restore the hotel, Dani's forced to accept help from Liam Stone—a big-city hotel developer whose sleek, modern vision is everything she's trying to avoid.

Meet Me at the Grand by Lindsay Harrel

We solve the problem of what to read next.

WHERE EVERY STORY IS A FRIEND,
AND EVERY CHAPTER IS A NEW JOURNEY...

Subscribe to our newsletter for the latest news, weekly giveaways, exclusive author interviews, and more!

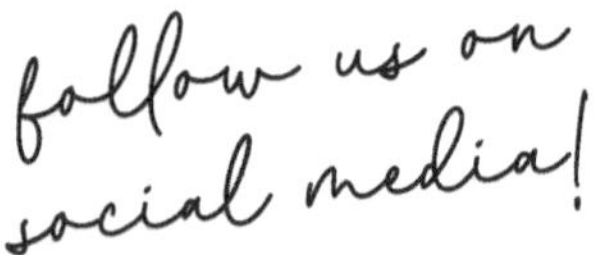

Shop paperbacks, ebooks, audiobooks, and more at
SUNRISEPUBLISHING.MYSHOPIFY.COM